3

The Ordinary Adept

Book 1

The Ordinary Adept
Book 1

Well, it's a Heck of a Mid Life Crisis!

P. T. Straub

authorHOUSE®

AuthorHouse™
1663 Liberty Drive
Bloomington, IN 47403
www.authorhouse.com
Phone: 1-800-839-8640

Published by AuthorHouse 12/13/2011

ISBN: 978-1-4634-2781-8 (sc)
ISBN: 978-1-4634-2782-5 (e)

Library of Congress Control Number: 2011911247

Acknowledgments

I would like to warmly thank Magda Nusink for her literary advice, Evelyn Kryt for her wonderful photo, and my husband, Michael, for his patience with the escapades that led to writing this book! Many thanks also to AuthorHouse and their skillful editors. I am also grateful for the encouragement of friends and family—including my cat—and also to Julia Cameron and her book The Vein of Gold, *which provided the necessary momentum to begin this project. Lastly, I remain in awe of spirit—the perfection of their guidance and their diligence in maintaining my free will.*

~Chapter 1~

The Tree Trunk

Wham!

Tess couldn't quite believe what she had heard.

"Uh, what did you say?"

Frank looked away briefly, and then looked back at her and said very carefully, "I am leaving you, Tess. I am going to go live with another woman."

He meant it.

She felt as if all the breath had been knocked out of her. She took a few steps back and bumped up against the living room carpet, which was rolled up against the wall. Her mouth opened, but no words came out.

"You can stay in the house. My things will be gone when you get back from work tonight."

Her eyes filled with tears as the full impact hit her. She regained her breath and let out a yell. *"Why?!"* And then she changed her mind about engaging Frank further in this battle and ran abruptly to the kitchen, dodging the stereo that was covered with a pink sheet, and past the ladder and assorted paint cans that were neatly sitting beside it. *This can't be happening*, she thought to herself, her heart hammering. She picked up her purse, sitting by the back door off the kitchen, stepped quickly into her penny loafers, and then yanked open the screen door and ran outside, her hair flying and tears streaming down her face. Frank was calling, saying something to her as she left, but it was too late. Tess simply could not bear to hear anything more. She jumped into the car and was quickly out of the driveway.

At the transit parking lot she swiped her metro pass in front of the ticket machine, and as the gate moved up, she stepped on the gas and screeched into a spot near the back of the lot. Her tears were done, but as she got out of the car, her legs were shaking. She closed her eyes, took in a deep breath, and let it out slowly. Her whole body felt numb. She grabbed her purse out of the backseat, spotted her jean jacket nearby and grabbed it too, then shut the door and aimed the remote at the car. "Bubeep," and the car announced that it was locked. She put on her jacket and walked to the subway terminal in a daze. Amidst the blur of commuter rush hour she felt as if she were in slow motion, in a kind of a numb bubble, unaffected by the chaotic activity around her.

Once downtown, she exited the subway station and walked through the connecting mall to her usual coffee stop. The barista handed her a cup of dark roast. "Here's your usual," said the handsome Latino, flashing a dazzling smile at her. She took the coffee and nodded numbly at the clerk, oblivious to his charismatic vibes, and fishing around in the pocket of her jacket, she produced her coffee card. "Great—have an awesome day!" he said as he took her card. He swiped the card and handed it back to her while turning to the next customer. She mumbled her thanks and turned toward the street exit.

Out on the street, the wind whipped by and the chill in the air forecast the imminent November snow. The blustery air blew Tess's dark shoulder-length hair back, revealing her pretty face, which had no wrinkles despite her forty years of age. The wind pulled open her worn and comfortable jean jacket, which she deftly grabbed and buttoned with her free hand. Even though she was clad in a jean jacket, white T-shirt, faded blue jeans, and penny loafers, she had an air of elegance about her—as if she were of royal blood transplanted from an exotic locale, incognito in the busy downtown core amongst the city crowds. She leaned her slim figure determinedly into the wind in order to keep afoot, moving her hand with the coffee a slight distance away in case of drips. She was aware that the wind was cold, but today she did not feel it, unusual for her, especially since she had left her fall coat hanging by the back door at home. She walked with the crowd across the downtown intersection and over to the nearby university buildings, where her employer, Muldack Inc., rented laboratory and office space.

With a *bing,* the elevator arrived at the third floor of a tall glass and steel building, where small biotech companies were housed. Tess stepped out, juggling her coffee and her purse in her right hand, and walked across the large hallway over to a door with "322" on a small brass plate affixed to the top frame and a larger brass plate engraved with "Muldack" on the middle of the door. With her free hand, she turned the large brass doorknob and walked into the laboratory office. It was deserted at the moment, as most of the other technicians were late starters. She set the coffee onto her desk and tucked her purse into the big wooden drawer. The technicians' office had seven big old wooden desks packed into an oppressively cramped space that most likely had once served as an executive office. Well—make that six desks— Tess could hardly see Bruce's desk, as it was strewn with all of his earthly possessions, including a big blue clunker of a hockey bag. Tess wondered why he didn't just take his stuff home. She took off her jacket and hung it on a heavy steel office chair at her desk, grabbed her black lab notebook and turned toward the door to the laboratories, ready to immerse herself in the latest round of experiments.

A short while later Tess was focused on her latest cloning reaction while seated on a tall laboratory chair on wheels, located directly in front of a biohazard hood. She had on her Muldack white lab coat, two layers of purple neoprene gloves, and safety glasses. Her long, curly brown hair was the only giveaway that this was indeed the same Tess who, only a few hours earlier, had suddenly learned about the recent intentions of her husband of seventeen years.

With a gentle touch, like that of a neurosurgeon, she carefully dispensed the last of her master mix onto the side of a small plastic tube that was about the size of the top of her pinkie finger and, with a deft flick of her wrist, ejected the micro-tip on her pipetteman into the small biohazard bag, which was supported by a tubular fluorescent-pink steel stand. This was exacting work, and sometimes Tess held her breath as she precisely dispensed her master mix.

She carefully laid down her pipetteman on the stainless steel surface of the hood and held up her small rack of ten tiny plastic tubes. Each of the tubes had a tiny lid that was attached by an even tinier plastic tab. All of the lids were carefully arranged to point to the back of the rack and out of the way. Each tube had a number written in blue marker from one to ten. She surveyed the small bubble of viscous clear liquid that now resided inside and near the top of each tube. She moved the rack up a little higher and peered through the plastic rack to view another tiny bubble of liquid that she had previously placed in the very bottom of each of these tiny conical tubes. Satisfied, she carefully placed the rack of tubes down again and gently closed the lid on each tube. She rolled back on her lab chair and peeled off the second layer of gloves, flipping them into the larger biohazard bag in the stand beside the hood. She took a deep breath and shook back her hair, ready for the next step.

Tess retrieved her rack of tubes and walked over to a nearby lab bench, which had various pieces of equipment neatly arranged on its black, shiny surface. There were rows of white shelves above, some with carefully labelled bottles of liquid, and others with neat rows of binders and books. By this time of day the lab was full and bustling with activity. Behind her, Sarah was working at her lab bench, busily pipetting solutions into fresh bottles and chatting to Fred, who worked at the bench across from her. Tess, intent upon her experiment, arranged her ten tiny tubes symmetrically inside a small centrifuge and closed the lid. She set the dial at one minute, just a quick spin, and pushed the On button. The familiar swooshing sound filled the lab momentarily and then ceased. She opened the lid and began to pick out each tube and re-place it into her clear plastic rack.

"Hey, Tess—it's for you," called Sarah from behind her. She turned around and caught Sarah's cheery "good morning" smile as she held out the phone in a gloveless hand. Tess smiled back, peeled off her gloves, and took off her safety glasses, allowing them to dangle from the supporting cord around her neck. Then she stepped over to Sarah and took the phone. "Thanks," she said, and then responded into the phone, "Hello?"

"Tess. It's Diane. I just got off of the phone with Frank; he thought I should know what's happened between the two of you." Tess's eyes immediately filled with tears, and the busy lab suddenly seemed far away. *How could he do this to me?* she thought, feeling an almost physical ache in her heart. The total body numbness reappeared, and her legs began shaking again. Tess turned to face the wall so that her lab colleagues wouldn't see her face. "Oh," she squeaked into the phone, and the tears now began snaking their way down her face, past her safety glasses, and splashing down onto her lab coat. She gave a hearty sniff and tried to talk, but nothing came out.

"You're crying and can't talk, right, Tess?" said Diane sadly. Tess nodded numbly to the phone. "Call me back when you can talk, Tess. I'm so sorry." That did it; she could not hold back the tsunami of tears any longer, and a full-blown crying jag was on its way. *I can't do this in the lab, I just can't …* she thought to herself, clamping one hand over her face and hanging up the phone with the other.

She ran blindly past her lab mates, still covering her face, and out the door, making a beeline for the washroom, which was, thankfully, just across the hall. Sobbing, she burst through the door, startling two coworkers engrossed in conversation in the locker area. They stared at her teary face with open mouths, and for an instant she stared back bleary-eyed, and with another sob, she lunged into a cubicle and slammed the door. She threw herself against the back of the cubicle door—somehow avoiding the chrome hook, sobbing uncontrollably into her arms. She heard the quiet whispers of Karen and Margaret from the locker area, and then a shuffling and footsteps as they discreetly left the washroom, kindly allowing her some privacy.

Sometime later Tess emerged from the cubicle and headed for the sink. She removed her lab coat and placed it on a nearby counter, turned on the faucet, and splashed cold water over her face, using her cupped hands. She took a couple of deep breaths and looked up at herself in the mirror. A puffy-eyed Tess stared back. *Thank God for waterproof mascara*, she thought wryly. She dried her face with a paper towel. *I can't go back to the lab— not yet; I'll probably start blubbering!* she thought to herself miserably. She peeked out of the washroom door—the door to the lab was closed, and the coast was clear. Tess headed toward the stairs to the library on the fourth floor.

Soon Tess was sitting in a cozy chair tucked into the corner of the library and was immersed in the current issue of her favorite journal, *Nature*.

"Tess, what're you doing here? Aren't you going to the meeting?" asked a voice from behind her. She whirled around in the chair to find Bruce walking out of the Current Journals section of the library, a stack of papers in one hand and his glasses in the other. Her heart started pounding again, and she felt the sharp prick of tears threatening to start. She threw the *Nature* journal on a nearby coffee table and jumped up from the chair.

"What meeting?" she croaked, and turned toward the door to the hall, hiding her face and opening the door for Bruce, hoping he wouldn't notice her brimming tears. She took a deep breath, felt a tiny bit braver, and turned to look him in the eye. Bruce glanced briefly at her face, and then with a curt nod he swept through the opened door.

He can see that you are upset.

Tess slowly let out her breath and took another deep one. She hurried to catch up with Bruce's brisk pace and walked beside him. "Stark has called an impromptu meeting in the lab at eleven," he said, without looking at her. "It's about all the rumors that have been circulating, you know, about layoffs and all that stuff. Everyone's been madly updating their CVs (curricula vitae; that is, scientific résumés) these past few weeks—haven't you noticed?" He stopped and looked purposefully at her. "Are you okay?"

"Yeah. Well, no, but I'm okay now," she said weakly but didn't look back at him.

"Well, let's go then," he said, resuming his long strides toward the stairwell, and Tess quietly followed behind him.

Downstairs, the lab was warm and packed with people, a mix of those with lab coats on and many that had taken their coats off, and noisy with chatter. Thankful that Bruce had headed to the front of the lab and was busy chatting with Norman, the lab director, Tess wormed her way through the crowded lab back to her lab bench, to her forgotten rack of tubes. "So much for *that* experiment," thought Tess gloomily. The temperature-sensitive experiment was designed to work at thirty seven degrees Celsius, and even though the lab was warm, it was a far cry from the correct temperature.

"Hey Tess—for you again." She turned around to find Sarah once again holding the phone out to her, this time with her hand over the mouthpiece.

"What?" she said numbly.

"It sounds like Stark," said Sarah and waved the phone at her. She took the receiver from Sarah.

"Hello," she said.

"Tess!" boomed the voice of Stephen Stark, the vice president of Muldack. "Can you come up to my office right away?"

"Uh, yes," said Tess, wondering vaguely why Stark wasn't down there in the lab with everyone else at the meeting that he was supposed to be giving. She looked over at Sarah, who was staring back at her with one hand on her waist, and a "what's up?" look on her face. "Stark's going to be late," said Tess numbly, hanging up the phone and turning to walk out of the crowded lab, leaving Sarah staring blankly after her.

She walked up the stairs to the fourth floor again, this time turning right, down to the executive offices. *What the hell does he want with me anyway*, she thought to herself. *I'm just a lab techie, and Stark never talks with the lab people.* She opened the door to Stark's office. The spacious and modern office was empty. She stepped cautiously inside. The morning sunlight was streaming into the windowed office, glinting off the various industrial awards proudly displayed upon the chrome and glass wall unit to the left.

Looking straight ahead, she saw that Stark's laptop was closed, and the glass desktop was paperless and spotless, not even a fingerprint! The door clicked closed behind Tess.

"In here, Tess," called Stark's voice through an open doorway on the right of the office. Tess strode over and walked into a small boardroom. Stark was sitting at the far end of the oval wooden table, and a woman Tess had never met was sitting in the middle, with a manila envelope on the table in front of her. Stark motioned to the empty chair at the front of the table, and Tess, with prickles now forming at the back of her neck, felt a chill go down her back and at the same time a flush of anger rise in her face as she slowly realized the purpose of this surprise meeting. She took a few determined steps and arrived at the chair, and stood behind it for a moment, looking Stark right in the eye, sending a silent angry message. Then she quickly looked away and took a seat, hastily composing herself and focusing her thoughts.

A short time later she was exiting Stark's boardroom with her manila envelope, a small banker's box, and instructions to collect her personal belongings and to kindly exit the building within the hour. She could hear the next victim entering Stark's office as she left the boardroom. The layoff rumors were indeed true, despite Stark's announcement two weeks earlier that all was fine, and that no one needed to worry about their job or go about updating their résumés. *He didn't even bat an eye. It was no skin off his back!* she realized angrily. *Lying bastard!* she thought to herself.

~*Chapter 2*~

Chumbawamba

"Diane, you are my really good friend, so I know I can be totally honest with you. I'm just not interested in going to some dreary old church, okay?"

Tess was sitting in her home office, her feet up on the desk, the phone cradled on her shoulder, chatting with Diane. Diane and Tess had met a year ago during a workshop on "Small Business—Mistakes to Avoid for the Entrepreneur," and they somehow just clicked together. Diane, along with her husband, Bill, and young boy, Christopher, often had dinner together with Tess and Frank, before their split. Tess and Diane often met on their own, holding brainstorming sessions on starting small businesses and many other topics that seemed common between the two of them.

Tess had always had the feeling that she could do something more than just earning a living working for someone else. She had always been lucky and able to work in fields that were cutting edge, like genetic engineering, gene transfer therapies, and, most recently, as a cloning technician at Muldack, a biotech company. Tess's passion was research and discovering the unknown in the frontiers of science. But as exciting as these fields were to Tess, she still felt there was something *missing*. Tess had thought about starting her own business; perhaps this might be what she needed in her life. But there was even more to it than that. Somehow, deep down inside there was this feeling tugging away at the back of her mind, a feeling that she was supposed to do something … that her life had a purpose. But she could not pin it down any further than that.

Tess had gotten a flyer advertising a small business workshop in her home mailbox last year, and had immediately registered, thinking it could be another possible lead in her "purpose." Diane, meanwhile, already had a few small start-ups on the go and was always on the alert for strategies that could help her expand them, which is what drew her to the same workshop. Tess and Diane had met at the break, both heading for the coffee and snacks and an opportunity to chat with others, and had bumped into each other literally—realizing that both were wearing the very same fuchsia-colored wool jacket. This was a prelude to the many hearty laughs they would experience together as their friendship deepened during the year. Diane had immediately put the workshop material to good use, but Tess—although the information was valuable—felt kind of lost and had no idea what kind of business to start, and still did not find any leads as to whether creating a small business was even where her inner path, her purpose, lay.

"Oh, Tess, don't be such a stick in the mud," exclaimed Diane, yanking her back to the phone conversation. "Maybe you'll meet a nice, handsome, young Christian guy!"

Tess rolled her eyes. "Yeah, like he'd be interested in a forty-year-old divorced and unemployed lab techie!" she exclaimed. "What is it about that church anyways, Diane? Why are you going there? You're not *religious* or anything, are you?"

"Hey, Tess, actually, I don't know why I've been going there; it's just kind of a feeling, you know? I went to a small fund-raiser there last month, and one of the organizers asked me to come to the Sunday service. I don't know why, but I went, and, well, I really liked it, Tess, especially the singing! So I went again the next week, and it kind of, well I don't know, recharged my batteries or something." Diane lowered her voice. "Look, Tess, it's time for you to buck up, you know. Get out there and put the painful past behind you; do new things. I think you should come, at least this once. Please, Tess, do it for me!"

Oh man! That Diane knows just how to get her way, thought Tess. *Do it for her ... well of course I'd do just about anything for her!* "Okay, Diane," said Tess reluctantly, "but just this once—d'ya hear me?"

"Yes! That's my Tess!" exclaimed Diane. "Gotta go. I'll see you on Sunday!" and Tess was left staring absently at the phone as a click followed by a dial tone confirmed that Diane indeed had hung up.

Tess was thinking that she was not in the least interested in hearing a religious sermon, and her mind immediately came up with a dozen fine excuses that she could pose to Diane to cancel on Sunday. Tess absent-mindedly hung up the phone and looked at the piles of paper sprawled all over her desk, and her thoughts turned to her situation with Frank. She really felt that she could make their marriage work after Frank's little "fling" about five years ago. But now—it was definitely over. Thank God they didn't have any kids (Tess had been unable to become pregnant); that would have made it so much more complicated and painful. She had firmly decided that she and Frank should be sensible and civilized about their divorce, and had insisted too that they divide up everything themselves, to save on lawyers' fees. Once they had figured out their remaining mortgage, at the state of the housing market, and what was left of their assets—it was looking more than likely they'd both be in debt by the time they were actually split. And just to add icing to her cake, her last job interview had really bombed. She still was not working, and Tess really disliked being unproductive. Still, before the layoff, Christine—a former college classmate who was now with Serokine Corp., a biotech company working in the infectious diseases field— was scouting for a laboratory manager and had approached her. And indeed that interview had gone quite well. Serokine was developing test kits that could detect highly infectious diseases like Ebola and Hepatitis, and Tess found such work to be both cutting-edge and fascinating, and was truly hoping that this possibility might work out. But she had not heard any news back from them as yet. Tess had supposed that they'd found someone else more qualified for the job, as she didn't have much managerial experience. And none of her other job leads were even resulting in interviews.

What's that? A scratching sound was coming from … somewhere … She flung her long legs off of the desk and jumped up. Very faintly she heard, "Ee-ow, ee-ow!" *What the heck is that? That's not my Spunky, is it*? Spunky was Frank and Tess's cat (actually now officially Tess's cat after Frank recently gave her custody), a beautiful five-year-old tortoise-shell, and quite unusual in that she could at one moment be sitting quite calm and still, the next moment be jumping straight up in the air, the next racing around the house, and the next climbing up the drapes. *Hmmmm, sounds like it's coming from this direction …* Tess walked over to the window and looked out. "Ee-ow, ee-ow!" Tess looked down and spotted a tiny, white, little fur ball of a kitten that was intently pawing at the basement window beneath the office! She tapped on the office window, and the kitten looked up. She blended perfectly into the snow, but those two big, beautiful, green eyes gave away the fact that there actually was a little creature sitting out there.

Tess ran out of the office, through the living room where the sleeping Spunky lay, and to the back door of the kitchen. She opened it up and peeked out. "Ee-ow!" She shoved on her boots and walked carefully into the frigid air. "Ee-ow!" Those big, green eyes blinked back at her. She carefully edged over to the kitten and crouched down with her hand extended. "Hey, little squeaky cat," said Tess, and the cute little fur ball touched her nose to Tess's outstretched hand. Then she stood up, arched her tiny back, and started purring! Tess's heart just melted. "Oh, yes, you're coming right in with me," said Tess, and scooped up the kitten, who just purred even more.

The following Sunday, Tess found herself in St Paul's resplendent church with Diane. The interior was quite incredible, decked out with stained glass and painted windows along each side; although they did not provide any sunlight, they did seem to be backlit, showing beautiful and ornate detail on each significant event in the life of Christ. The baptism of Jesus by Saint John was quite striking, and Tess stopped, gazing in awe at this window as she and Diane were on the way to their pew. The huge front altar had a domed arch adorned with magnificent paintings of angels and archangels, and also a scene depicting the conversion of Saint Paul, which struck Tess as quite cosmic looking. Tess briefly wondered why she felt so odd about this painting, and continued down the aisle. All of the pillars inside of the church also had either angels or the apostles carved onto them. The choir's singing had been extraordinary, and Tess had thoroughly enjoyed herself—until pastor Green came out onto the altar to speak.

She took a deep breath. *I'll try to keep an open mind, to try and understand just what Diane sees in this,* she said to herself.

> *"And gavest them bread from heaven for their hunger, and broughtest forth water for them out of the rock for their thirst, and promisedst them that they should go in to possess the land which thou hadst sworn to give them. But they and our fathers dealt proudly, and hardened their necks, and harkened not to thy commandments."*

Tess stifled a yawn and wondered why a man so scholarly and credentialed could be presenting such archaic literature to modern-day people? Pastor Green told how this passage related to recent events and provided lessons for everyday life. Tess glanced around the splendid church; every pew was packed, and most eyes were fixed on the pastor. *And what was he up to now?* The tone of his sermon had changed, and he was telling everyone to *ask Jesus* and that he would *call* you. *Just how would He "call" anyways?* Tess wondered to herself. Now people were standing, and some were walking to the front of the church, standing below the altar, where the pastor was now waving more to "come forward, brothers and sisters."

Tess glanced over at Diane, and was shocked to find her in tears! "Diane, what ..." Tess started to say. Diane jumped up and quickly brushed past her, sobbing! "Wait, Diane—what's wrong?" asked Tess, staring at her friend who was walking quickly down the aisle with the others to the front of the church. Tess immediately grabbed her purse and chased after Diane. She gently pushed past a few others, also crying, and found Diane right at the edge of the altar, still crying, but listening intently to Pastor Green.

Tess gently grabbed Diane's arm, and she turned around and embraced Tess in a huge hug. Tess hugged her back, and stepped away a bit, wondering what on earth was going on. Diane turned back toward the pastor, listening intently and dabbing at her eyes with a soggy ball of Kleenex.

Tess looked around her—most people had tears in their eyes and were either intently listening to the pastor or hugging the person beside them. Tess felt shaken by the whole thing, and tried to understand what the pastor was saying. Tess thought he said something like, "accept Christ into your heart," and then he said, "accept this commitment to Jesus from this moment forward." Everyone, including Tess, made the commitment, the "sinners' prayer," line by line as the pastor spoke it. When they were done, people were hugging one another, and some still had tears in their eyes, but all apparently realized that they had just had a significant experience. *This must be what it's like to have a spiritual experience!* Tess thought. As Diane and Tess turned with the crowd and started walking back to the pew, an earnest young man standing in the aisle handed each of them a pamphlet that seemed to provide some guidance on their new commitment. Back at their pew, Tess quickly tucked her pamphlet into her purse and looked over at Diane, who seemed quite composed again and was putting on her coat. Tess was surprised at how quickly Diane had composed herself.

"I've got to go, Tess" she said. "Oh, by the way, Christopher says to say hi to Aunt Tess. She smiled and whirled around and headed quickly away, leaving Tess standing at the pew looking at the back of Diane's bright red coat as she rushed out the front door of the church.

Diane's son, Christopher, was a real cutie pie. He was about five or six (Tess could never remember his age exactly) and loved to dance. Shortly after she and Frank had split,

Tess had dinner together with Diane, Bill, and Christopher. Afterwards Christopher had asked his dad to put on his favorite tune from a nineties group called Chumbawamba, a cheerful tune called "Tubthumping." Away he went, dancing all over the living room, and when he heard, *"I get knocked down,"* down on the floor he went, and then, with, *"but I get up again—you're never going to keep me down,"* he jumped back up and laughed and laughed. So Tess had danced with him; around and around the living room floor they went until they were both gasping and giggling on the floor.

Smiling to herself at the thought of Christopher's sandy curls bouncing up and down and the sparkle of his laughter, Tess shrugged into her winter coat and joined the crowd in the aisle of the magnificent church, feeling a lot brighter than she had in some time. *What brilliant lyrics*, thought Tess as the song "Tubthumping" played in her head. *Don't let life knock you down*, she thought. *Just get up again!*

Tess arrived home, and as she put the key in the lock of the front door she hear, "Ee-ow, ee-ow!" coming from inside the house. Smiling, she opened the door to find her little white fur ball meowing and pacing, and the more refined Spunky sitting nearby aloofly watching. "Hello, my Squeek!" exclaimed Tess, and dropped her purse on the floor and scooped up the kitten, who immediately began purring up a storm. Tess kicked off her boots and looked over at the answering machine in the kitchen—the red light was blinking. She walked over with Squeek in her arms and hit the play button.

"Tess, it's Christine—please call me as soon as you can. Bye!"

Finally! thought Tess. *Odd that she would call on a Sunday, though. I wonder if they work a lot of overtime.* "Okay, Squeek, down you go!" She carefully placed Squeek on the kitchen floor and took off her coat and laid it on the small chair from the kitchenette. She glanced at the twelve beautiful long-stemmed yellow roses in the crystal vase on the kitchen table. Her dad had sent her those for her fortieth birthday this past Monday. Tess smiled. He was so sweet to do that. The flowers and his birthday wishes had really cheered her. She leaned closer and sniffed—yes! She could still smell their sweet fragrance.

She grabbed her phone out of her coat, flipped it open, and scrolled down the menu looking for Christine's number. Both Squeek and Spunky had started rubbing up against her legs and purring, but Tess was totally engrossed in her mission to find Christine's number, unable to give them any of her attention. Ah, there it is! Shortly she heard Christine's cheerful voice.

"Hey Tess—thanks for calling me back so quickly!"

Oh, yeah! Tess thought to herself. *Like I'm going to take my time calling her back on my only job offer!*

"So—when can you start?" asked Christine excitedly, not allowing Tess to get a word in.

"Oh, Christine, I can start next week, if you like," said Tess. "This is really great of you; thank you so much. I'm very excited" she added.

"Great, Tess, see you tomorrow morning then. We have flex hours so anytime before ten is okay. Oh, and don't bring your lunch, there's tons of places to go out to eat here. We'll go grab a bite together, okay?" said Christine. "Bye now!"

"Bye," echoed Tess into the dial tone, as Christine had already hung up. *Whaddya know?* thought Tess, and she smiled to herself. It felt good to have a job again, and the prospect of doing some work in an exciting field like Ebola virus detection just gave her soul that lift she had been waiting for! She heaved a deep sigh of relief and hung up the phone. Chumbawamba indeed!

~Chapter 3~

Who's That Talking?

Tess got on the subway—there were no seats, and there also was no access to grab a handrail, as the subway was quite full that morning. She was subway surfing again; her laptop case and purse were slung over her left shoulder. The latest edition of *Nature* was in her right hand, and she was standing in the middle and sideways to the flow of the subway train with her knees slightly bent, trying to keep her balance and read a few snippets from her journal at the same time. With much of her focus on keeping her balance, Tess certainly wasn't getting much reading done. Thoughts of Frank tugged at her, and she could hardly believe that six months had passed since he had announced he was leaving. The train came out of the underground tunnel into the bright, blazing sunshine, and Tess looked up and peeked over the shoulders of her subway mates to see the outside world rush by.

Frank and Tess had sold their house, unfortunately at a loss, and Tess was now in her own apartment, which was close to the subway line in the upscale Lawrence Park area. She shared her new digs with both Squeek and Spunky, and

Tess found them to be such loving companions. That little white blessing of a cat, Squeek, was such a delight to Tess! They played a little game each morning; Tess would awaken slightly when she felt Squeek jump onto the foot of the bed, and determinedly Tess would keep her eyes shut. Squeek would slowly and delicately tiptoe along the side of the bed, ever closer and closer to Tess's face. It was all Tess could do to not open her eyes and smile at Squeek, who by now would be so close she could hear her purring. And then Squeek would bring her nose right up to Tess's face; Tess could feel Squeek's breath on her face. Then Squeek would carefully place the tip of her front paw over Tess's mouth, and it would be all over. Tess would "awaken" with a smile, beaming at Squeek, her little white angel of the morning!

Tess and Frank had split all of their belongings in a very civilized fashion. They kept in good communication with one another without letting negative emotions like anger and frustration get in the way of their ability to work together on their separation. Tess reflected back at how calm she was during that time, and thought that perhaps she didn't get angry because she had totally let go of him emotionally. She knew that she could not trust him, not after two indiscretions, and because of this also knew that she could no longer be married. To Tess, trust was a huge part of the marriage commitment, and if this was gone there was really no sense in trying to make the marriage work.

Tess sold many of her belongings during a garage sale in the spring just before selling the house. She'd even sold her treasured *Star Trek* collection, the *original* series, for two hundred dollars. Tess was a confirmed Trekkie and very much into science fiction. Tess felt that Shatner and the original gang had the best chemistry in the original *Star Trek* series, and she was now sorry that she'd sold her collection. But, she was moving on, putting her past behind her, getting a fresh start.

"Oops!" The train lurched, and she sidestepped to keep her balance, jostling a teenage boy who was immersed in his MP3 tunes. He didn't seem to notice, and Tess quickly glanced at his face. His eyes were closed, and he seemed totally unaware of the world around him. Tess stepped back and resumed her surfing position in the middle of the train, which was once again inside the underground section of the subway approaching the next stop. She tucked her journal into the side pocket of her laptop bag as the train stopped, and a new batch of commuters got on. She spotted a well-dressed and really quite exotic-looking African woman who had her small black Holy Bible open. Tess had tried reading the Bible—but just couldn't get past all of the thees and thous. The language was too archaic. After her experience with Diane at St Paul's, Tess had read through the brochure, and came to the realization that they had made a commitment of sorts, a spiritual commitment, to Jesus. In Tess's forty years, she had done many things, including skydiving and motorcycling (Tess claims to her friends she did these daredevilish things because of a "fun gene" that she inherited), but she had never done anything spiritual before.

As a matter of fact, Tess was quite the neo-Darwinist. "Show me the proof" was always her retort whenever the subject of religion or spiritual things came up in conversation. To Tess, science was always able to explain everything, even the evolution of humankind. She always kept current in the field of genetics, and observed the evidence of how closely related the DNA of certain species were, including man and primate, and the overwhelming belief regarding the existence of the human species was that humans arose through the process of natural selection. This was Tess's firm belief, and her very work, in the biotech area in the field of molecular biology, to her was validation of those beliefs. The proof of evolution was in the DNA of all living things! Or at least that was what Tess had thought, until now.

Tess really didn't quite know what to make of her spiritual experience, but did feel a certain *je ne sais quoi*. Perhaps it was desire to learn, know, and understand exactly what she had done at St Paul's that day. This was a turning point in her life, a shift in direction so that she might discover her special purpose in life! In following up on her commitment, Tess had gone to a Christian bookstore to look for a Bible, thinking she'd purchase one written in current language. All of the traditional Bibles had language that was too archaic for Tess. So she wandered around the store, and seemed drawn to a shelf at the back that carried Christian novels. She slowly scanned the book titles, and then stopped in the middle of the row.

That's the one.

She was staring at a book called *The Message. Hmm, that one seems interesting*, she thought. She pulled it out. It had a funky kind of night-time metropolis-type picture on the front, and in wavy text across the picture was, "The New Testament in Contemporary Language—Like You've Never Read It Before." She flipped open the book and scanned one of the pages. It seemed quite friendly to read, and did seem to be speaking about biblical events. Tess felt that this was the right one.

"Bloor," the train operator called, and Tess was back in the world of the commuter. The train stopped, and half the people exited the train. Tess moved her way through the crowd to the closed doors on the other side of the subway car. A throng of people was trying to get onto the train.

That contemporary Bible was quite interesting to read though, remembered Tess, and she felt that something on the edge of her awareness was spurring her on to read more. So, every day she read a chapter or so. And she'd even found a church close to her new apartment, and was attending most Sundays. The pastor's sermons were quite good, with contemporary language, and he put his heart into his sermons. And it did seem that each time she learned something, even if it was just one little tidbit that seemed to fit with what was going on in her life at that moment.

Tess focused on working her way to the opposite side of the train and walked out amongst the throng of other morning commuters. She went in the opposite direction of the crowd to the east exit, where her coffee shop was.

Soon Tess, with her steaming, tall, bold concoction, was in front of a tall, glass, modern, high technology tower. This innovative high-tech center was located in the downtown core, and Tess was working in the research and development lab of another biotech company, Serokine Corp., which had facilities on the tenth floor. Tess marched in as the automatic glass doors opened, and strode purposefully through the spacious foyer over to the bank of elevators. Once on the tenth floor, she walked to the entrance to Serokine and placed her left hand on a letter-sized biopad atop a waist-high stand, balancing her laptop case and purse on her shoulder and her coffee in her right hand. The pad scanned her handprint, and a low beep confirmed her security ID, and the entrance doors whooshed open. She stepped into the hallway, lined with glass walls and doorways to various laboratories and offices, and headed toward the end of the hallway. She heard voices and the sounds of lab equipment running as she walked briskly down the hall.

"Oh, there you are, Tess," exclaimed Sheila, whose elegant figure had emerged from one of the lab doorways on the left and now stood right in front of Tess. "You won't believe what Philadelphia has done now," she said, shaking her head and tossing her red curly hair. Sheila was immaculately dressed and had her lab coat on over top. She was the head of viral research, and she still insisted on keeping her hand in the lab, often staying long hours into the night to complete the final touches on experiments. Serokine was developing a kit to detect Ebola in human bodily fluids and various other substances, as part of a biodefense contract. They had worked up a research process for making a small number of kits and were in the midst of developing it into a large-scale manufacturing process, the *d,* or development, part of research and development. The manufacturing plant was located in Philadelphia, in a facility that Serokine had purchased two years previously.

Tess stepped around Sheila and said, "Good morning, Sheila," on her way past, and kept on walking, knowing that she had a ton of work to get to and didn't have the time to engage Sheila and her latest gripe with the Philadelphia team. She called back, "Sheila, whatever the issue is now, why don't you speak with Mark? He's the liaison between your lab and Philadelphia; it's his job to transfer the process that your lab has developed, and also to keep the transfer itself going as smoothly as possible." Tess was now at the end of the hallway, and she turned the corner, hoping that Sheila would not follow her.

But Sheila would not be put off. She quickly caught up with Tess and put her hand on Tess's arm. Tess stopped and turned to look at Sheila, whose face was flushed with anger.

"Tess, they've completely bastardized our process; they'll never be able to make a kit that runs! You've got to listen to me. They are changing a critical enzyme just because it's cheaper, and they've also swapped nucleotide manufactures to a generic version. The kit will never work! How come they didn't check with us first? We could have informed them before they started doing their production runs! And, Mark doesn't listen to me anyways, his ego is just too damn big, if you ask me!" retorted Sheila. Tess calmly sipped on her tall bold until Sheila had finished. She had fielded similar complaints from other research scientists about the changes required to create the manufacturing process for kit production.

Tess's short time as operations manager in this R+D lab had been unbelievably busy. It had been a ton of work for the research team to bring their lab up to GLP or Good Laboratory Practice standards, and for the development lab to turn their work into GMP or Good Manufacturing Processes. The development team burned the midnight oil on a number of occasions as they did the due-diligence work to bring their lab up to current standards. When these midnight sessions ended, Tess often sent the staff home in cabs. Tess also found that keeping a steady supply of chocolate in her office worked quite well to relieve stress for the lab staff (they'd often drop in when stressed out and whisk away a handful of dark chocolate kisses). GLP and GMP were the "lingo" of the biotech-manufacturing world, about which Tess was quickly learning. It was a real culture change for the researchers, used to working creatively and not within the strict confines of GLP and GMP regulations. There was quite a lot of conflict with the Philadelphia facility, which is why Mathew McGuire, Serokine's president and patriarch, had brought in Mark Lancaster, a systems engineer who had experience in transferring processes from small research scale to larger manufacturing scale. But no one seemed to be really communicating with each other to try and work things out; instead, they all seemed to simply be pointing fingers and placing blame. All except Mark, that is.

"Sheila, we've been through this already. They have to make compromises in order to scale up the process. Yes, the substitutions will cause a loss in performance, but you can't create a manufacturing operation out of a ten-kit process. Mark knows what he is doing. Please just *listen* to him."

"Oh, Tess, we're not trying to create a manufacturing operation—we're creating a kit that does a damn fine job of detecting Ebola." Sheila's hands flew to her hips, anger evident in her voice. "Don't you get it, Tess? The kit that Philadelphia's making will miss the virus more often than it will hit it! You just don't give a damn, do you?" Sheila exclaimed, and wheeled around and stormed back into the lab.

It's going to be a fine day, Tess thought to herself as she strode over to her office. Through the frosted glass Tess could see a tall, distinguished figure waiting inside her office. Mathew McGuire was inside, looking quite striking in his steel-grey Armani suit, arms folded on his chest and a stern look on his face. He was leaning on Pearl's desk, waiting for Tess as she stepped inside. Tess could feel the tension in the air. "Good morning, Mathew," said Tess pleasantly as she placed her coffee on her desk, inwardly bracing herself for what likely would be a verbal onslaught. Tess shared her office with Pearl, one of the development scientists. Pearl had come to Canada from India ten years ago and had worked her butt off to gain Canadian status as a PhD, even though she already had stature as a medical doctor in India.

"What's going on with Arlene?" asked Mathew angrily. He stood up and walked around Tess to close the office door. Tess knew what was coming. Mathew could be loud when he was angry. He turned around and took a step closer to Tess; his normally friendly blue-grey eyes had turned electric blue in anger. "She's bringing a suit on us, against Gregory, for sexual harassment." Why didn't you tell me earlier that something was going on?" he boomed at Tess. Tess stood her ground; her hands flew to her hips, and she stood tall, although she was only as tall as Mathew's shoulder.

Her eyes were fiery. "She's doing that just to piss us off, Mathew," retorted Tess loudly. Loud was the only way to get through to Mathew in his current state. "Look, Mathew, Gregory didn't even raise a finger to her. It's not his fault—it's Arlene. She's gone too far this time. Gregory is not in the wrong here," said Tess emphatically.

Tess had taken each of them aside when she heard that trouble was brewing between them, and it was clear to Tess that none of Arlene's complaints were valid. Arlene had been in Sheila's lab for about a year, and had launched complaint after complaint against Sheila. For no good reason as far as Tess could see, and she had assumed it was a personality conflict. After discussing the situation with Sheila, they thought it best for Arlene to try again in another department. Arlene had agreed to accept a position in the development department, under Gregory's direction. But the complaints simply shifted their focus from Sheila to Gregory.

"We've got to fire Gregory, Tess. There's no ifs, ands, or buts about it. Serokine can't deal with any kind of lawsuit right now; the stock is in the cooker, and it'll plunge if word gets out that we have a court case against us." Mathew was both pacing and yelling now. Tess kept her ground. She knew that she was right, and Mathew was wrong. All she needed to do was get his attention. Right now he was venting, letting off steam, and inside he was trying to figure out the right thing to do. But outside he was on a tirade and wanting to take action, any kind of action.

Shake him.

That's a good idea, she thought, and wondered momentarily where that thought had come from. He had turned around, ready to let out another blast. His eyes were blazing with anger, and he ran his hands through his hair in exasperation. She stepped right up to him, reached up, and grabbed his shoulders and shook for all she was worth. "Listen up, Mathew," she yelled at him. His mouth opened—but nothing came out. It was like the tail shaking the dog—Tess, a slight wisp of a woman, actually being able to shake Mathew, who was pretty solid at six foot five, 240 pounds, and five times a week at the gym. He stepped back a bit, eyes widening in surprise, and just looked dumbly at her, and Tess saw her chance.

"Just listen, Mathew, please," said Tess quietly and firmly, still standing right in front of Mathew, an earnest look on her face as she looked him in the eye. "I *understand* that you are angry, and I *also understand* that you are worried about what happens to Serokine. But you can't fire Gregory; he is not in the wrong here. Arlene is in the wrong. It is her that we need to go after." She paused for a moment to see if this had sunk in. His face softened, but the eyes were still angry. He folded his arms and leaned back against Pearl's desk, not breaking his steely gaze, waiting for her to continue.

"It's been going on for over a year, first with Sheila in research. We thought it was a personality conflict, so we arranged a transfer into Gregory's department, but the trouble continued. We didn't tell you because we thought we could handle it ourselves with some guidance from the human resources department." Tess took a deep breath. "I had taken her out to lunch yesterday to get her out of the lab, away from work, to try and get to the root of the issue. She didn't say anything at all about sexual harassment, Mathew." *And, she must have already been making arrangements with a lawyer,* thought Tess. Otherwise Tess would not be having an angry Serokine president in her office just now.

"All right, Tess," barked Mathew. "I'll leave this with Norman Brentworth, our lawyer. Don't talk to Gregory," he said curtly. "Arlene's ID card will be wiped." He whisked past her and opened the office door and quickly walked down the corridor to his office without looking back at Tess.

Tess took in a deep breath, and let it out slowly. She didn't particularly like confrontations, and certainly did not like to yell. Tess rarely yelled, and really only remembered yelling at her twin brothers when she was younger and growing up in suburban Toronto. Born in Montreal, Tess and her family had moved to Toronto when she was two, and then the twins were born. Tess grew into the ringleader of troublemaking, always getting her younger brothers into trouble but never getting the blame because she was the girl, even if she was a tomboy. However, over this past six months at Serokine, Tess had the occasion to yell at least four times, and two of those times were at Mathew McGuire. The first yelling match was in the midst of a research group departmental meeting that got way out of control. That was a month after Tess had first joined Serokine, and she had dropped in on their meeting (with Sheila's permission) to inform the research group of the GLP regulations that their department needed to meet in order to avoid being fined or even shut down by Canadian regulators. Meeting the regulations in essence meant that a ton of work had to be done to get their instrumentation up to specifications, and then to maintain that state. And then they had to repeat critical experimentation to ensure their results were repeatable and thus valid. The scientists were quite ruffled at the prospect of having this kind of formality and rigidity placed upon their work. They felt that it stifled their creative efforts and that it would take them much longer to accomplish their goals. "That's bullshit," exclaimed Rod McLaherty, Serokine's lead research scientist. "You can't make us do all that," he added loudly, his face flushing.

"Yeah," chimed in Dolly, one of the lead technicians in

the lab, "that will take years to do; we'll never get our kit finished!"

"Listen, gang" Sheila chimed in. "We have to do this; we'll never be able to sell our kit if we don't have a qualified lab," she said loudly but firmly.

"Bull," repeated Rod, standing up. "I'm not doing it, and we're wasting our time here. Let's get back to work everyone," he said, pushing his chair away from the meeting room table.

"Sit down, Rod," yelled Gregory loudly. "We need to talk this through."

"Like hell we do," retorted Rod, and the meeting went to hell in a handbasket, with everyone shouting at each other.

Tess had been aghast, not knowing what to do. Her first formal meeting at Serokine was totally out of control. So she did the only thing she could think of; she sucked in a deep breath and yelled back, "*Stop it*," banging her fist on the table. Her coffee cup jumped, and the projector rattled. They were still going at it. Tess briefly wondered if they were loud enough for people outside the meeting room or even in the offices upstairs to hear them. "Shut up—everyone!" And she banged both fists on the table. The room fell silent, and all eyes were on Tess.

Just at that moment Mathew had opened the meeting room door behind Tess and peeked inside. "Just what is going on here?" he said loudly.

Tess whirled around, and the words were out of her mouth before she realized who she was looking at. "We are under control here. Please leave—now," she said sternly. *Holy crap!* She thought to herself, her heart pounding. *I've just told the president of the company to essentially take a hike!* He turned those steely eyes on her and paused for a moment, assessing her demeanor. Tess didn't dare to even blink, and looked right back at him. Her hand had started shaking, so she steadied it on the meeting room table. His eyes softened. Mathew seemed satisfied with that; he gave her a curt nod and closed the door. And now, Tess had just experienced her second yelling match with Mathew!

"Morning, Tess" said Pearl, breezing into the office with her briefcase in hand. Her long and beautiful black hair was woven into a beautiful braid, and she wore a colorful silk scarf that matched her top.

Thoughts of the stormy meeting dissolved, and Tess replied, "Morning, Pearl—love your braid!" Pearl smiled brightly back at Tess, and then Tess turned to her laptop, still in her bag, ready to finally begin her day.

She put her laptop on her desk. *That laptop is the best investment I've ever made,* Tess thought to herself. It had put her further in debt, but it was worth it. She'd been able to take her work home with her, and after a bit of arm-twisting of the director of the information technology department, she could also do Serokine e-mails from home using a corporate secure log in. She was logging in a ton of hours, but the pay was good, and she was steadily working her way out of her half of the debt that she and Frank had amassed. Tess enjoyed the challenge of managing the lab, and the work that the research and development (R and D) groups were doing was really quite exciting, and gave her a sense of purpose. Tess heard the familiar Windows theme as Pearl's computer was also setting up, and Pearl sat silently in front of her computer.

Tess hauled a few papers out of the side pocket of her laptop bag and scanned them as she placed them on top of the piles of paper already stacked on her desk. She sat back in her chair and looked into her computer screen as her e-mails loaded up. Looks like about fifty e-mails since last night, she reckoned, and started sifting through them.

Sometime later she felt a now-familiar presence, and it felt insistent upon getting her attention. She stopped in the midst of answering one of her last e-mails. *Wow … that feels like … well, it feels just like the Holy Spirit …* Tess thought to herself, remembering back to the first time she felt this spiritual presence. She'd heard the pastor at church talk about the Holy Spirit, and how it could make you feel like a million bucks once you *had* it.

Tess wasn't sure exactly what that was at first, never having had any previous spiritual encounters in her forty years, but a few weeks after her visit to St Paul's with Diane, Tess had been walking to the subway one morning with her MP3 on. She had read a few paragraphs from *The Message* just before leaving for work, as she had been doing every morning, and a certain part had really stuck with her. Jesus was teaching his growing following of disciples and had left the house of a girl who was reportedly dead. Jesus claimed that she was not dead—just sleeping—and woke the girl up. As he left the house, two blind men followed him. He asked them if they really believed that Jesus could heal them. They said, "Why, yes, Master!" Jesus had touched their eyes and said, "Become what you believe." And the blind men could then see.

It was the "become what you believe" that struck Tess. The words had seemed to almost jump off of the page and speak to her heart. "Become what you believe," she said out loud as she walked into the subway. It felt good to say that. "Yeah, I can do that," she said. And a recent favorite tune came up on her MP3; "Shout, shout, let it all out," sang Tess happily along with the group Tears for Fears, feeling quite marvellous. It was like she was as light as a feather, and her heart was gleeful—as if she were a kid again, singing her favorite song. She couldn't help but have a huge smile on her face, and she sang all the way to the subway station and then merged with the throng of commuters. She couldn't quite figure out why she was feeling so damn good, when it suddenly struck her. "It makes you feel like a million bucks," the pastor had said. *That must be it! It was the Holy Spirit!* Tess wasn't quite sure what that exactly was, but she sure felt great! Tess remembered thinking that maybe this Holy Spirit was letting her know she was on the right track or something.

Thinking back, Tess remembered another encounter after the yelling match with the research department. Back at home, Tess had unwound with a steamy lavender essence bubble bath (Tess's favorite stress relieving activity). As she sank slowly into the bubbles, she had felt that presence again, only much stronger, feeling almost euphoric, and this time she could see something in her mind's eye, a white ball of light that seemed, well, so exceedingly *compassionate*. Back in her office with Pearl, it was this certain presence, this *compassionate* presence, that Tess was noticing. Tess looked around her office. Pearl was silently engrossed in the report on her computer screen. Tess closed her eyes and could see that marvelous white ball of light. *Hmmmm, I wonder why it's here now? Maybe that's where I got the idea to shake Mathew this morning,* she thought. *So I could get his attention and make him listen.* She could have sworn there was a voice that actually said, "Shake him," to her. *But I really don't know,* she thought. *Perhaps I'll file that one away in the I'll-learn-what-that-is-about-later box,* she thought to herself and turned back to her e-mails. In her short six months as a Christian, Tess had a fair number of items already in that box.

~Chapter 4~

Go Talk to That Man

"Oh, come on, Tess, you will like this. And, there's someone I want you to meet."

Oh-oh, Tess thought. Her new friend Helen was imploring her to come on this singles hike. Meeting a single man was the last thing Tess wanted right now. She simply wanted to immerse herself in her work and not complicate things with dating.

Tess had met Helen at the church evangelism group. Tess really didn't like the idea of evangelizing anyone, and especially not going outside the church into the public and knocking on doors. But she'd started the evangelism course just to see what it was all about. Tess loved to learn and wanted to know more about her new spiritual experience, and she now found herself in the middle of an excursion. That's where she and Helen had met.

"What do you mean—we're going out to visit someone?" asked Tess incredulously.

"Well that's why we're all here, isn't it?" said Helen.

Tess was taken aback. "I'm not sure I want to go along ...

can I pass on this one"? Tess didn't like the idea of forcing religion down anyone's throat.

"Oh, it's all planned, Tess" said Helen firmly. "You've taken enough classes to know what we are to do. Sparky is picking out a house for us to visit. Come on, now, we'll all pray together that there will be someone at this house that needs to hear what we have to say." Tess joined in their prayer, and when they were done the four of them went to see Sparky. Tess tagged behind them, secretly hoping the heel on her shoe would break so she'd have to stay behind.

"Okay, Sparks," said Helen with a smile, "let's see what you've come up with." Sparky, a former electrician, now retired, organized the visits for the evangelism teams. Tall and greying, with a very friendly smile, Sparky was a devoted man. He took the tall stack of friendship cards that were filled out by those attending the church over the past few weeks, and recited a prayer over them, that those persons that were truly in need would be visited by the right team, which could say just the right thing in just the right way, that would help those persons to come to understand that Jesus could *save* them. Tess always hesitated when she heard the words *Jesus saves*. Although she was being taught that Jesus saved us from sins, to Tess it felt different than that—more like, *Jesus awakens*. Tess felt more alive, with a sense of wonder at this new spiritual journey that she seemed to be on.

Sparky handed the group four handpicked cards, and they were on their way. The evangelism excursion had been quite the experience for Tess. They'd driven to the east end of the city, and the occupants of the first three houses either were not home or did not answer the doorbell. All four of them were now standing in front of a very large and elaborate home. Helen determinedly pushed the doorbell again. "I'm sure it didn't ring the first time," she said. This time they all heard it ring. Then they heard footsteps, and the door opened. Music was playing softly in the background, and a woman with a very friendly face was saying hello to them. Helen dutifully gave her statement about why they were there, following up from the church on the friendship card that the persons at this address had recently filled out.

"Oh, you're all from the church—please, come in," she said pleasantly. The music was a bit louder once they were inside the house, and Tess recognized the music as one of the contemporary Christian songs that the choir liked to sing, "Here I Am to Worship." Tess smiled to herself as she realized that the people in this home were already Christians. This was just the right place for a novice evangelism team to come and practice their skills. Sparky had picked just the right card! Tess marvelled at this spiritual coincidence, and she now understood the purpose of the prayers of Sparky and the team. Their prayers were a spiritual request sent to God or Jesus or the Angels, or perhaps to all of them, and—voila! The right connections were made.

Tess's attention came back to Helen on the phone. "Well, Tess, what'll it be? Are you coming on this hike or not?" asked Helen again. Tess had left Helen's question unanswered and was staring down at the floor. Squeek was curled up at her feet with her head resting on Tess's left foot. Tess could feel her purring in her sleep and wondered momentarily how cats could do that. "Tess, are you there?" Helen was insistent that Tess come with her on the singles hike this Saturday. "We're all meeting just down the street from you at Lawrence Park. How much easier can it get—it's only a two-minute walk for you?" she quipped. Tess gave in.

Saturday morning found Tess on tiptoe peeking out of the high window of her basement apartment. It was clear and sunny; the air felt warm on her face—no need to take a jacket for the hike! Tess stepped away from the window and stopped suddenly. *What the heck is that?* A low jarring kind of noise seemed to be coming from—well, it seemed to be coming from all around her. To Tess it almost sounded like what a roar from a Tyrannosaurus would be like, powerful—but at the same time muted as if it were far away. Listening to this jarring noise was somehow making her think that this particular sound would originate from two very large things being forced together or forced to slide past each other. Then she felt it, a slight shaking—an earthquake! Tess could feel the floor vibrate ever so slightly, and she caught sight of the vase of fresh flowers on her kitchen table—they were trembling slightly as well. And then just as quickly as it came, it was gone; the vibration and the roaring sound had stopped. It had all happened so fast! Tess felt that she had actually heard the jarring noise before the floor started to shake—but that couldn't be right. She shook her head as if to clear it. Toronto didn't get very many earthquakes; in fact, Tess had never felt any tremors until now. It had all happened so fast! Tess made a mental note for later, to check for news stories about the quake.

Her hair brushed across her face, and she turned back to the open window. A light breeze was still coming in, and Tess's thoughts switched to the morning's hike with Helen that she had reluctantly agreed to. A gentle wind was good; it would keep the summer's heat from becoming unbearable. In fact, it was a perfect day for a hike. Tess grabbed a bottle of water from her fridge and picked up her purse by the apartment door, and then she headed out, hoping that there wouldn't be any more earthquakes.

A few minutes later Tess saw Helen on the northwest corner of the main intersection. About forty or so were gathered on the corner, and it was nearing 10:00 a.m., the start time for the hike. There was a sturdy-looking woman heartily talking and laughing with some others as she handed them their tickets in exchange for thirty dollars. Tess was uneasily watching as the woman handed Helen two tickets. Helen walked over to Tess.

"Good morning, Tess. Here you go!" She handed the ticket to Tess, and Tess took it absent-mindedly.

"Oh, Stanley!" yelled Helen suddenly, giving Tess a start. "Here we are!" she called to a tall and handsome man. She grabbed Tess's arm. "Here he is—come on!"

Oh, man—that Helen. I just knew it—I don't want to meet anyone just now, Tess thought bleakly to herself. *I'm not ready for dating yet!*

Helen introduced Stan to Tess, and Tess shook his hand. "Hullo," said Tess.

"Nice to meet you, Tess," said Stan, and gave her a slight nod. He was nicely dressed in a gold-colored golf shirt and designer jeans; his dark hair had a touch of grey. Tess felt as if he were a more distinguished man that normally wore a blue banker's type of suit. *Hmph,* thought Tess. *Seems nice enough, but I'm not interested in meeting you or anyone else,* she thought firmly to herself as she smiled weakly back at him and then looked quickly away.

The light had changed, and everyone was crossing south, and both Helen and Stan had disappeared into the throng of people. Tess hesitated, and then crossed, lagging behind the crowd a bit. By the time she got across the street the light had changed and was now green in the other direction, and she moved together with the crowd to cross the street to the entrance to Lawrence Park. She waited on the corner for a bit as the rest of the crowd moved past her. *Where's Helen?* thought Tess. Then she spotted Stan's tall and distinguished form; he'd crossed the street and was just ahead of her on the sidewalk. He was looking the other way and didn't see her. *I'll just stay here, and wait for Helen,* thought Tess.

Go talk to that man.

Tess felt like she had been shoved firmly forward. *Huh?* she thought, looking around. No one was behind her. It felt as if she just had someone right behind her, whispering into her ear with hands on her shoulders that had pushed her toward Stan. Bewildered, she looked forward. Stan was still in view but was moving quickly ahead.

Go!

Okay! thought Tess, wondering just who was speaking to her, and started moving ahead before she was shoved again. Tess walked quickly up through the crowd and caught up with Stan.

"Hey, Stan, do you mind if we walk together?" asked Tess. Stan looked over at Tess and flashed a brilliant smile back at her.

"No, of course not." Tess couldn't help but smile back, and she resolved to herself to get to know this man.

It was a gorgeous day, and Tess kept walking and chatting with Stan. Tess learned that Stan had owned a landscaping company for ten years, along with a business partner. Tess was surprised that Stan had such a physical job, because he seemed to have such an intellectual demeanor. Stan was living with his dad, and this allowed him to keep a low overhead for running his business. The group of hikers arrived at Sunnybrook Park, where they all stopped for lunch. She lost sight of Stan as the hikers scattered—some over by the lunch counter, some finding benches in the shade, and others heading over to the washrooms.

"There you are, Tess," exclaimed Helen. Tess whirled around to find a smiling Helen behind her, holding two lemonades. "I was watching you two, you know—you look good together," said Helen excitedly, handing Tess one of the lemonades. "Oh, look, here he comes." Stan strode lankily toward them.

"Hello, ladies," said Stan, a smile in his deep voice. "May I sit with you two?" he asked politely, motioning to the bench that was nearby, and sat down before either Tess or Helen could answer. Stan had brought a sandwich with him and started opening it. Helen motioned with her hand and mouthed silently that Tess should sit beside Stan, and then indicated she would sit beside Tess. Tess hesitated. Helen looked exasperated at Tess and then pushed her in front of the bench beside Stan. Tess sat stiffly down and found herself sandwiched between Stan and Helen.

Helen was smiling like a Cheshire cat. "Well, Stanley, isn't it a lovely day to be walking with a lovely woman," said Helen, leaning around Tess to catch his eye.

Holy smokes! thought Tess. Helen was making her feel like a mouse that was dangling from a cat's mouth, and she stretched her arms a bit to try and relax her tense muscles.

"It certainly is," said Stan, nodding at Tess and then smiling at Helen. Tess opened her lemonade and took a big swig to try and distract herself. Tess could feel Helen getting ready to make another comment about Tess to Stan, and she couldn't stand it any longer.

"Well, guys, I'm going to find the ladies' room. I'll catch up with you later, okay?" she said as she stood up. She nodded to both of them. Helen's mouth was open, but no words came out. Stan smiled back at Tess and nodded. Tess hurried off to the nearby washrooms, glad to have made her escape.

A short while later the walk had resumed, and Tess found herself on her own, in a space between two groups of people walking together. It was really quite pleasant walking in the warm sun, in and out of the forest. The smell of the fresh forest air was almost intoxicating as she walked over the footbridge crossing over the Wilket Creek (which looked more like a river to Tess). It was also nice to be alone with her thoughts. Tess felt uncertain about engaging in a relationship with Stan—or anyone else right now. She was determined to make a new career for herself at Serokine and felt that she didn't have time for dating right now. It had been such a great opportunity for Tess, her first management position, although quite challenging, but she was so close to paying off her debt. The hours she'd put in there had been quite ridiculous; there was even one morning recently she had gotten to the office at 6:00 a.m. to try and get an early start on the fifty to one hundred e-mails that she usually had to respond to every morning. But she felt a deep sense of purpose in her work there, and maybe, Tess thought, immersing herself in her work was helping her to find out who she was and what she was capable of achieving. Concentrating on her career was also a way of letting go of the old Tess that was formerly married to Frank, and of embracing the new career-minded Tess.

Tess recalled an unusual event that had taken place the morning of the 6:00 a.m. start at work. The sun was just up, and it was actually quite beautiful being downtown exiting the College Park subway into the small park surrounded by office towers. She didn't normally exit there, but her regular exit wasn't open yet, and she had to exit through the courtyard. The sun was glinting off the towers and through the trees; the birds were announcing that the day had just begun. As Tess had strode back toward Bay Street a young black fellow had caught up with her. Tess was taken aback to find a homeless person panhandling on the street so early, but he seemed a little different somehow. His appearance was very clean, and he tried to ease her apprehension by reaching inside of his T-shirt to produce a very simple wooden cross.

"Please, Miss," he said earnestly to Tess. "I just need enough money to get the bus to Sudbury. Please, will you help me?" Tess's heart had warmed at the simple wooden cross that hung by a suede thread around his neck. It was the cross from a Christian boys' school.

"What's your name?" asked Tess.

"Valentino," said the young man, smiling brightly, and then suddenly he became very serious again. "Please, I need your help. The bus station is just down the street, and I need to be on a bus to Sudbury this morning. I have a job waiting in the mine there." He stopped and pleaded at Tess with his eyes.

Tess was weighing everything Valentino was saying to her. She felt he was genuine, even though he could have easily been making it all up. The Greyhound Bus Station was just down the street, so that was true. She knew that there was a mine in Sudbury, the "Big Nickel." But why was he here on his own without any money?

"How much is the bus fare?" Tess asked him. He gave her a big smile in return.

"Eighty dollars," he said.

Whew! thought Tess. That's a pile of money to be giving away. She looked carefully into Valentino's hopeful eyes. He looked unflinchingly back and gave her another big smile. Well, he was obviously in need. Who was she to judge his situation? As Tess recalled her meeting with Valentino she felt good about just being able to help someone in need. Somehow being able to help those in need seemed to be a part of the new Tess, as if this were in sync somehow with her purpose.

"Oomph." She was back in the world of the Sunnybrook Park hikers, and the group that was behind her was walking faster than she was, and one of the members of the group had accidentally bumped into her as they passed by.

"Sorry 'bout that, Miss," he called without even turning around to look at her to see if she was okay.

Tess found herself to still be walking on her own, and she sauntered across another footbridge in the bright sunlight. Remembering the Valentino incident, she did not know what made her give so much money to a person she'd only just met. Somehow she just seemed to know that she could trust that he was genuine. And now, what about Stan, this man she had only just met? Should she begin dating again? Was Stan the right man to be dating right now? How could she trust any man after being dumped by her ex for another woman? Could she take time from her work to date? All of these questions were whirling through Tess's mind as she walked back into the forest, smelling the musty natural scents from the trees and the moist ground. She inhaled deeply, and detected a faint whiff of cedar amongst the myriad of scents.

Then, Tess felt that *compassionate* presence again. Without hesitating, she asked with her thoughts: *Is Stan the right man for me?*

She got a warm, euphoric, glowing feeling, and could see the white ball of light clearly in her mind's eye. It *felt* right. He *felt* right. The feeling stayed with her for a few more moments, and she basked in this euphoria and this knowing presence, and was thankful to God, Jesus, the Angels, and whoever else might be present with her just now.

"Hey, Tess," called Stan suddenly from behind her. Tess stopped and whirled around to find Stan's tall, handsome form striding toward her. She paused and watched him move purposefully toward her, hands in his navy blue windbreaker. She tried to assess his character by watching him carefully as he caught up with her. *He's quite handsome,* she noticed. *And, he's so very pleasant, but deep and thoughtful at the same time,* as she remembered their conversations from that morning. They were again walking side by side.

He feels like a genuine person, that he's being honest with me, she discerned.

"Want one?" he said aloofly, and held out a roll of wintergreen-flavored mints. Tess smiled; she loved those mints. Her grandmother always had some of those in her purse when Tess was visiting as a little girl. Those particular mints always made Tess feel that warm, special feeling that she had when visiting her "granny" in Montreal during the summer months off of school.

Tess politely took a mint and immediately started crunching on it. Stan looked over at her. "You're not supposed to chew those," he said. Tess looked over at him, and Stan was giving that special smile of his. She crunched down on another bit of mint and smiled back at him.

"I just love to crunch them," she said. Stan laughed, and quietly slipped his bigger hand into her smaller one as they walked through the forest together, and Tess's heart gave a leap of joy.

~Chapter 5~

Rampa

"Your mother is sick, Tess. She's been on the living room couch for the past week," said Harold.

"What?!" exclaimed Tess into the phone. "How come I didn't hear about this?" she asked Harold heatedly. Her heart was racing. Her mother was so far away, all the way across to the other side of the country, in Vancouver. Tess felt panicky. It was unusual for her mother, Rose, to be ill and to have been off of her feet for a whole week already! Tess's parents had divorced when she was twenty-one, and her mother had eventually remarried, to a wonderful man—Harold, and moved from Toronto to Vancouver. Harold was six feet tall, broad shouldered, big boned, and as strong as an ox. Being an engineer and owner of an international engineering organization, he was quite often out of the country. Rose kept busy running a designer fashion boutique in Vancouver's city center. And this gave Rose a chance to travel too, to New York, Paris, Rome, and also back to Toronto, to gather the latest fashions for her shop.

"She didn't want to bother you, Tess," said Harold in

his quiet but authoritative voice. "But I'm worried about her; she's been in quite a lot of pain."

"What?" exclaimed Tess again. "Why? What's going on? This sounds serious!" demanded Tess.

Harold described the events of the past weekend, where he'd taken Rose to the hospital, and she'd endured a battery of tests and been given some kind of painkiller that had given her serious side effects, including nonstop vomiting. She was back home again but with no information on what was wrong, and she was still apparently in a lot of pain, as she could not tolerate the medication.

"I'm coming out there," said Tess firmly to Harold. "I want to see her."

"Wait, Tess, we're going to Dr Moffat's tomorrow; let's see what the test results show first before you come all the way out here," said Harold. "Rose does not want you to worry."

Tess could not help but worry. She had an uneasy feeling. Her mother had never been ill like this, at least nothing other than an occasional flu. Her work in the boutique was her *passion*; she loved her store, and the clientele just adored her. In the twenty years she'd had the shop, Rose developed many devoted clients. Tess felt Rose's passion for her work; the shop is what had kept her healthy. Tess admired this and, at the same time, wondered about how to ignite her own passion and purpose.

"Then at least let me talk to her, Harold!" exclaimed Tess again.

"Yes, Tess, of course," he said, and Tess could hear him walking with the cordless phone over to the living room. She heard Harold explain to her mother that Tess was being insistent and that she should talk to Tess.

"Hi, Tess," said Rose. Her mother's voice sounded so very far away. "It's so nice of you to call."

"Mum!" exclaimed Tess. "What's going on?" she asked Rose. Tess listened to her mother recount the events of the weekend. She had severe pain in the middle of her back, and also in the front on the left side, under the rib cage. She had undergone rounds of scans and tests at the hospital, and was now at home firmly implanted on the couch, where she felt the most comfortable.

"Missy, please don't worry so much. We'll let you know tomorrow what the doctor says; don't go jumping on a plane for no reason," her mother implored her. Missy was Rose's pet name for Tess as a child, one that had stuck with her into adulthood.

Tess relented, and then said her good-byes, but wasn't very happy about it. *Might be her gall bladder,* Tess was thinking. If that's the case, it'll probably need to come out. Hopefully it's nothing worse than that, she thought to herself as she put down the receiver. She turned around to find Stan standing quietly behind her in the kitchen.

"Rose is sick?" he asked, a worried look on his face.

Stan and Tess had married on a beautiful Caribbean island, Antigua, only two years previous. Just the two of them flew down, and they were married in a gazebo by the water in a beautiful resort. They had spent a magical two weeks together on this lush tropical island. Tess couldn't believe how time had truly flown by for the two of them. When they first married, they were living in a low-rise apartment that was "no pets allowed." Tess had relinquished custody of her beloved Squeek and Spunky to her ex, Frank, who was kind enough to take Spunky back and adopt Squeek. They now lived in a house that she and Stan had purchased together. It had worked out well. Stan was older, unmarried (until meeting Tess), and had saved quite a bit of money from his years in the landscaping business. Combined with Tess's biotech income, they could afford a very nice but moderate-size house in the Toronto north central area. However, when they moved into the house Stan had told her in no uncertain terms that he wasn't ready for a pet in the house.

"I'm just not a cat person, Tess. Let your ex keep Squeek and Spunky," he had said. Well, that was that, thought Tess. But Stan was such a caring and respectful husband. He knew that Tess was building a career and worked long hours at Serokine, and that she also enjoyed volunteering at the church, but he did ask her to stop working on weekends so that they could spend some quality time together. He'd even come to church with her once in a while, but not as often as Tess would like. Stan was so completely different from Frank. He was so *interested* in her, asking about her work, engaging her in such lively topics of discussion, including surprising discussions on aliens, which he acknowledged that he'd been interested in since seeing a UFO during his childhood. Tess was so drawn to him not only intellectually but also romantically. Stan was an incredible lover, and they both loved to lie together naked and embrace, just holding each other afterwards. And he was so respectful. Stan never made any remarks about her church activities, but at the same time he made it clear that he was not interested in becoming a churchgoer or Christian himself.

Stan was still standing in front of her with a quizzical look on his face, waiting to hear about Rose.

"Yes, and I'm really worried about her, Stan," she said, and her voice cracked a bit. Immediately Stan embraced her in a bear hug. Stan's hugs always made Tess forget about whatever it was she was doing or thinking before the hug, and she squeezed him heartily back.

A few weeks after Tess's phone call, they found out that Rose had lung cancer. And it looked bad, because it had already spread to her brain. At least that's what the MRI was telling Dr Moffat. Tess had flown out to spend time with Rose and Harold. Stan, who did not like to fly, had instead sent his love and best wishes to both Rose and Harold. *Maybe it was all those years smoking,* Tess thought. Her mother had smoked most of her life, but had quit cold turkey five years ago. Although Rose never really said what prompted her to quit, Tess wondered now if she had the beginnings of some kind of health issue and was keeping it to herself. She never liked to bother Tess or her two twin brothers, Ron and Reggie, about her own health, but of course was very motherly about inquiring and caring about the health of her children.

Although Rose had gained some weight after she quit smoking, she still was such a very pretty woman, and combined with the many fashionable dresses that she wore to advertise her boutique, she was always so beautifully *together* somehow. Tess found her in a chocolate brown and beige designer robe and flowered beige silk pajamas, her sandy-colored hair up in an elegant bun, reclining on the living room sofa. Tess could see the pain in her pretty face as she kissed her hello upon her arrival. She had new medication that didn't have the terrible side effects of those she was given in the hospital, but it was obvious that they only took the edge off of the pain.

It seemed that it was too late for chemo, and that surgery was also out of the question, as the lung tumor that was causing the pain was also accompanied by many smaller satellite tumors, *too* many. However, they were considering radiation to shrink those in the brain and prolong the inevitable for a while. The prospects looked very grim indeed, and Tess was shocked.

Harold had really opened up to Tess when she was visiting Rose. He had always been so very busy at Emmiorp, his engineering company; he'd never really been around to chat much when Tess came to visit her mother. And

Rose's shop was in the care of the store manager, Ruth, who had given firm instructions to Rose not to worry about the shop. But now he had curtailed his traveling to be with Rose. Rose had been instructing Harold on how to cook, calling instructions to him from the living room while he was clunking about in the kitchen. It was now her mission to transfer all of her culinary knowledge to Harold. Rose was an amazing cook, and Harold was in the kitchen concocting her most fabulous recipe—Rose's spicy minestrone. Tess remembered this hearty soup from winter days as a kid, coming into the house on a cold and blustery day, and warming up on the wonderful concoction. The hot Italian sausage was sautéing in a humungous saucepan that Tess had named the Hercules of saucepans, while the soup itself was being concocted in a large pot at the back of the stove.

While the soup was simmering, Rose, Harold, and Tess had a chance to chat. Tess was so surprised to find that Harold had an interest in a Tibetan monk. "He's not a monk," affirmed Harold. "He's a lama; that's something quite different altogether. And, his writings are so aligned with what I've learned as a Mason."

Tess was shocked. Although she wasn't exactly sure what a Mason was, she had an idea that it involved spiritual activities, and she had no idea that Harold had a spiritual side. He had always seemed to be so business oriented and quite a logical thinker. Tess had asked Harold a plethora of questions, and had completely engaged Harold in this topic. Tess still was keeping one eye on Rose closely from her perch across the way on the loveseat. Harold sat close to Rose on a kitchen chair that he'd brought into the living room and parked close to Rose's new living quarters on the sofa. Rose had a small table near her on the other side, which had a glass of water, a half-nibbled cookie, her pain medication, and a small vase with a fresh pink rose in it.

Harold explained what a Freemason was, and Tess listened curiously. Rose had turned her head away and had fixed her attention to the television, which was on, but the sound was muted so they could all chat. He explained that there was a lodge in Vancouver that he attended regularly when he was in town. There was a body of work that they studied, which involved moral, philosophical, and metaphysical themes, and, yes, their works were kept secret—to preserve them, as when bodies of work become public they always seem to become distorted. It was the metaphysical works that Harold said were so aligned with the writings of Rampa, this Tibetan lama.

"Oh, Harry, dear, please stop it now. Don't be going on about your *funny* stuff to Tess. You know I don't like you to talk about it. *Please!*" said Rose emphatically, looking at Harold and shifting her position on the couch slightly to ease her back pain.

Harold immediately stopped, not wanting to upset Rose, and then got up to stir the soup, but he winked at Tess on his way back to the kitchen. "I have a book for you to take back with you, Tess. You'll find it quite interesting," he whispered to her. Tess smiled, happy that Harold was opening up and also about their common interest in things spiritual.

That had been three weeks ago, and now Tess was back at work on a cold, blustery December day. And not only was it quite a busy time at Serokine, there were rumors flying about a corporate merger—none of which had been confirmed by upper management. Morale was low, especially for Tess now with the news about Rose's health. Stan had been so great over these past few weeks, always there to encourage her and to offer his shoulder for her to cry on. But it was the book that Harold had given Tess that was on her mind right now.

The book that had captured her interest was called

The Third Eye, written by a Tibetan lama whose name was
Tuesday Lobsang Rampa. It was quite a weird title for a
book, thought Tess. It was really quite beautifully written
and so inspiring to read, this story of awakening, Tibetan
spiritualism, and the Buddhist way of life, in the truly
remarkable culture and country of Tibet. Somehow the
romance of the young sage's early life really allowed Tess
to forget all of the stresses upon her mind and truly absorb
herself in something completely different. And the advanced
metaphysical approach interwoven into the daily life of a
lama-in-training was truly astounding. It was so different a
culture and so incredible to read about Tibetan mysticism.

Tess realized that the Tibetan teachings were so outside
of the Christian realm, and many of the teachings would
be condemned as devil worship. Astral projection, crystal
gazing, aura deciphering, and such were some of the magical
or metaphysical techniques presented by Rampa—presented
as being a natural part of life for those who chose to pursue
the development of these techniques. For some reason, it
had totally captured her interest, and she had immersed
herself in the book. What especially resonated with her was
the death process, and that to Tibetan Buddhists, life did
not end with the death of the physical body. Physical death
liberated the spirit—or soul, which was the real carrier of
life. The soul had a life to go back to on another plane
of existence, and then would reincarnate again and have
another physical life. "The Wheel of Life" is what Rampa
called it, and it seemed to be just so *romantic* a notion to
Tess, kind of like having one adventure after another from
life to life. When your clothes are worn they are discarded,
and in much the same way the soul discards the body when
it is worn and torn, was the way Rampa described it. Death
is birth. Dying is part of the process of being born into

another plane of existence. It was starting to dawn upon Tess that many of the questions in her little I'll-learn-what-that-is-about-later box were being answered by the information in Rampa's book. Tess was realizing that life is—well, just so *immense*! Tess's neo-Darwin days were firmly behind her. Christian awakening had certainly opened her mind to the spiritual realm, and now the Tibetan teachings were opening doors to a vast storehouse of knowledge. Tess was so excited—there was just so much more to learn!

Just then her phone rang and jolted her back into the realities of working life once again. But it was not a colleague on the phone.

"Tess, its Harold." His voice sounded tense and curt. "You have to come right away. Rose is in the hospital." His words hit like stones, and Tess sank back into her office chair, her heart sinking. "Just a minute, Tess; I'm passing you to Rose."

Harold passed his cell phone to Rose, who briefly spoke, but her voice was so weak she was just whispering. Tess couldn't quite catch what she was saying—something about whispering tumbleweeds.

The words tumbled out of Tess all at once: "I love you, Mum. I'm coming soon; I'll be there tonight, okay?" said Tess cheerfully, but inside her heart was breaking. Harold was back on the phone, and his voice was shaky.

"Tess, she had a really bad spell, and I called nine-one-one. They've had her on morphine because the pain was so bad, and since then she's gotten so weak. It doesn't look good, Tess. You should be here as soon as possible. Please, Tess." Harold didn't need to say anything more; Tess was already at the airline website looking to book the next flight to Vancouver.

A few hours later Tess was on the plane with Ann,

Rose's sister and Tess's only aunt, and both were worried and pensive about Rose. Stan had slipped while going down the stairs to the basement a few days previous, and had a badly sprained ankle. Tess had insisted that Stan stay home and not fly out with her. Although he was distraught that he would not be with Tess during this family crisis, Stan had reluctantly agreed.

Tess and Ann had met Harold at the hospital, and Rose's situation was indeed quite bad. She was slipping in and out of coma. The spread of the cancer in her brain was causing her body to totally shut down. At one point Tess was holding Rose's hand, and Rose's eyes popped open. She looked at Tess, and Tess could see a spark of recognition. Tess smiled warmly back and squeezed her hand, and then Rose sank back into coma again. For Tess it was truly heart-wrenching to see her slipping away like this. Tess fought back her tears, worried that Rose would suddenly open her eyes and catch her crying.

Hours later, Harold had just returned from a walk to get a breath of air, and he put his hand on Tess's shoulder. "You and Ann should go back to the house; it's getting quite late. I'd like to stay for a bit, and I'll join you both at home soon, okay?" Ann came over, and both Tess and Ann gave Harold a joint hug, which made all of them teary-eyed.

"All right, Harold," sniffed Tess. "Love you." Ann nodded to Harold but couldn't speak. They each stood silently for a moment, watching Rose, sending their silent prayers and their love to her. Ann had brought Rose's favorite pink flowered shawl and had spread it on top of the bed and tucked it around Rose. She looked almost like a delicate china doll swathed in an elegant pashmina, her chest rising and falling ever so slightly. They turned away and left Harold by Rose's side.

At home a short while later, Tess had fallen asleep in Rose's bed, and it seemed like she had been asleep for only a few minutes when Tess was suddenly and totally awake. *Huh?* She had lifted her face from the pillow. *Why am I awake?* she wondered, and realized that she was on Rose's side of the bed in her home in Vancouver, and she had been lying on her stomach, something she never did normally. She turned around to find none other than Rose floating in midair above her!

"Mum!" cried Tess. Through a kind of an energy cloud, Tess could see Rose's head and part of her shoulders, enough to see that she had her green hospital gown on. It was like looking inside of a clear crystal; there were many facets and angles through which she was seeing her mother's face. There seemed to be a hint of a green haze or energy swirling around her as well.

Tess squeezed her eyes shut, and she could still see Rose in front of her. She popped them open again, and Rose was still floating in front of her. Tess glanced at the digital clock—3:33a.m.! She looked back at Rose, who seemed to be saying something to her. Tess closed her eyes in an effort to concentrate on hearing her.

Love you, Missy!

Tess sent her thoughts to Rose. *Mum, I can hear you! I love you too, Mum,* thought Tess, quite astounded by what was going on. Then Tess remembered something important that she had read in Rampa's book. *Mum, there are Angels or helpers waiting to guide you to the other plane—listen to them, Mum, they will take you into the light,* she thought emphatically to Rose. And slowly, ever so slowly, the green light faded, and Rose disappeared.

Tess lay awake in the bed, still absorbing what had occurred. A shiver ran through her body. She felt truly blessed, in so many ways. It was real—everything she had read! We truly do have a spirit, a soul; we are indeed more than just a physical body! It was Rose's spirit that had come to visit Tess on her way to the "other plane." Tess was grateful for this gift that Rose had given her.

A few hours later the buzzing of the phone woke Tess, who had slipped back to sleep after Rose's departure, and she hopped out of bed knowing what would happen next. She could hear Ann getting up in the spare bedroom as she walked to the kitchen phone. She picked up the phone, and Tess could faintly hear Harold's voice. He was breaking the news to her, news that Tess already knew. The knowledge that Rose's spirit was definitely alive kept her calm and collected as she heard Harold pour his heart out to her.

A short time later, Tess and Ann arrived at the hospital to comfort Harold and to help with the necessary arrangements. Dawn was just breaking, and the sun was peeking in the windows of the hospital waiting room, where they found Harold looking quite haggard. They each gave him a big hug, which he gratefully returned. Tess walked apprehensively to Rose's room and walked inside. Rose still had the flowery pashmina tucked around her, but there was no rise and fall of the chest, and her mouth was slightly open. It felt so strange and scary to Tess to see her mother's body so lifeless and still.

It's just a husk …

Tess was riveted by those words. The thought was clear and quiet, and was definitely not her own. She could *feel* that. Tess knew the words were from Rampa's book; a husk was one way in which Rampa described the physical body once the soul had departed. This reminder comforted her, and she also realized that she had heard something outside of the normal realm. Tess was also very much aware that she had been hearing these thoughts on and off for some time now. She was on the verge of asking just *who* it was that was sending her these thoughts, when Harold and Ann came into the room, and Tess became embroiled in the task of gathering up Rose's personal belongings.

~Chapter 6~

Ximon

"I didn't get any middle-of-the-night visitors, and just what do you mean by *visitors* anyway?" Reg's e-mails were usually just one-liners and straight to the point. Tess decided it was best not to answer. She'd been on the phone with Ron earlier and had tried asking the same question in a roundabout way, and had determined that her brothers had not been visited either.

It seemed that Tess was the only person that Rose had visited the night she died. Tess preferred to think of it as "passing" rather than dying, as she was now utterly convinced that Rose was still alive and now living on the other plane. But neither Ron nor Reg, or Aunt Ann had noticed anything unusual that night. And although Harold was actually with Rose when she passed, he had not seen her spirit at the time. Tess knew that Harold was open to hearing about spiritual experiences, and so she had told him the whole story. Harold was quite astounded to hear Tess recount the events of Rose's visit, and seemed greatly comforted by this knowledge, the knowledge that her spirit was seen and spoken with by Tess. Tess found it to be such a relief to be able to share that powerful event with someone who understood. Harold advised Tess that she had a gift of clairvoyance and that is why only she had seen Rose. She decided not to mention anything about this to anyone else—except perhaps Stan when she returned home. Tess had called Stan with the news, and he was quite upset to not be there with Tess during this sad time. Tess had asked both him and her two brothers to stay put for now, as there would not be a funeral.

Tess and Harold had agreed to follow Rose's wishes and did not make any arrangements for a service. Harold remembered the Tibetan way, to leave the body in state for three days in order for the spirit to fully detach from the body. And then Rose was cremated, as per her wishes. Harold and Tess decided to split her ashes between the two of them, and agreed that each would plant them with flowers in their own garden in May, when the weather permitted.

~

The following months were a blur to Tess. She was incredibly busy at Serokine and worked long hours during the week. Weekends were precious time to spend with Stan, and they often would go out of town for a romantic dinner an overnight stay in a quaint inn. Tess and Stan were quite smitten with each other and still felt as if they were honeymooners. Tess so admired Stan, who was so respectful and considerate, and he always seemed to be thinking about Tess—bringing her flowers (three single red roses) every so often. They had great discussions on any and all topics, including Stan's interest in aliens and Tess's expanding spiritual awareness. Stan was adamant about keeping any issues about their relationship aired and out in the open so that nothing would fester and come between them. And so Tess had little time to herself, but she did manage to squeeze in some reading. Harold was inspired by Tess's experience with Rose's spirit, and had given Tess all of his Rampa books to take home and read—and there were nineteen of them!

Rampa had such a romantic writing style; his descriptions of his early life as a lama-in-training, and his experiences with his guru and mentor, Lama Mingyar Dondup, were filled with life and wonder, and were so incredibly mystical. It was the mystical aspect that kept Tess riveted to his books, and she devoured one after another. Rampa described the spiritual teachings of the Tibetan lamas, which revealed that not only did our soul undergo multiple reincarnations, but it was actually one part or one-tenth of a higher being, or oversoul. There were nine other souls that were also connected to this oversoul, and all of these souls had a very cosmic connection to each other—they were all part of the same "soul group." Often the members of soul groups liked to reincarnate together and share life experiences and learnings.

Tess found herself especially drawn to Rampa's experiences with his beloved mentor after he had passed from physical life into the spiritual plane. Rampa was still receiving guidance from him, but now from the other side as a spiritual guide. Lama Dondup seemed to visit Rampa during the times when he was most in need of advice, and Rampa could both see and hear his guide in his spiritual form on these visits. Lama Dondup seemed to be able to pick out just the right things to say to Rampa, and this was really making Tess think about the thought experiences she had been having, and who or what might be sending them. Tess was toying with the idea that her voices were actually from her own spiritual guide that was here to help. At the moment Tess had been reading about Rampa's life in North America, and he had settled down in Canada to begin his book writing. He had two cats that were, incredibly, quite telepathic, and Rampa seemed to love them so. And the cats seemed to just adore him. *What an incredible life it must have been,* thought Tess dreamily. She remembered her beloved Squeek and imagined being able to talk with her and how that could have so enriched their lives.

Stan, that wonderful man, had called Tess one morning at work. It was that messy time in the spring where the snow was just melting, and the bulbs were just barely peeking out of the ground, and Stan had not begun his spring landscaping contracts as yet. He was able to take his time in the mornings, and on this particular morning he had just gotten off the phone with his dad, Otto. He had been a widower now for ten years, and was currently dating a woman, Lily, that he had met, interestingly enough, in the same singles hiking group that Stan and Tess had met on. Lily was upset about a cat that she had found in a friend's apartment building, and had been unable to find a home for her, and today was the day to take this cat to the humane society. And so, this was the subject of Stan's call to Tess.

"Hi, Tess. Am I calling at a bad time?" asked Stan, who could hear the noise from the lab just outside of Tess's office. The maelstrom around Tess suddenly seemed so distant and far away, as if she were in a special kind of bubble, in which only she and Stan existed.

"No, Stan, you can call me anytime; you know that," said Tess softly into the phone, smiling at how courteous Stan still was even after three years of marriage.

"Well, something has come up, and I need your opinion on this," said Stan so seriously. Tess braced herself; from his tone it sounded like something heavy-duty. "Lily has a stray cat that she hasn't been able to find a home for, and she's really upset because now she has to take her to the humane society." Stan hesitated. "Well, what do you think, Tess, would you like to have a cat again?" Tess could hear the smile in his voice now.

"Ah, well that'd be a no-brainer, I think, Stan!" exclaimed Tess, and her heart was now leaping at the prospect of having a cat again. They were such dear animals and great companions. Each cat seemed to have its own distinct personality, and Tess had been so lucky to have had a few very unique cats in her life. "But how are you with this, Stan? I thought you weren't ready for a pet in the house." she said, suddenly concerned, remembering his firm stance when they'd moved into the house a few years ago.

"Well, I was thinking that since your mom has passed, it's a good time for you to have a cat now; so if you are willing, she'll be in the basement tonight when you get home from work." Tess was ecstatic! She'd definitely have to leave work early, or, rather, on time for once.

"What's the cat's name? What's she like? What color is her coat?" The questions were coming fast and furious now, and Tess couldn't get all the words out fast enough; she wanted to know all of the details about this new member of her family, the family of Stan and Tess.

A few hours later, Tess burst through the front door and dropped her purse on the floor, looking around anxiously for the cat. *Oh, right!* thought Tess. Stan said he was going to keep her in the basement … and she made a beeline for the basement door, which was indeed shut. She opened the door slowly and walked down the first few steps and turned on the landing and then peered into the basement. "Hello, little cat. Where are you?" No noise, no movement. She ventured slowly down the stairs and looked around. The main room in the basement served as a shared office for both her and Stan. Tess's desk on the left-hand side of the room had piles of papers and stacks of books, both on top and underneath the desk. All nineteen of Rampa's books were sitting in some of the piles on the top of the desk. A few plants were also on top and one plant—a philodendron—had snaked its way up the many pictures above her desk and all the way over to the wooden bookcase, which was filled to brimming. Some shelves had two rows of books, one behind the other, and there were books stacked on top reaching the ceiling. Stan's desk on the other side was neat and tidy, with an old Pentium I on it. Her eyes adjusted slowly to the darkness; she didn't want to turn the light on and scare the cat.

There! Just under Stan's desk was a pair of unbelievably big yellow eyes. Tess crouched down and moved slowly closer. She felt somehow that the cat was deathly afraid, but it didn't move a muscle when Tess came closer. She stopped about two feet away to find a beautiful smoky gray cat, full grown, blinking at her with those big yellow eyes. She held out her hand, and the cat gingerly sniffed it. On a hunch, Tess gently scratched the top of her head—she knew from her previous cats that this was a favorite spot for "noogies." The cat didn't move, and Tess stroked her fur and was pleasantly surprised to find a double coat—she was so unbelievably soft! "You're soooo beautiful, you know," said Tess to her new furry companion. "I think we are really going to like each other, beautiful cat," she said with a smile. She could feel the tension melting in the cat, and finally it ventured out from under Stan's desk. She was a shorthair with smoky blue-grey coloring, quite thin but very sleek, and she had such elegant poise, kind of a refined demeanor about her. *What a beauty she is,* thought Tess and went upstairs, calling the cat to follow her and explore her new home.

A few days later she and Stan were relaxing on the living room sofa at the end of a long day. Tess was trying to find a name for their new cat. "Mitzi," said Stan, and Tess agreed, happy that Stan would think of a name for her. The vet had estimated that she was about two years old, and had given her a treatment for ear mites. The mites and malnutrition were her only difficulties, both easily solved. Tess looked at Mitzi, who was on the floor and now head-butting her leg, looking for some more cat noogies. Tess bent down to accommodate "The Mitz," as they were now calling her, and suddenly a sharp pain went through her abdomen. She quickly stood up off of the sofa, and her hand went to her right side.

"What's up, Tess?" said Stan, looking worriedly at Tess.

"I don't know, just a stitch in the side, I guess," she said and walked around a bit. It hurt to walk. "I think I'll have a hot bath, Stan. That'll make me feel better," said Tess. But it did not. In fact, the pain got much worse as the night went on. Tess did doze off, but was instantly awake at about 1a.m. The pain was in her lower right abdomen, and it was so intense that she couldn't even get out of bed. Tess was wrestling with her thoughts, trying to figure out whether this was serious enough to go to the hospital. Caution won out.

"Stan," said Tess, nudging him in the side.

"Mffff."

"Stan, wake up. I have to go to the hospital," said Tess emphatically.

"Huh?" Stan immediately sat up and looked over at Tess, who was white in the face and holding her right side. "It's worse?" he asked.

"Yeah, Stan. Let's go to the hospital," she said. "It feels like something serious."

A few hours later they were in a small curtained room in the nearby hospital emergency ward. Tess was lying on her left side on a hospital bed, and an IV with antibiotics was dripping into a needle in her right arm. A surgeon had just come in to look at Tess. He was tall and distinguished looking, fiftyish, with black reading glasses, and had walked into the room while reading her chart. He nodded curtly to Stan, then glanced at Tess and introduced himself as Dr Smith and said that he was her surgeon. She could almost feel Stan tense up even more with the words "her surgeon."

Tess blinked back at him. She was slightly more comfortable since they started some high-dose antibiotics, but was still in pain.

"We suspect it's your appendix, and I'm going to schedule you for emergency surgery in a few hours," Dr Smith said in a kind but serious voice. "Do you have any questions for me?" he asked while peering over his glasses.

Tess thought about it a bit. "Well, I just find it so interesting that I'm not throwing up or having diarrhea or anything," she said matter-of-factly.

The surgeon hesitated for a minute, then looked at Tess and nodded and left the room.

Tess looked over at Stan, who was sitting on a nearby chair. He's just beside himself, she thought. I feel so bad to be putting him through this.

Another hour passed before the emergency room doctor came in.

"Hello, I'm Dr Westabe," said a beautiful East Indian woman. She was about as tall as Tess, with long black hair tied up in a bun. She had very striking hazel-colored eyes and a bronze lipstick that made her look quite exotic. "How are you feeling?" she asked Tess, putting her hands and Tess's chart behind her back for a moment.

"Actually I'm beginning to feel a little better," she said, and it was true, the pain was easing up. "What about the surgery?" she asked the doctor.

"Well, if it was your appendix you'd still be in pain," she said, looking intently at Tess. Tess felt as if Dr Westabe were doing a visual assessment of her condition by the way she responded to questions and how she was lying on the cot.

"I think the antibiotics are helping you now. You probably have an infection, and the antibiotics are starting to clear it." She had brought the chart around in front of her, and she scribbled on the chart.

"How will I know for certain?" asked Tess, secretly relieved that there would be no surgery but still wondering just what was going on, and "an infection" just wasn't enough information.

"We've scheduled some tests, starting with an ultrasound, first thing in the morning, which is—actually in an hour or so," said Dr Westabe, quickly glancing at her watch. "I'll check back with you after we see the test results," she said, and nodded, first at Tess, then at Stan, and quickly left the room.

A few days later Tess was home with a large bottle of horse-size antibiotic capsules. She and Stan were thankful that it was nothing serious that had needed surgery, but there was no clear answer from Dr Westabe other than, "It's an infection, possibly in the fallopian tube. Take these antibiotics, and it should clear up in a week."

Stan was doting on Tess, making sure that she was comfortable at all times, bringing her tea and whatever else she desired. She was wrapped up in a nubbly blanket on the TV room sofa, a steaming cup of Earl Grey on the table beside her and the remote in her hand. An episode of *Star Trek Next Generation* was on the TV. Tess found that watching *Star Trek* always relaxed her no matter how stressed she was. The episodes always provided such a positive outlook on the future and usually left Tess in such a good mood after watching them. Stan settled in beside her on the couch, and they snuggled next to each other, both glad that Tess was home.

"Ooof …" exclaimed Tess suddenly. An extremely sharp

pain went through her side—and then just as suddenly left. Stan sat up quickly and looked at Tess.

"Okay, Tess, what's happening?" he asked. "Tell me."

Tess sat up. The pain was gone. "I don't know," she replied. "It's gone now." It was kind of weird, almost like an intense gas pain that instantly appeared and then disappeared. She had a sudden urge to urinate. "I'll be right back, Stan. Just going to the bathroom. I'm okay, honest," she said reassuringly.

A few moments later Tess could not believe her eyes. She was standing up in the bathroom staring down at the toilet bowl. Inside she saw a centimeter-size oval—something, with a long thin cord on both ends. She blinked and looked again. It was still there. *Holy smokes—what the hell is that?* she wondered. And it slowly dawned on her. It was a fetus, very young, likely six or seven weeks, and it had just popped out of her fallopian tube and found its way out. This is what caused the infection, she realized. It must have become non-viable while lodged in the fallopian tube, and an infection had set in. *That's pretty wild!* thought Tess. Never becoming pregnant in forty-four years and all of a sudden this … Tess wrestled with this realization, and whether or not to tell Stan, or anyone else, for that matter. Stan and Tess had many discussions about Tess's inability to become pregnant. They had explored options such as in vitro fertilization clinics and adoption. But they had not come to any decision. Hmmm … Tess was thinking, realizing that any minute now Stan was going to wonder what was taking her so long. Decision made, she flushed the toilet and washed her hands. *Stan would file a lawsuit against the hospital*, she thought. *I don't want any part of that hassle. I just want to get better and put this behind me.*

Over the next few weeks Stan and Tess were preparing

for a family event, the burial of Rose's ashes in their garden. Keeping busy was Tess's way of recovering from any traumatic event, and Tess had immersed herself in this project. She had found a beautiful plant—of course a rosebush, called Lovely Lady Rose, with the most gorgeous pink flowers. There was a perfect spot, right in the front of the garden, for this special plant. She'd planned a buffet lunch and had arranged for Harold, her brothers Ron and Reg, their children, and Aunt Ann all to attend. Tess and Harold decided that something simple but elegant should be read after they planted the rosebush, but not to fuss so much. Rose wouldn't have wanted all that bother.

The day arrived, a thankfully sunny day in June, and the house of Stan and Tess (and Mitzi) was buzzing with activity and chatter. Mitzi was observing it all from under the dining room table that was off to the side, full to brimming with a variety of delectable treats. Stan was navigating a tray filled with smoked salmon sushi through the living room, and they were disappearing off the plate fast. Tess had brought the last tray, containing a huge Caesar salad, to the dining room table. She'd planned to do the reading first, and then they could all dig in afterwards. Tess was so excited to have everyone gathered together at the same time, especially her niece and nephews, who just seemed to be growing up so fast.

"Okay, gang, let's head outside now," chimed Tess, and everyone piled outside into the warm summer sun.

The Lovely Lady Rose bush was sitting in the garden beside the hole. Rose's ashes were already inside, discretely placed there the night before by Tess and Harold. They didn't want the neighbors to figure out what was up. They were all dressed in their finest summer attire and gathered quaintly around the front of the garden. Tess cleared her throat and held up a flowered page with a script that she and Harold had picked out:

"I'm Free!
Don't grieve for me, for now I'm free,
I'm following the path God laid for me,
I took His hand when I heard Him call.
If my parting has left a void,
Then fill it with remembered joy.
A friendship shared, a laugh, a kiss.
Be not burdened with times of sorrow.
I wish you the sunshine of tomorrow.
My life's been full; I've savored much.
Good friends, good times, a loved one's touch.
Lift up your heart and share with me.
God wanted me now, He set me free."

"That was quite beautiful, Tess" said Harold huskily after a moment. Tess couldn't answer. Her entire head was tingling. She had tears in her eyes, but they seemed on hold as the tingling was getting more intense. She just stood there awkwardly.

"Let me, Tess," said Harold, and Tess stepped back while Harold placed the rosebush into the hole and then shoveled some peat around it. Her head was tingling big-time. She didn't know what to make of it, but it didn't feel bad. As a matter of fact, Tess was wondering if she was sensing something—perhaps Rose was there! Tess closed her eyes. Hmmm … She didn't see anything; but she felt—well, warm and cozy, like Rose had just given her a big hug.

Love you, Mum, Tess sent by thought.

The rest of the day had gone very well; everyone engaged in lively chatter and ate absolutely everything that Tess and Stan had put out on the table. *Mum would have been pleased,* thought Tess. *It wasn't such a big fuss, but at the same time we elegantly marked her passing!*

A few months later the summer was almost over, and Tess had not done a stitch of gardening, which was unusual for her. Their backdoor neighbor was a retired woman, Gladys, who was always out in her beautifully manicured garden in the summer. She had approached Stan when he was out cutting the grass. She commented on the Lady Rose, which had grown two feet and had twenty or thirty roses either in full bloom or about to bloom on it, and also on the fact that there were no other plants in the garden. "Oh, she's been busy," said Stan, but he knew better. Tess had been feeling pretty funky of late. She was always tired, and seemed to have a nagging pain in her abdomen. And, she was in bed for the whole day when getting her period, not at all like her usual self. And, she almost never wanted to have sex anymore; she said it was too painful.

Tess had been to her family doctor, but got no answers other than she did not have another infection. But she was still in pain. Her family doctor had finally referred her to a specialist at Women's Hospital, where it took two months to finally get an appointment. Tess was in this fellow's office for a total of about two minutes, and then he'd prescribed high-dose birth control pills. "That should fix you up," he said. And then he buzzed for the next patient. Just like that, an assembly line, thought Tess.

But the pills only made her feel nauseous and didn't stop the pain; they just took the edge off of it. She tried them for four months and then threw them in the garbage.

Her condition was really affecting her concentration, and her work at Serokine was slipping. Tess was considering getting a second opinion and had been doing some research on the Internet to try and figure out what might be going on. From what she'd read so far it really looked to her like she had a condition called endometriosis. But when she had mentioned this to her specialist, he had waved his hand and said that it was difficult to diagnose that condition, and to simply continue taking the high-dose pills. Tess wasn't the type to wonder "why me?" when in the midst of tough times; instead, she preferred to try to get to the root of her circumstances. But right now she felt like she was between a rock and a hard place and didn't know where to turn.

Finally Stan had had enough, and he decided to talk to Tess about something unusual. He was reluctant to reveal this information to Tess, but enough was enough, and it was time to do something completely different.

They were in their favorite restaurant, Sunshines. As a matter of fact, it wasn't just their favorite restaurant, it was where Tess and Stan had their first date. It was a little on the expensive side, but the food was quite excellent, and the restaurant had a salad bar that was second to none. Tess was just picking at her cedar-planked salmon; she hadn't really been hungry but wanted a night out with Stan.

"Tess, do you remember me mentioning the changes that my dad and I made when my mom was sick?" Stan asked Tess.

Tess looked up at him. It was unusual for Stan to be talking about his mother. Tess felt that even though it had been ten years since Frieda had passed from cancer, Stan was still very emotional, still grieving over her. "Well, I know it was a pretty rough time, from what you said. Chemo is never an easy treatment." She tilted her head and raised her right brow slightly, sending a questioning glance to Stan.

"Well, we did a lot of research, my dad and me," said Stan in a low voice, putting his fork down. "We checked out books on diet, the environment, herbs, and all kinds of alternative therapies. We stopped eating beef and gave away the barbeque. We brought home all kinds of teas and herbal remedies. But she would only try them once and then wasn't interested anymore." Stan paused and looked carefully into Tess's eyes. "There was this one interesting fellow, Ximon. He's a herbalist, but maybe a little more than just a herbalist. Anyways, we took Mom to see him. It turned out that he wasn't able to help her because she had already had chemo."

"That's a little arrogant, don't you think," exclaimed Tess.

"No, Tess, that's not it. The activity of his herbs is blocked by the chemo for some reason. So he said his treatment would not have worked for her."

"Oh, that's too bad, Stan," said Tess.

"But my dad and I each went for kind of a checkup with him after," said Stan. "It was quite interesting. He had me hold out my arm and try to keep it out while he pushed down on it. Well, of course I couldn't hold my arm up with him pushing down on it. And then he gave me two bottles of herbs to hold in my other hand." Stan paused. "And then I could keep my arm up even when he was pushing down on it. He said the herbs give my body balance and strength."

"That's pretty wild, Stan," said Tess.

"I know." Stan reached over and held Tess's hand. "Tess, I'd like you to go and see him. I know it's not a mainstream treatment, but I think he might be able to help you. At the very least you could just go and talk with him."

Tess perked up at this new prospect. She certainly wasn't getting anywhere with the medical system, and really didn't know what to do next. "Okay, Stan, actually that sounds like a good idea. I'll do it."

The following afternoon Tess had left work early to visit Ximon. She had arrived at his office close to the end of his day, and she was his last patient. He was very congenial and took the time to explain everything to Tess. He explained that his herbs were more than herbs; they had healing energy, and they could target the specific source of the problem. He also said that a type of energy blockage caused most problems in an organ or body system, and the herbs would bring about balance and remove this blockage.

Tess chatted with Ximon for over an hour, and she found herself laughing and feeling better than she had in quite some time. She left Ximon's office with four bottles of herbs, two for her endometriosis and two for the hypothyroidism that she'd had for fifteen years. Tess was worried that the herbs would all interact with each other, but Ximon reminded her that they would each specifically target the root cause. He said that you might as well fix two birds with one stone, and he predicted that in three months she would be free of both diseases!

~Chapter 7~

The Lower Astral

Sure enough, three months later Tess's pain was gone. And, she had to start backing off on her thyroid medication; she was periodically getting a racing pulse and feelings of anxiety—symptoms that she had too much thyroid activity now that her own thyroid was beginning to kick in. When she went for a checkup with Ximon, he suggested that she stop her thyroid meds altogether, and that her thyroid was now back in action and functioning normally. Both Stan and Tess were ecstatic! Tess was so glad that she had listened to Stan's advice about Ximon, and thought that Stan's timing was so good—Tess realized that she might not have listened to Stan if she thought there were still options within the medical system. Tess noticed a pattern about herself in that she really had to be in a bind, between a rock and a hard place, before her mind opened to options that seemed so far-fetched. A good lesson learned, and that is exactly how Tess was viewing the whole experience.

Tess had taken an interest in learning how to meditate. She wasn't quite sure why, but Rampa's writings had really opened her mind. There seemed to be so much more going on in life, and Tess had decided that she wanted to learn about the spiritual-metaphysical world. Meditating seemed to be a good way to start—and it was also a good way to learn how to dissolve stress. She'd cruised through the bookstore and found *Mindfulness for Dummies*—which had provided some good tips on mindfulness meditation, and she'd gotten in some introductory lessons one hour a week at a yoga center close to work. She wasn't quite sure if she was actually meditating, but she felt a peace of mind about making a venture into the realm of the metaphysical.

Stan had decided that now that Tess was feeling better, this was the time for Tess to learn how to golf. They'd dabbled at playing tennis and had a number of very good rounds; but Stan's ankle was flaring up after each game. Golf was such an ageless sport, and Stan had seen players ranging in age from five to eighty-five. You could keep active in golf well into your retirement years, and this really appealed to Stan. Stan was thinking that now that Tess was feeling so much better he'd get her out onto the fairway!

Tess loved the idea, and so did Otto, Stan's dad, when they mentioned that they were heading to a little par three executive course just northeast of Toronto, and so the three of them went out on a cool fall day. The sun was bright, and a hint of color was in the leaves. It was early morning, just after the sprinklers had watered the greens, and they were lush and true to their name.

Tess had fallen in love with her five-wood, and this was the only club she would use off the tee and for her first shot on the fairway. Stan just shook his head at her, but Tess didn't care. At least she could get the ball into the air and down the fairway a little ways. It felt so good to be able to just whack the ball and hear that sweet "ping," and see it soar up into the air down the fairway. But when it came to her irons, the ball would just go wherever it liked, mostly

P. T. Straub

into the sand traps—and rarely into the air. Stan had told Tess that this was typical for a beginner, and he added that her drives were not so typical, as she could really whack them off the tee, but getting the ball into the air off of the fairway would simply take practice.

Otto was also doing well for a new golfer at seventy-five years of age; he could keep his ball on the fairway, and they were all having a glorious morning. Tess noticed that not too many other golfers were around, which was great—they didn't have to worry about the pressure of faster golfers catching up to them. The first few holes had been higher up on the course and out in the sun, but now they were down on the lower edge of the course by the forest, and it was much cooler. Tess had zipped up her vest and wished she had worn a jacket, but she was enjoying herself too much to go back to the car for it. She could smell the musty forest odor beside the ninth tee, and she breathed it in deeply. The blue jays were squawking and calling to each other, and Tess spotted a hawk circling lazily above them. A wind had picked up, and she could hear the rustling of the leaves in the forest, almost as if they were dry and ready to fall, even if they hadn't changed their color yet.

Tess watched Stan ready his tall, athletic form for his drive off of the ninth tee, and was thinking to herself that she was so fortunate to know Stan. He was such a caring husband and there was this—well, something between them. Something that Tess couldn't quite put her finger on. But it felt special. *Almost cosmic*, Tess felt, like they were supposed to be together in the greater scheme of things.

She thought back over recent months. It had been tough going with the pain of the endometriosis, or whatever it was that she'd had. And during that time things had deteriorated at work. A huge multinational pharmaceutical company called TSK Inc. had bought Serokine, and morale was pretty

76

low. Many had been let go, including Serokine's president and Tess's boss, Mathew McGuire. Those remaining were shocked and saddened, and also were wondering if they would be next. All of the research and development group's work had been put on hold (Tess thought more likely they were shelved and not really on hold), and the products that they had developed together at Serokine were being evaluated as to how they would fit into TSK's business strategy.

It had been such a culture change, going from a small start-up laid-back atmosphere to a big pharma's big business atmosphere. And such a stressful change too. The meditation lessons seemed to be helping her keep her mind calm with that, though. Tess remembered her former office mate Pearl, who had been the lead scientist on one of Serokine's high-profile research projects. She and her team had really put their heart into their work on the West Nile Virus project, and they took it quite hard when it ended up on TSK's cancelled list. And Tess's role was changing from coordinating research and development activities to coordinating projects, monitoring their progress to quarterly goals using Gantt charts and spreadsheets with dashboard markers. If a project moved into a red-flag zone they would quickly undergo a reevaluation by TSK executives, and to Tess it seemed most likely that red flags were the demise of a project. Tess felt that it was a coldhearted approach, but she also knew that it wasn't easy to mix science with business.

However, Tess really thought highly of her new boss, Danton. He was a charismatic man, kind of Egyptian in appearance with his jet black hair and tanned skin, and he had a very friendly deep voice with a gravelly edge. He really had a way to finesse the management of all of TSK's projects, thought Tess. Danton could deliver the bad news of a cancelled project to the lead scientists and technicians, and yet at the same make them feel that each one of them was special and that their special talents would still be needed but in a different venue.

Danton Rousman was based out of the head office in San Francisco, and Tess warmly remembered their first meeting. The remaining scientists had put together a summary of all of their research and development work to present to Danton on his visit to Toronto, and they were all in the midst of a presentation in the boardroom when the fire alarms went off in the MaRS building. Tess was on the Joint Health and Safety Committee and was one of the fire wardens. She hadn't formally met Danton, but as they all stood up and headed to the front exit of the boardroom toward the stairwell she saw Danton standing aside, watching the crowd with a curious smile on his face. Tess marched over and introduced herself.

"Hello, Mr Rousman. I'm Tess, the operations manager here, and also the fire warden. You'll have to follow the others down that stairwell." Tess pointed to the open door of the boardroom and the stairwell across the hall that the scientists were all marching into.

"Well, hello, Tess," said Danton in a warm, gravelly voice, and he reached out with both hands, shaking her right hand with his right and covering it with his left hand. "Please call me Danton." He gave her hand a firm squeeze and looked directly into her eyes with a friendly smile. "I'm so glad to finally meet you, Tess." Tess looked back at him, noticing—something, she wasn't quite sure what.

You know him.

Her voice was guiding her. That was it! She had some kind of a connection with Danton, almost like she had met him before somewhere. She squeezed his hand in return, still trying to figure out the déjà vu feeling that she was having and wondering if it was connected to her voice saying that they knew each other.

"Glad to meet you also! But really, you have to go—and I have to go and check that everyone has left the floor."

He smiled warmly at her. "Of course, Tess. I'll touch base with you later." He turned and headed out with the others, and Tess watched him stride purposefully out and call to Pearl, who was just entering the stairwell. He must have cracked a joke because Tess could hear Pearl's laughter floating out from the stairwell as Tess headed out of the boardroom to begin her check of the floor. That made Tess smile, as she began her sweep.

That had been a month ago, and now Tess was feeling that things might just turn around a bit at their changing workplace. Her mind came back to the ninth green, and they putted out. The round of golf had been just wonderful, and Tess, Stan, and Otto had thoroughly enjoyed themselves, most especially Tess. The next day, however, Tess got up feeling sluggish with a slight headache. *Damn!* she thought. *Why didn't I wear my coat?* She was worried. There was a flu epidemic of sorts in the city at the moment, a virulent type that seemed quite often to lead to pneumonia. Many people were ending up in the hospital from this bug, and hospitals had to take extra precautions to limit their staff's exposure to the public, to reduce the risk of them coming down with it. It was early in the season for the flu; they were only at the end of September.

Stan was quite the health nut, and he had Tess take some extra vitamin C and made some tea with ginseng, and then he prescribed a hot bath followed by a nap. After her nap, Tess actually felt worse, with alternating hot flashes and then cold chills. Stan took her temperature, and it was high, at 37.8 degrees Celsius! Both Tess and Stan were worried.

Later that night Tess awoke with a start and realized she had an almost excruciating pain in her lower abdomen. *Not again!* thought Tess. She clamped her hand over her side and rolled slightly over to look at the clock. It was 1:11a.m.!

"Stan," called Tess. Tess had asked Stan to sleep in the spare room to limit his exposure to her bug. Tess heard the rustle of covers and squeaking of the floorboards as he hurried over to their bedroom.

"What's up, Tess? How are you feeling?" he asked her as he hurried to her side.

"I dunno, Stan, my side hurts, and I feel really crappy."

"Your side hurts?" Stan repeated. "I thought you had the flu." He sat down on the bed beside Tess. He put a hand on her forehead. It felt comforting to Tess to feel Stan's cool hand on her hot forehead. "You're still hot, Tess." And then it suddenly dawned on him. "Tess, maybe your infection is back—that's why your side is so sore, and that's why you feel so bad." He stood up. "Can you stand up, Tess? See if you can get out of bed."

Tess tried to sit up but immediately fell back on the bed, both hands on her lower abdomen. "No way, Stan. I can't get up."

"Okay, Tess. I'm calling nine-one-one right now. You stay put," he said firmly and marched out to the kitchen phone.

A short while later Tess had been delivered by ambulance to a hospital just north of Toronto. Poor Stan, thought Tess. He had to stay at home; the hospital would not allow anyone other than her into the emergency room while the flu alert was on. The paramedics were gloved and masked; and so were the emergency staff. They had placed her into one of the curtained rooms in the emergency room, and so far Tess had had four visitors, three nurses and one doctor. The last one, a nurse, had given her a shot of morphine for the pain. Within a few minutes Tess could actually feel the powerful drug begin to work; at first the edge of the pain seemed to diminish ever so slightly, and then as the full effect of the drug took hold her whole body just seemed to relax all at once, and the pain was gone. She could still feel a dull kind of ache in her lower right abdomen and was now quite sleepy.

When she awoke she was in another room that seemed to be partitioned off from the emergency room. There was one other stretcher and a curtain separating them. A friendly nurse was adjusting a one-liter IV bag that hung by her bed; it was attached by needle to Tess's left wrist.

"Are you cold? Would you like a blanket?" asked the nurse.

"Uh, yes, please," said Tess weakly. "What time is it?"

"Oh, let's see." She lifted up the edge of her glove and peered at her watch. "It's about 6:00 a.m."

"Has anyone called my husband?" asked Tess, concerned about Stan. "He must be worried to death about me."

"The emergency room nurse would have called him," she said pleasantly. "But if you'd like to speak to him, I'll wheel you over to that phone." She pointed to the phone on the counter across the room. "Come on." She unlocked the stretcher wheels and maneuvered Tess alongside of the counter so that Tess was right beside the phone.

"You are scheduled for an ultrasound in about an hour, as soon as the technician starts," she said. "An attendant will come and take you up—okay?" She smiled and left Tess by the phone.

Stan had been grateful that she called and told Tess that he had been notified by a doctor to let him know what hospital she was in. Tess promised to keep Stan posted herself or to at least have someone call him regularly.

As it turned out, Tess had peritonitis, a very serious infection, and the surgeon on duty was standing beside both her and Stan, who was now allowed into the hospital, since Tess was formally admitted and was about to head into the operating room. He had explained to Tess and Stan that he wasn't sure how extensive the infection was, but that he would try to do as minimal an incision as possible. But he warned that if the infection was widespread, he'd have to do a larger incision in order to get at everything.

As he turned to head into the antechamber to gown up, another nurse came by with a blanket and placed it over Tess. It was toasty warm! The pain in her abdomen was momentarily forgotten. "Oh, man, that feels incredible," said Tess, feeling the lovely warmth spread deep inside her body. The nurse smiled at her.

"We keep them in an oven," she said. "We find that it helps relax patients before they go in for surgery." She looked at Stan. "She's in good hands," she said reassuringly. "Dr Black is one of our most excellent surgeons." She patted Stan's shoulder and hurried off.

Sometime later Tess was slowly awakening and felt as if she were inside of a dark, woolly cocoon. She could hear voices around her but couldn't quite make out what they were saying. She knew that she had to wake up and tried moving her legs and arms. "She's coming around," Tess heard someone say.

Tess opened her eyes but couldn't see so clearly. It felt like there was a nurse standing beside her. Her body felt really bloated, especially her abdomen, almost as if she were ready to burst at the seams. And she was having trouble catching her breath. She could see a near empty one-liter IV bag hanging beside her bed and another full one hanging in readiness beside it. Suddenly she felt something wet underneath her bottom.

"Something's wrong," she exclaimed. "I'm bleeding!" She looked at the nurse.

"It's okay; you are not bleeding. You've had some surgery, and you're now in your own room. Here, you can look at the incision and see for yourself," and the nurse drew back the bed cover and partially opened the gown to reveal Tess's bloated tummy. Tess was horrified—she looked like the Michelin man! Her abdomen was a huge, distended, yellowish dome dabbed with red patches of iodine, and a silver row of staples down the middle was holding her incision together—just barely, thought Tess. Tess felt more wetness come beneath her.

"I'm exploding!" she exclaimed. "Something's wrong! I want to see the doctor. Please go and get him *now*!" yelled Tess. She felt as if things were out of control, and no one understood that something was wrong.

With a gloved hand the nurse pulled her gown back all of the way. "Oh—you have your period, Tess, that's nor …"

"I want to see my doctor *now*," interrupted Tess emphatically. She was terrified! They didn't understand—she felt as if her body were about to blow apart!

The nurse beside her waved to another nurse just outside the door and then pulled out her cell phone. In a moment the nurse put her cell phone to Tess's ear.

"Its Dr Black, honey. Now don't worry," he said comfortingly. "Tess, I am so sorry that I forgot to tell you that when I took out your ovary, you would immediately get your period. You will be okay. Do you understand me, Tess?" said Dr Black in a kind but firm voice.

Tess relaxed a bit. His voice was so reassuring.

"Okay, Doctor. Thank you," she added weakly.

Tess awoke the next morning to find Stan's handsome face looking down at her from beside her bed. She could see that he had been wearing a mask, but it was partially off and dangling around his neck. There were circles under his eyes, and Tess thought that he probably had not slept a wink. She smiled at Stan, and he took her little hand in his bigger ones.

"Glad to see you are awake, Tess," he said huskily. "I've been so worried about you."

Dr Black had taken out her right fallopian tube, ovary, and appendix. All had been affected by the peritonitis, which had evidently arisen in her fallopian tube, likely damaged from the tubal pregnancy and infection, and had burst, spreading the infection into the surrounding abdominal cavity. None of this really had sunken in yet with Tess because of all of the medication she was on; it felt like some kind of a bad dream.

"There you are, Tess," said a young black nurse, who had just come in. She tugged on a mask that was over her face and released it so that it hung down from her neck. She looked over at Stan. "I'm Christina, and I'll be looking after your wife." She smiled and then turned to Tess.

"We're going for a walk, ma'am," she said with a smile, taking off her gloves.

Tess was aghast. "What?" both she and Stan said in unison.

"Yep! Doctor's orders for all patients. Gotta get them walking the day after. That's what starts the healing!" she said cheerfully.

She shooed Stan over to the other side of the bed and put down the metal guardrails. Tess was staring at Christina, not really believing that she would actually be able to get out of the bed, much less walk.

Christina picked up the bed controller and raised the head of the bed. "This'll help give you a bit of leverage," she said.

Tess felt that same out-of-control feeling from yesterday. *They just don't understand; this doesn't feel right,* Tess thought to herself. But she was powerless to stop Christina's determined efforts.

Christina reached over, grabbed both of Tess's hands, and started pulling.

"You can do it; help me now to get you up—just swing your legs over to me," she said heartily. Tess tried to move her legs but could really feel the pull of the staples in her abdomen as she tried to sit up. A dull throb made its way into Tess's awareness. She felt like a bloated blimp and definitely not in control of her body at all. And then, somehow, she was sitting up at the side of her bed with her feet just above the floor.

"Here are your slippers," the nurse said, and plopped them down just under her feet. "Just hop down; I'll hold you. You can do it, now; come on!" she encouraged.

Tess absolutely doubted that she would be able to stand, much less walk. Christina grabbed her hands again and tugged, gently sliding Tess down off of the edge of the bed.

Tess felt her slippers beneath her feet and, somehow, she was actually standing! She looked in amazement at Christina, who had now let go of her hands.

"You can do it; come on, take a step," she said, smiling at Tess.

Tess shakily took a step forward, and then another one. She couldn't go any farther because there were several small tubes in her way.

"Here, I'll help you fix those," the nurse said, and she wheeled over the IV stand that had Tess's ever-present bag of IV fluid, and also had a urine bag hanging on it. "Here, hold onto this and just wheel it beside you as you walk. You can hold onto it to keep your balance," she instructed Tess.

She took a few more shaky steps and smiled back at

the nurse. Stan had appeared beside her, and he was also smiling.

"Wow, that's kind of cool," said Tess. It felt really wild, being swollen to what felt like the size of the Michelin man, and up on her feet and out of bed, knowing that she had a large incision in her abdomen, and the only thing holding her insides inside of her were a few shiny staples. "But I'd like to go back to bed," she said quickly.

Stan was only allowed to visit once per day and then only for an hour or so due to quarantine rules imposed by the hospital. So he would come by in the mornings to sit and chat with Tess until time was up—or until Tess fell asleep. Then he was off to work.

One morning as Stan came in, Tess decided to tell him about what happened to Christina, her nurse.

"I think the police came to take her away," said Tess. Stan just looked blankly at her. He'd brought Tess a copy of one of the magazines she liked to read, *Scientific American*, which had the title of the feature article blazing in blue: "Multiverses—Multiple Universes, do they exist?" He placed the magazine carefully on the side table.

"I heard the nurses whispering about it," said Tess, and she raised the head of the bed with her remote. She swung her legs over to the side of the bed and pushed herself up, and then slowly slid out of bed into her slippers below. Her abdomen was not quite as big as the first day, and it was marginally easier to get out of bed. She grabbed her IV stand and shuffled over to greet Stan, who was now by the end of the bed.

"Good to see you up and about, Tess," said Stan, ignoring her comment about the nurse, and pecked her on the cheek. "Why don't we go for a walk down the hall together?" Tess nodded. She was trying to walk as much as she could, knowing that this would facilitate the healing process and also seemed to help relieve her swelling. Her kidneys were initially not working after the surgery, and Tess was given a diuretic to stimulate them. The IV drip was changed frequently, and it contained saline and some powerful antibiotics to control and wipe out the infection in her abdomen; but still her kidneys were struggling to keep up. And now that her catheter was removed, she was up and down quite a bit to the bathroom.

Stan walked slowly along with Tess as she shuffled down the hall. They each donned masks and gloves while outside of her room as per the flu quarantine rules. The walk was a blur to Tess, and when they arrived back at her room she quickly laid back down in bed again.

Sometime later Tess awoke. Stan had gone, and her breakfast was untouched on the side table, her *Scientific American* beside it. A small white meds cup contained her Tylenol with codeine. "Number three's" the nurse had said they were. The morphine was stopped once she was able to walk, and now the codeine was handling her pain.

She glanced over to the bed beside her—the curtain was drawn, and it seemed to Tess that her roommate had company. It was almost as if the two of them had made a small tent and that there was a light glowing inside. It looked very romantic to Tess—almost like they were having a quiet night together by candlelight in a tent! She blinked and then looked away, feeling kind of funny, as if she were in a dream world. Directly ahead of her a kind of a pale orange membrane was floating, surrounding her. The membrane seemed to be made of many cells. She looked around, feeling calm but wondering just what it was. Then Tess saw through the membrane and saw some weird cartoon-like figures, and they were all just kind of sitting around. When she looked directly at one of them, the figure jumped up and started making lewd gestures at her. She looked away, and it stopped. Tess looked back again, and her eye caught another cartoon figure, and it started jumping up and down, and whirling about. The motions were odd, kind of like a film that had several frames removed from section to section, jumpy and discontinuous.

"Psss psss sss, Tess, whsss whsss trouble ..." it said to her.

Tess felt nauseous and didn't like these odd characters. She pushed herself up and slid out of bed, into her slippers, and shuffled out into the hallway. *Maybe a walk will do me good*, she thought. There was something familiar about them, but she couldn't quite remember.

Tess spent the rest of the day and well into the evening shuffling around the corridor until she was exhausted, and then getting into bed and trying to sleep, and then seeing the cartoon figures. She tried not to look at them because they would start in again as soon as she gave them her attention, but it was hard—she seemed to be surrounded by them.

"Hello, Tess" greeted Christina, and Tess's eyes flew open. "I've brought the head nurse with me, Adriana." Tess blinked at Christina and then looked over at Adriana.

"I thought she was in jail," said Tess.

"What are you talking about? Give me your hand," said Adriana sharply, who looked at Tess's wrist where her IV had been inserted. The IV needle slipped out of her wrist as Tess lifted up her arm.

"We'll have to put it in on your other wrist, Tess," she said.

"I don't think so," said Tess, getting that out-of-control feeling again. No way was she going to let either of them touch her. "You'll have to go and get the doctor because I don't want either of you to touch me." Tess had heard them plotting something about her. Those whispers had been going on all night. "Whsss whsss trouble psss sssss, Christina," they had said to Tess.

"You cannot go without your IV, Tess. If you will not let us place it back in for you, then you will have to call your husband to come and speak with us." Adriana had passed a meaningful glance over to Christina, who nodded, and they both left Tess.

Damn right—I'll call Stan, that's the thing to do! thought Tess, and she pushed herself up and slid out of bed. She dialed her home number, and Stan's deep voice was on the phone.

"Hullo?"

"Stan, it's Tess. Can you come to the hospital? I need to see the doctor. The nurses here are plotting something, and it has to stop now. You need to help me, Stan!" Tess exclaimed.

"Tess, I don't know what you're talking about, honey, but I will come out right away."

Tess relaxed. *Stan will fix things; he'll understand*, she thought.

"Whssss ssss whsss, Tess," they said.

A short while later her phone rang. "Tess, I'm downstairs; they won't let me in," said Stan. "Get one of the nurses on the phone, Tess, to explain just why it is that I'm here in the middle of the night."

"Okay, Stan." She put down the receiver and shuffled to the door and stuck out her head. One of the nurses at the nursing station looked over at Tess. "My husband is downstairs. Can you talk to security to let him in?" she called.

In a few moments Stan was in her room by her side. He gave her a big, warm hug, and Tess just melted. "It is okay, honey. Whatever is happening, we will figure it out." He pulled away and gently stroked her hair away from her face. "What's going on, Tess?" he asked with concern.

"They are plotting against me," said Tess. "I've heard them whispering about me all night. I won't let them touch me, and I want my doctor, Stan," said Tess firmly.

Stan looked at her. "Okay, Tess, I will go and speak with them," he said and gave her a quizzical look. "You stay right there," he added.

A few minutes later Stan was back. Tess could not believe what she had heard.

"Tess, are you okay?" Stan asked.

"Stan, I heard you plotting with the nurses," she said matter-of-factly.

"Now, Tess, don't you think that's just a little ridiculous?" he asked her, putting his hand on her shoulder.

Tess shrugged his hand away. He didn't understand. Something wasn't right, and Tess now knew that they were all against her!

"Tess, I'm going to go outside and speak to Christina. Why don't you try putting your fingers in your ears, and see what happens?" he asked with a smile on his face.

"Don't be silly St ..." she started to say. "Well, okay. I'll try it, Stan," she said with a change of heart. Still uncertain of what she was doing, she plugged her ears. "Go," she ordered Stan.

"Whsss whsss whsss, Tess, trouble whsss sssss ..."

Omigod! thought Tess to herself. Those voices have been in my head. And suddenly she was overcome with this realization. It was the painkillers! Now she knew why the weird membrane and the cartoon characters were familiar—she was in the lower astral!

Tess remembered Rampa's teachings about a place called the astral plane that existed in the nonphysical realm, where a whole spectrum of entities lived. At the higher or more positive end were delightful elementals like faeries and plant devas. But the lower end was a very nasty kind of place, where entities of a very low vibration existed. Usually we would not be aware of these "thought forms" unless we were very sick or under the influence of drugs that had lowered our vibration down to a level where we would be able to detect them. Normally there was a kind of a membrane or a veil that shielded our consciousness from becoming aware of them. It was the voices of these thought forms that Tess had been listening too—they had been giving her delusional ideas that the nursing staff, and now Stan, had all been plotting against her!

Stan returned with a worried look on his face. "Tess?"

"It's okay, Stan. I could still hear the voices with my ears plugged. The voices have been in my head. Must be the drugs!" She smiled at Stan. "I'm so sorry, Stan, to have been such a troublemaker," she said apologetically.

~Chapter 8~

The Chi of Life

Dr Black had prescribed five weeks of rest before returning to work, and had given her some high-dose oral antibiotics to take for the next ten days. It had been pretty rough going; she was unable to sleep for the first week until the effects of all the narcotic painkillers had worn off. And the new antibiotics had really given her a sore stomach. But she was glad just to be alive, now that the reality of her situation had time to sink in. Certainly Dr Black had saved her life, and Tess was grateful. *And, thank God, I'm out of the lower astral as well,* thought Tess. That was a place she did not want to go back to!

She walked when she was unable to sleep, pacing quietly through the house like a little mouse, not wanting to wake Stan and The Mitz. It was too cold for Tess to be outside, so each morning Stan started taking her to the nearby mall to walk. Tess was still walking ever so slowly; the members of the seniors' morning walking club were all passing her, much to Tess's chagrin.

At Tess's urging, Stan had taken Tess to see Ximon. Tess was wondering how she could have gotten so sick so quickly and thought that Ximon would have some answers for her. Ximon was kind enough to see both Tess and Stan together.

"What happened to you, Miss Tess?!" Ximon was stunned that she had been through such an ordeal. "Why didn't you call me? Just look at you! You are not in very good shape!" His face was serious, and he shook his head at her. Ximon's concern for Tess was clear.

"Ximon, I uh …" Tess was at a loss for words.

"It was a Sunday, Ximon; we couldn't contact you. And we thought it was the flu; we couldn't have come to see you anyways."

"Oh, the flu—you could have called me. I can fix that over the phone!" he quipped. Those words caught Tess's attention, and she was just thinking about how remarkable that was, and wondered how healing over the phone would work.

"But it wasn't the flu—it was a pelvic infection, Ximon. I don't understand why this happened," said Tess.

"Let me see," said Ximon, and he hovered his left hand over Tess's abdomen and stood quietly for a few moments.

"Yes, and the infection is still there." Tess was shocked to hear that. She'd had massive doses of intravenous antibiotics while in the hospital. "You need some healing. We'll schedule you in for first thing tomorrow."

"But, Ximon, why does this keep happening?" Tess asked, determined to get to the root cause of her issue.

"You have a weakness there, Tess. Once you have an infection like that it's much easier to reoccur." He looked sternly at Tess. "You must call me right away when you feel it coming on, Tess."

"But, Ximon, what happens on the weekend when we can't reach you?" asked Stan, worry in his voice.

"Ah!" he turned to Tess. "There's no other answer. We

have to make you a healer." He smiled at Tess. Both Stan and Tess looked quizzically at Ximon. "We'll schedule that session once we've removed your infection," he said matter-of-factly. Tess smiled to herself. An extraordinary turn of events, and now an opportunity to learn about energy healing!

Stan had dropped Tess off at Ximon's office the next morning. Ximon's waiting room already had a few people in it, but the receptionist had hurried Tess to a special room off to the side. The small room was darkened slightly; there was a recliner, a small stool, and a massage table with a blanket and a pillow. These were the only pieces of furniture in the room.

"Just sit here and relax," said the receptionist and motioned toward the chair.

"Thanks," said Tess, and she eased into the chair. She took a couple of deep breaths and felt her mind become quiet. She had not been able to meditate until the effects of the narcotics had worn off, and now she was grateful to feel the peacefulness seep back into her.

It hadn't been easy to learn how to meditate—but her teacher at the yoga center had a good method of teaching. "First you relax the body," he said. "Then you can relax the mind." He had taught them to do a relaxing body scan first while lying down, and then right after to repeat the same process while sitting up. This helped to teach the body how to relax in a sitting-up position. Sitting up was the best way to meditate—you couldn't fall asleep. But then there was the issue of all her thoughts whirling around in her mind. But, with time and repeated effort, Tess was able to learn to let go of these whirling thoughts and not follow them. She was able to quiet her mind and enter that peaceful state.

Tess had noticed a vision would appear whenever she became peaceful in her meditation state—an "eye" would appear out of a mist. It was an ancient eye, with an appearance very much like that of an elephant's eye. Tess thought it was kind of weird but didn't think too much about it.

After a few moments a thought entered her mind—*Where is my voice?* Tess had been wondering about the source of her voice and the fact that she had not heard it in some time, and was just thinking that if it was a spirit guide, perhaps it's harder to hear them when you are taking medication, and she certainly had quite a lot of meds both while in the hospital and out.

The room door opened. "There you are, Miss Tess!" greeted Ximon. He quickly closed the door and sat down on the stool beside her. "Let's get you started," he said warmly.

He placed both hands on her lower abdomen and became still. "Just relax, Tess, this will take some time," he said with his eyes closed.

Tess relaxed but was curious as to exactly what he was doing. His hands had immediately become quite warm. Almost hot! And it felt, well, really quite comforting. "Your hands," said Tess. "How come they are so hot?"

"It's the energy. It's working on your infection."

"What kind of energy?" asked Tess.

"Healing energy, of course," said Ximon, still with his eyes closed. He lifted his hands slightly and moved them to another section on her abdomen. They were still incredibly hot!

"Where does it come from?" asked Tess.

"We are surrounded by it. I simply channel it through my body and my hands, and send more of it to you. It's the life force energy, chi."

Tess wasn't quite sure what chi was but certainly was going to look that up. She wondered if this was the same "prana" energy that Rampa talked about in his books, or even the same chi from Tai Chi, something Tess had been thinking about doing.

"The herbs contain the chi too," explained Ximon. "That's how they heal." Tess nodded. She remembered that the Tibetans were also experts at using herbs to heal.

"The herbs are a bit slower though," Ximon continued. Right now we need to treat you with direct energy healing to clear your infection more quickly." He opened his eyes and looked at her. His eyes were hazel colored, warm, and kind. "You are going to be all right, Miss Tess," he reassured her. "You know the medical system is good for broken legs, heart attacks, and trauma. But for chronic disease, you know they are really just using a baseball bat, don't you? Don't you feel like you've been beaten up a little bit?" he asked Tess gently.

Tess certainly agreed with Ximon.

During her remaining three weeks at home recuperating, Tess spent all of her waking hours researching this mysterious chi energy. She'd been all over the Internet and had found some really interesting books at her local library. Tess devoured the books and was starting to notice some interesting patterns. It seemed that most cultures outside of North America already knew about chi energy, and that each culture had its own unique way of referring to chi and how it was used. Many cultures had practices that Tess had previously considered to be mystical and kind of airy-fairy, and these practices had been around for thousands of years! Most North Americans, like Tess, had never heard of chi. And, for that matter, most North Americans looked upon themselves and their body as purely physical, nothing else. North American medicine was all about "show me the proof" via clinical trials and studies that dissected each part of the body into its parts and considering the part itself, aside from the whole.

But what all of this research was telling Tess was that we were certainly more than a physical body. That we were a kind of a compilation of a physical body, an energy chi body, and, somehow, there was a mind body too. The mind body seemed to Tess to be a kind of an interface between the physical and energetic portions of the self, or the whole enchilada. *Kind of a holistic self,* thought Tess. All of Tess's recent events seemed to be suddenly clicking together. *This really seems to fit with my experiences—being able to see Rose when she passed, and hearing my guiding voice; feeling Ximon's energy during his healing session; and feeling that compassionate presence of the Holy Spirit.* Tess was thinking that all of these nonphysical experiences were being sensed somehow by a higher or second set of senses aside from the physical.

Clairvoyance, thought Tess, remembering Harold's advice to her about her gift. These were the psychic senses! They were indeed very real, and Tess was only just becoming aware of them.

During Tess's last week of recuperation, she visited Ximon again, this time to apparently learn how to channel this healing chi herself. The procedure was similar to her healing session except that he had placed his hands over various positions on her head, and she didn't feel any heat coming from Ximon's hands. Instead she felt a kind of tingling sensation, and almost like a magnetic pull coming from his hands.

After about twenty minutes Ximon said, "Okay, Miss Tess, your energy channels are open, and you are now in tune with the chi."

"What do I do now?" asked Tess.

"Right now, every day you should do your self-healing on

your abdomen. Just place your hands in different positions for about twenty minutes each day. After a few weeks you can cut it back to a couple of times a week. This will help strengthen you. Eventually once a week should be okay— but if you feel another infection setting in, make sure you treat it right away. Go for an hour if you need to. And call me if you are worried. Oh, and don't forget, you can do it anywhere. If you are at work, just go into the bathroom for a few minutes to do the healing. Got it?" asked Ximon.

Well, this all sounded kind of vague to Tess, but she nodded her head. "All right, Ximon, thank you very much." That was that. Very simple, with no mumbo jumbo, no magical incantations, no wand waving. Just use your hands and your own chi energy. *Hmph!* thought Tess. It was kind of hard to believe that it was as simple as that!

The next few months were a busy time for Tess. Upon her return to work she had found that several new projects had started, and all of them had accumulated a pile of data that needed inputting into schedules and assorted planning documents. Tess's role was evolving into that of a project coordinator of sorts, helping the various teams to understand where they were in the project time line, and using the planning indicators to determine if they were moving into a red-flag zone or not. All of this was like another layer over top of the science that was driving each project and developing each of TSK's products.

She found a nearby Tai Chi center and had started taking classes once per week. Tess really enjoyed the classes, and after about six weeks or so she found that she could actually do a few of the forms from memory, and also, most importantly, she could do them without falling over! Her balance seemed to be improving. The "sensei," or master teacher, said that this was because the Tai Chi was like a walking meditation, and that with time and practice this would improve her mental focus. As well, he said that the chi she was circulating by performing the slow and steady movements would actually strengthen her body.

Tess was now doing her self-healing using Ximon's technique once per week and was quite amazed at what she was beginning to feel. At first she didn't feel anything, but Tess was determined that she would learn how to do this. She kept at it and tried to keep an open mind. She could actually feel a tingling sensation coming from her hands—it was pretty wild!

Stan was agreeable to Tess embarking on the Tai Chi classes but wasn't interested in joining himself. He also wasn't saying much about Tess's self-healing sessions, and this was unusual for Stan, as he liked to engage in discussions with Tess. Tess felt that perhaps Stan was thinking that she was taking things a bit too far. Tess had wondered about this herself. She'd noticed a bit of a pattern in her own behavior in that each time she discovered something new she would immerse herself in it. When she had become an evangelical, Tess had spent quite a lot of time volunteering at the church. When she became ill with the endometriosis, Tess had spent quite a lot of time researching this illness. And now, with these interesting revelations about the nature of chi and what an integral part of life it was, Tess was yet again immersing herself in chi-related activities. She tried to put herself into Stan's shoes and look at her activities from his point of view. Tess had really undergone quite a lot of changes in the few years they'd been married. Tess felt that these experiences were part of a plan, perhaps a part of her life purpose or to prepare her for something bigger, but realized that to Stan it must look like she was going every which way, without much focus in her life.

Hmmmm, Tess mused. *But these experiences happened to me, not to Stan,* she reckoned. *Each of them has been so real, so powerful. How could I not change after having gone through them?* Tess was realizing that she had a powerful desire to learn and to grow from each of her experiences.

~Chapter 9~

The Being of Light

It was Saturday and New Year's Eve, and Tess was looking forward to a quiet night cocooning at home with Stan. A bottle of Henkel was chilling in the fridge, and Tess had bought an assortment of their favorite treats to munch on while they counted down to the new year. Staying at home having a romantic evening was now their New Year's Eve tradition. Tess had bought an assortment of elegant crackers, salmon mousse, brie, and jumbo shrimp for them to snack on, and Stan was sure to be picking out an assortment of DVDs for them to watch until it was time for the countdown. Last year's celebration they'd planned on watching all three of the Crocodile Dundee series one after the other, but they only got halfway through the first one (Mic and Sue were kissing after their swim in a freshwater lagoon), and they found themselves making love on the sofa under a blanket in their TV room, and then both falling sound asleep. Tess smiled as she remembered Stan waking up with a start and poking his nose out of the blanket to spy the remote, and they caught the countdown in the Big Apple just in time!

Tess was staring into her computer screen and daydreaming. She glanced down in the bottom corner of the screen—it was five thirty already! She looked at her Gantt chart; it still showed a late finish date for this particular project. No matter how much tweaking she did, the end result was the same—the project was moving into the red-flag zone. She rubbed her eyes and realized that she was getting a headache.

That's enough! thought Tess. Time to go home. She saved the file and started the shutdown process on her computer. Standing up for the first time in a couple of hours, Tess stretched and felt a tweak in her abdomen.

Oh-oh! All of Tess's attention was immediately galvanized on the reason for the tweak, and also on the reason for her growing headache. *It's back!*

Her pelvic infection was returning. Tess realized that it had been over a week since she did her last self-healing session. And it had been quite a tough week; she'd worked until seven or eight on a few nights, and here she was in on Saturday as well, trying to keep up with her growing workload. The stress must be bringing it on!

I'll call Ximon! she thought, thankful that he had been there when she needed him. *Oh, Damn!* She remembered that he would leave at noon on Saturdays and that he wouldn't be back in his office until Monday.

She sat in her chair, her thoughts whirling around, wondering what to do. *Well, I'm sure there will be a walk-in clinic open somewhere tomorrow, even on New Year's Day!*

You can do it.

There it was. That quiet, still voice. Her guide. Tess sat still for a moment. Then—*Okay!* thought Tess, and she stood up and somehow felt and understood what she needed to do. She gathered her coat and purse and thought out her plan.

The subway was packed with New Year's Eve partiers on their way to an evening of fun and excitement, but Tess—an experienced subwaygoer—wormed her way through the throng to the centre of the subway car and managed to find an empty seat. She carefully arranged her purse and laptop case on the floor behind her legs, and placed her hands casually in her lap, with her palms facing inwards toward her lower abdomen. She slowly took three deep breaths, letting each of them out slowly, and felt the tensions of the day release—and her body relaxed. Her meditation practice had allowed her to essentially enter that peaceful place in her mind wherever she happened to be, in this case on a busy subway. She closed her eyes, feigning a nap, and started her chi flowing the way that Ximon had taught her.

A short while later, Tess was sitting quietly in a kind of an energy bubble, which to Tess felt like she was surrounded by a golden Teflon eggshell filled with gold-colored sparkly energy. The loud chatter and movement of people felt far away, as if all of the party-goers' energy were simply sliding off of this protective eggshell and not impacting her at all. Her hands were still casually resting over her abdomen, and she could feel the heat from her chi literally blazing out of her hands and heating up her lower abdomen. Tess was totally impressed at the intensity of the energy! But at the same time she kept calm and focused on the flow of her chi. She could feel the heat continue to grow in intensity as the energy did its work on the beginnings of her infection.

Twenty minutes later the subway train pulled into its last stop at Finch station, and Tess opened her eyes. The subway-goers were all exiting the train, and Tess hesitated for a moment. *Namasté, divine ones*, sent Tess by thought, in a prayer of thanks to the universe for the healing energy. She collected her purse and computer bag and was off to the parking lot to find her car for the drive home to Stan.

Stan and The Mitz greeted Tess at the door. "Happy New Year's Eve, Tess," said Stan and gave Tess one of his famous big bear hugs even before she had her coat off. Tess allowed her purse and computer bag to drop to the floor and returned Stan's hug. The Mitz was head-butting her legs and purring loudly. *It felt so good to be home!* she realized.

Tess looked up and mentioned to Stan that she was feeling a bit off and wanted to just take it easy that evening and go to bed early. But Stan knew better. He stepped back with one eyebrow raised. "You aren't feeling good, are you, Tess?"

"Well, I don't feel bad; it's probably just a cold or something," replied Tess. But she could see from the look on Stan's face that he didn't believe her. Somewhere in the back of Tess's mind she was remembering how in sync she and Stan were with each other—he could read her like a book.

"You are going to bed right now, and we're taking you to a clinic first thing in the morning," he said firmly; thoughts of romance and a night spent cocooning together had evaporated. "I don't want another visit from nine-one-one, thank you!"

Neither did Tess. She wasn't quite sure what to do, but did think that it was best to take the time to rest and allow her body to complete the healing process that Tess firmly believed she had just initiated on the subway ride home.

The next morning Tess felt The Mitz stirring beside her. Her beloved cat had been curled up in the crook of her back all night. Tess slowly turned over as Mitzi stood up and did a perfect arch with her back and headed toward the foot of the bed. Tess looked over at Stan, who was also awake and looking right at Tess with one eyebrow raised. "God, Stan, have you been watching me sleep?" asked Tess with a start.

"So, Tess, how are you feeling?" asked Stan, ignoring Tess's question.

"Well I ..." Tess was now fully awake—and felt better! She was amazed. No headache, no body aches, no fever, no pain! Her healing had worked! She smiled at Stan. "Stan, I feel fantastic! I'm okay, dear. You don't have to worry!" She was ecstatic!

But Stan was still worried. "Tess, we should still get you checked out. I'm taking you to the walk-in clinic."

He had propped himself up on one elbow and was still looking quizzically at Tess with the raised eyebrow. Tess looked into his eyes and could feel his concern for her safety. It certainly was a "thing" with Stan—his protectiveness of her. Perhaps it was his upbringing; Otto had been very protective of Stan during his childhood, and this had carried over into adulthood as Stan had continued to live with his dad after his mother had passed over.

Tess was busy formulating a plan as she threw off the covers and bounded after The Mitz, who was now meowing loudly for her breakfast. "Okay, Stan, we'll go," she called to Stan on her way to the kitchen, with Mitzi "mrrrowing" loudly at her heels. Tess agreed to go to the clinic with Stan—a compromise. It couldn't hurt to be safe. But, inside, Tess knew that something dramatic had occurred.

She had healed herself, and that realization was huge!

The physician at the walk-in clinic had prescribed antibiotics after hearing Tess and Stan relay the history of Tess's recent hospitalization, and that she had been feeling off yesterday. Tess reluctantly started on the medication—she knew that it would only upset her stomach and that it was entirely unnecessary, but it was important to Tess to keep her relationship with Stan on an even keel. This was Tess's way of trying to keep balance in their relationship. Tess was learning and growing at a different pace than Stan. And she was still determined to call Ximon in the morning, to find out for sure if the infection was indeed really gone.

The next morning, promptly at ten, Tess had dialed Ximon's number. "Yahweh Healing," answered the voice of his receptionist.

"May I speak with Ximon, please?" asked Tess.

"Oh, hello, Tess—hold on," she replied, recognizing Tess's voice, and Tess heard the clicking of the transfer button, and then after a moment more clicking as Ximon picked up the phone in his treatment room.

"Ximon here."

"Ximon, it's Tess. I'm sorry to bother you."

"Ah, Miss Tess, it's good to hear from you. What is up?" asked Ximon with his friendly voice.

Tess got to the point quickly, as she knew that Ximon often took important calls when with a client and didn't want to cause too much of a disruption.

"Good that you called; just let me check," said Ximon, and there was silence for a moment. "Way to go, Tess," said Ximon, and Tess could hear the smile in his voice. "You do not have any sign of infection. And you don't need to take those antibiotics; they will only upset your stomach," he said. Tess smiled. She had already known Ximon's answer.

"Thank you, Ximon. That makes me feel so much better. Have a good day!" wished Tess.

"Bye, Miss Tess," said Ximon, and Tess slowly put the phone back on the receiver. But Tess knew that Stan would not understand. He loved her dearly and would still want her to follow the traditional route, to be safe, even though he had encouraged her to see Ximon in the first place. So she would do both, take the antibiotics and continue her self-healing. To Tess it was the only way.

The next few months flew by, and before Tess knew it,

it was the end of March already and the cut daffodils in the laboratory beaker on Tess's office desk were blazing a brilliant yellow harbinger of spring. Tess was at the office making arrangements for a two-day meeting in May at the head office in San Francisco. TSK was doing a review of all projects and was flying all key personnel into San Fran to attend. And, Tess would also be able to spend some time with her new boss, Danton. She'd really only met him once in person last summer just after TSK had taken the reigns from Serokine, but had talked with him often by phone and sometimes during project meetings, and she had just gotten off of the phone with Danton, discussing the fine-tuning of the upcoming meeting. His voice was gravelly and warm, almost as if he were giving you a great big hug with his words. But he could be firm and to the point if things were not going the way he liked during his meetings. There was just something about him, Tess thought. She wasn't exactly sure what that something was, but deep down inside Tess thought that he felt just so familiar, and their working relationship was great, almost like they had known each other for years. But Tess was certain that they had not met before, and was wondering if perhaps she had dreamed about him and was having déjà vu experiences. Her fingers flew over the keyboard as Tess fine-tuned the notification e-mails that she would send out regarding the May meetings, but her mind was still on that familiar feeling about Danton. Perhaps it was something she had read—but what? It was eluding her just now.

Tess was a voracious reader, and a pile of books was always beside her bed. Quite often Tess would have four or five books on the go at the same time and would switch from one to another. Tess loved to read just before going to sleep, sometimes picking up one book, reading it for a while and then putting it down and picking up another—and occasionally would fall asleep amongst her books. Once when nodding off, the book she was reading had fallen on Stan's head (who was asleep beside her), and he'd awakened with a retort about this bookworm who was trying to knock off her husband for the insurance money, before turning over and going back to sleep.

Tess kept several journals written back to front (Tess didn't know why, but it just felt right to create them in this fashion), with some journals recording her daily experiences and others recording her thoughts about some of the research she was doing. Right now all of Tess's books centered on the themes of healing modalities, spiritual awareness, and the nature of human consciousness—as she was seeking to learn more about her experiences of late. Tess had been pleasantly surprised by some of Carl Jung's writings. She'd picked up an older book, *The Basic Writings of C.G. Jung*, in the bargain bin of her local bookstore that had his writings on a number of fascinating topics on the nature of the psyche. Tess found that not only was he such an expert on the nature of human consciousness, but he was keenly interested and knowledgeable on the nature of man's spiritual experiences. Jung's archetypes, or patterns of behavior, were quite fascinating to Tess. Also, Jung seemed to have been the first person to coin the phrase "synchronicity," or meaningful coincidence, which Tess found extraordinarily interesting. It had been occurring to Tess just how phenomenal it was to have met an incredible healer such as Ximon just when she was at her wits end about her health, and what an amazing turn her life was taking as a result. It didn't feel like a lucky break or a chance encounter—Tess was learning and growing as a result and felt that somehow Ximon was meant to be a part of her life just now—a hugely meaningful realization to Tess.

Tess was also becoming quite the researcher, and in her

spare time, usually just before going to bed, Tess would do some research about energy healing on the Internet. From her readings of Rampa's work, it seemed that the Tibetan Lamas were quite advanced healers, but you had to be a Lama before being taught their healing techniques. Tess realized that there was little chance of her learning Tibetan healing. There was also a Japanese system called Reiki that seemed to be a little more organized in that there were masters that could teach the technique to others, and some of them were actually in North America. A Chinese system called Qi Gong also seemed to be quite interesting, and there were also teachers in North America. But from what Tess could determine, it seemed that Ximon was kind of an independent healer. He had his own method of healing that was unique to him. Tess only knew this one energy healing technique—Ximon had many more but did not plan on creating a school to teach his other techniques. After Tess had asked Ximon about learning more, he revealed that he had actually only taught this one technique to Tess out of kindness, to help her out of the spot that she had been in. Ximon was so busy with his healing practice that he had no time to develop a school or to teach it to others in any great depth. *No wonder his office is full every day*, thought Tess. *He truly is a miracle worker!*

Tess had spent a bit of time researching a technique called Chios; for some reason this healing method appealed to her. This method looked unique; it was developed in California and had a well organized structure and system, with all information available on the Internet. This appealed to Tess; they were very forthright about their teachings, and it looked as if they were on the leading edge of creating a standardized system for energy healing. She had scrolled through the list of master teachers and found a few located nearby, and had bookmarked them for future contact. It was quite tempting to Tess, to learn more about this incredible technique.

As Tess's attention came back to her work e-mails about the meeting requests, she put the final touches into her messages and hit the send button on each of them one by one. Tess could see the hourglass whirling on her screen as the messages were queued through TSK's e-mail server, and she took a deep breath and tried again to bring her attention back to her massive to-do list. As she began to focus on her business tasks, she could still feel that magic only felt by seekers such as Tess—that there was so much out there to learn and to do!

A few weeks later it was Easter, and the Good Friday tradition for Tess and Stan was to spend some time with Tess's dad, Cameron. Cameron had remarried shortly after he and Rose had split, to a wonderful woman—Susan—that he had met while on a business trip to Montreal. Susan was also very creative, like Rose, but in a different way—she had a gift with home decorating and cooking, and it was always like a warm homecoming to visit, as the décor was a cozy-elegant country style, and such appetizing aromas were always coming from her English country style kitchen. Stan and Tess had arrived in the early afternoon to find Susan and her next door neighbor, Tara, cooking up a storm in the kitchen. Susan waved at Tess and Stan from the kitchen. "Your dad's out cutting the lawn!" she called to them, smiling, and then pointed to the kitchen window with her wooden spoon. Cameron was out in the backyard on the lawn tractor, way down at the far end, which they called the "back nine." There was a fog of green behind the tractor as Cameron trundled through the thick grass on his Lawn-Boy; Cameron didn't use the lawn bag and instead liked to refertilize the lawn with the cuttings. They had a beautiful spot just north of Toronto on ten acres, and at least one of those acres was the back lawn. Cameron kept it neatly manicured, and Stan had sauntered out toward the back nine to flag him down.

Susan and Tara were back in the kitchen busily concocting that most heavenly of desserts, a tiramisu, and Tess could smell the wonderful aromas of rum and chocolate. "Mmmmm, can I sample?" asked Tess, wandering in and leaning on the countertop with a hopeful grin on her face.

"Nope—no tasting 'till after dinner," smiled Susan. "So, how are you, Tess? Tell me what's going on with you and Stan these days," Susan said, giving Tess a sideways glance as she carefully stacked the rum-laden ladyfingers into a circle on an ornate glass cake plate. As Tess updated Susan on the latest news, Tara—who was not only Cameron and Susan's next-door neighbor but also Susan's best friend— was humming as she whisked the cream into a foamy froth. It was a familiar tune, and as Tess was chatting with Susan she felt the familiarity of the tune but couldn't quite place it. Suddenly it hit her, and she broke off her conversation with Susan.

"Uh, Tara, is that 'Morning Has Broken' that you're humming?" inquired Tess. Susan looked over at Tess, then at Tara, and then went back to carefully arranging the ladyfingers, forming the base of the tiramisu.

"Never heard of that title," said Tara. "But it's a hymn, my favorite one at that. 'Christ Beside Me' I think it's called." She put down the whisk and picked up the rubber-tipped spatula and started spooning the cream on top of the rum-soaked ladyfingers that Susan had finished arranging on the glass cake plate. She went back to her humming.

"Hmm ..." Tess thought to herself. Sure sounded like a Cat Stevens song to her. Tess sneaked a finger-full of cream from the glass mixing bowl that Tara had momentarily put

P. T. Straub

down as she and Susan straightened a couple of runaway ladyfingers that were starting to roll down from the top of the carefully arranged dessert. Tess had been playing that very tune a few days earlier. She and Stan had been having a discussion about the type of music that they each had listened to while in high school, and, much to Tess's surprise, Stan had never heard of Cat Stevens or even listened to any of his music, so Tess had played Cat's best hits CD for Stan. Much to Tess's dismay Stan displayed no interest in the music and had given Tess the raised eyebrow and a polite, "It's okay, I guess," in response.

The back door swung open at the far end of the long open style country kitchen as Cameron and Stan walked inside from the backyard. Cameron flipped his boots off one by one, looking hot and sweaty in his khaki green lawn-mowing sweats, and walked quickly over to plant a kiss on Tess's cheek.

"Hey, Cam, don't be dragging any grass in here with you," quipped Susan, peering up at Cameron, who was now pulling something out of his hip pocket.

"How are ya, honey?" asked Cameron to Tess, then winked at Susan while wiping his brow with a rather bedraggled-looking hanky.

"I'm good, Dad," said Tess with a smile, feeling her dad's contentment with a good morning's lawn-mowing. His obsession with a neatly mowed lawn was a sharp contrast to the disorganization of the garden shed, which was threatening to explode each time the door latch was unhooked, as it was stuffed so full of lawn care implements—and even, to Tess's chagrin, two pink flamingoes.

"Stan tells me that you're quite busy at work, Tess" said Cameron, stuffing the now soaked hanky back into his hip pocket. "That's good! And how's the stock doing?" he added.

112

Tess headed out of the kitchen back to the backyard with her dad, racking her brains for any memory of the latest TSK stock prices, stalling her answer with a few ums and well—uhs. Stan was still standing by the back door, and he stepped around Tess and Cameron as he headed inside of the kitchen. Tess smiled and caught his eye. Stan grinned back. He was after a taste of the dessert too, Tess knew. She could hear Tara still humming away, and she and Susan put the finishing touches on their creation.

A few hours later the dinner table was noisy with the sounds of a good meal—forks and knives clinking, and comments of "great salmon, Susan" murmured from lips muffled with the delicious cuisine. The meal was quite excellent, a gourmet dinner of salmon marinated in a lemon-maple syrup sauce, wild rice, carrots mixed with parsnip, sautéed mushrooms, small slices of warmed focaccia bread, and a Liebfraumilch, whose fruity flavor totally enhanced the culinary experience. And the pièce de résistance was the tiramisu, which they had all eagerly dived into alongside steaming cups of cappuccino sprinkled with nutmeg.

It had been great to catch up with Dad and Susan, Tess thought to herself when she and Stan were driving back home. Tess really admired their home—it was just so beautifully together somehow, and still so cozy at the same time. Tess thought it could easily win a home decor contest, and it was Susan's gift to have just the right touch in coordinating the elegant country look that their home had. Both retired, Susan and Cameron kept busy on the ten-acre hobby farm—some of which was rented to a nearby farmer, and some was worked into a huge garden, beautifully manicured lawn, and a small replanted spruce forest at the very back end of the back nine. It always felt so comfortable to be there.

Stan had gotten up first the next morning and announced

to Tess that he'd like to go to church. "What did you say, Stan?!" asked Tess blearily, just about falling out of bed as his statement started to sink in. "Did you say you wanted to go to church or something?" she replied. Stan was already on his way out the door, and he turned to give her the raised eyebrow and a smile and muttered something about a "feeling" he had.

Stan had a history of trusting his feelings about certain things and had told Tess about how sometimes he would get a feeling about taking a certain route home or even avoiding his usual route and would find out later he'd avoided a traffic jam or accident. Stan had even told her that he had decided to go to the hikers' outing at Lawrence Park where he and Tess had met because he'd had a feeling about it when Helen had invited him to meet Tess. And so Tess knew that Stan really was following up on another one of his intuitive hunches.

Once showered and dressed, Tess was quite happy to accommodate Stan, and they attended that morning's contemporary service. It had been quite some time since Tess had been to church because Tess's recent holistic and metaphysical adventures had been satisfying that inner longing for "something more" that she had looked for previously in church services.

Tess found that she had missed listening to the choir, and felt entirely caught up in the energies of worship by song, and was standing and clapping to the music along with the crowd of churchgoers. They had a temporary replacement for the church's regular pastor, who was away on a six-month assignment, and this new fellow seemed quite young. But his sermon was very down to earth and elegant at the same time, thought Tess. The young pastor won Tess's heart with a personal story about his family, and he made a passing comment that he would routinely sing while washing the dishes, and Tess had smiled to herself as she pictured this elegant young man with his wife and a kitchen full of playing children, singing delightedly while he did the most mundane of household activities.

The pastor in his sermon had touched on the healing that Jesus had performed, and he made special mention of the woman with the bleeding disorder, and how Jesus had not only healed her but had elegantly let the townspeople know that she was purified and that it was now okay for her to rejoin them as a member of society, implying that she had spent the last twelve years cast out of the town because of her disorder. Tess had never caught that deeper meaning before and found it interesting that the pastor chose a story about healing, especially when Tess was just now dealing with issues around healing.

And then at the end of his sermon the pastor was telling a story about his visit to Ireland when he was a young Christian (*and that must have been very young*, thought Tess to herself). He said something about being out for a walk in the country fields and had come across an unusual celebration that was taking place on a Saturday. This was interesting because his sermon dealt with Colossians 2:16:"Therefore do not let anyone judge you by what you eat or drink, or with regard to a religious festival, a New Moon celebration or a Sabbath day." He relayed his humorous story of being caught up in the throng of the crowd as they made their way through the country path, singing songs that seemed quite unchristian-like, and the pastor said that he was quite worried to be associated with this crowd of potential pagan worshipers, who seemed to be celebrating the new moon. Then apparently they had arrived at their destination, and the crowd circled around a particular knoll and began to sing this song. Just at that moment the choir in the church started up, as did the contemporary band, and to Tess's and Stan's surprise—it was none other than "Christ Beside Me."

Tess was staggered! Stan looked over at Tess in surprise—both eyebrows were raised, and his mouth was slightly open as if he wanted to say something but was too surprised to talk. He looked back and forth from the pastor to Tess, and Tess felt that he recognized the music not only as Tara's hymn from the day previous, but also as the Cat Stevens tune "Morning Has Broken" that Tess had played for him a few days ago. Tess was happy to notice Stan's awareness that something quite significant was occurring, and for a logical thinker like Stan to notice a major synchronicity, Tess realized, represented a paradigm shift for him. Tess believed that whether he was aware of this or not, he may be shifting from a "life happens to me" belief to an "I am a part of life" belief.

Now the pastor was singing (*quite beautifully,* Tess thought) and waving his hands, urging the crowd to stand and sing; and before they knew it the whole church was singing this beautiful hymn. Tess was overwhelmed, and she put her hand to her mouth, tears now running down her face. It was so beautiful; the whole church was united in song, and the feeling was indescribable—as if the room were also filled completely with angels showering gold sparkles down on the whole congregation! She couldn't imagine how such a series of coincidences could have occurred. It was clearly a mystical occurrence. One of Jung's synchronicities! God, Jesus, Angels, spirit guides—whomever were around Tess and Stan just now, Tess was grateful to them all for such a clear message presented to both her and Stan. And to Tess, the message was that this was her calling, her purpose—healing!

A few days later Tess was back on the Internet doing some more research on healing, and she reflected back on the events at the impromptu church visit. It was just so damn fascinating! All these years in the high-tech science industry looking for documentation, creating analyses, and documenting proof of hypotheses, and now she was learning on the complete opposite side of the scale that the meaningful coincidences and her other mystical experiences, as intangible as they were, were just the tip of the iceberg. She was realizing that there was so much more out there in the world of human consciousness and experience if you could find a way to just keep an open mind. Tess realized that she had to be between a rock and a hard place with her health before being ready to openly look in new directions for relief from her endometriosis—before being willing to open her mind to alternatives like energy healing, which science had always dismissed as quackery. And this openness, combined with her miraculous experiences, had also propelled Tess out of the box of Christianity, allowing her to step into the realm of the metaphysical and the infinite world of human consciousness.

Tess noticed on the Chios website that there was quite a lot of information about this healing technique, and she was passionate about getting started. A number of teachers worldwide were listed, and … Yes! She scanned a contact list of teachers. Teachers were located close by! She excitedly wrote down the name and number of each teacher, and then reviewed the curriculum. This particular course of study involved studying and practicing the healing at home, and then completing a series of workbooks, which would then be sent to the teacher for review. It was a little disturbing to Tess that she wouldn't actually be in a classroom, but the material was very well structured—and then again this wasn't a conventional field. *Why should it be taught in a conventional manner?* Tess thought to herself.

Tess had spoken to Roger, a soft-spoken young man

with a wonderful Australian accent. "Actually I'm from New Zealand," Roger had clarified when they had spoken over the phone. "I'm a Kiwi." Tess loved hearing Roger talk and wondered what had brought him halfway around the world to Toronto.

"Well, it's the energy here," he said. "It's right for diversity, and for explorers in human consciousness." Tess wanted to learn how human consciousness was connected with chi or energy healing, and she was certain that she was going to find out! The first step in learning Chios was an "attunement." This seemed to Tess to be a kind of opening and a connecting process, kind of like turning the big dial on her stereo to look for the right "station" for the Chios energy and then making the connection so that Tess could now be the receiver for this healing energy.

Astoundingly, Roger was able to do the attunement remotely, which meant that Tess stayed put at home while Roger connected to Tess's energy field from his studio in downtown Toronto. He had previously arranged for Tess to send to him by mail a recent photo of herself, which Roger used to visualize Tess's energy field and connect with it. At the prearranged time, Tess was to be ready and very relaxed, sitting down while keeping her mind quiet. Tess had waited, a little skeptical that she would feel much of anything, but after a few minutes, much to her surprise, she could feel her scalp gently prickling! And then a gentle warmness spread from her neck down her spine. She also felt a little euphoric, as if she'd had a whole bar of her favorite dark chocolate! At the end of the thirty minutes Tess was so relaxed—and refreshed, all at the same time.

As she spoke with Roger by phone afterwards, he explained that there were exercises for Tess to practice on her own, many of which involved developing a certain kind of focus and intention with her mind. Tess knew that her meditation practice would help her to develop this focus.

During the weeks following, Tess found that she could start the energy flowing simply by using her thoughts, in a kind of a visualization of the energy pouring into her body from the universe, and out through her hands. Much to her surprise, she could actually feel the difference between the Chios energy and Ximon's healing energy. It was wild enough to be feeling the energy moving invisibly through her hands, but the Chios energy felt somehow more refined, almost like the way a swatch of linen cloth would feel as opposed to that of silk. After a few weeks of practicing, Tess was able to start the energy within a second or two of visualizing the energy flowing.

There were also meditation exercises, and Tess had a small, flowered, sitting cushion that was quite portable and allowed her to sit in a half lotus position to meditate for a length of time without her legs falling asleep. On one particular evening Tess, sitting cross-legged on her cushion dressed in her purple tie-dye T-shirt and black yoga stretch pants, her hair tied back with a matching purple flowered scarf, was doing the exercise of following her breath. This exercise was the perfect way to let go of her thoughts and quiet her mind as she breathed slowly and deeply in through her nose, and slowly let the breath out through her mouth—feeling all the sensations of her breath, tickling in on her nose and hot on its way out over her lips. This exercise always made Tess feel so peaceful, and that's exactly what she needed on this particular evening at the beginning of May, just prior to her big meeting in San Fran, when recent activities at TSK were getting to be so crazily busy—peace of mind was exactly what she sought. The Mitz had quietly walked into the room and sat next to Tess, curling her tail elegantly around her sleek form, calmly watching Tess breathe.

Suddenly Tess felt something stirring, something deep inside her soul. It felt beautiful somehow, but she could not narrow it down any further than that. Her eyes started tearing up a bit. *Must be a divine presence,* she thought to herself. *Perhaps it's an Angel?* Tess had felt these divine presences before during church services but had never felt them during a meditation. Then suddenly—what is that? Ever so slowly a light was appearing on her right side, slowly enough so that Tess wasn't startled. Her eyes were firmly shut, and she was wondering just what to make of this light, and noted to herself that her strongest metaphysical skill seemed to be hearing and feeling these spiritual presences. "Who is here?" she asked finally, out loud.

I am Jason.

Wow, thought Tess. *I got an answer!* She didn't know what to say at first, and started to notice what she was feeling … she could feel that this Jason was benevolent and—ancient! *Are you an Angel?* asked Tess by thought, addressing the light. Her heart was skittering with excitement, and she realized that she was losing her relaxed meditation state. She took a few deep breaths, in, then out, and felt her body relax again, and her heart calmed. The light was still there. She sneaked one eye open—nothing physically in front of her. She clamped it shut—the light, this "Jason," was still there.

I am here to help you.

Holy smokes! she thought to herself. She had never had a conversation with a being of light before.

What shall we do? asked Tess to Spirit Jason.

Practice.

Practice what? asked Tess.

Everything, and nothing.

Somehow Tess understood; she had felt his meaning. The "everything" part to practice was the energy-related exercises, and the "nothing" part to practice was the meditating.

Thank you, Spirit Jason, said Tess by thought. And then the being of light was gone.

~*Chapter 10*~

Penelope

San Francisco was absolutely beautiful. Tess had been attending TSK's annual project meeting at the head office in downtown San Francisco, and it had been a busy but successful two days. The second day's meetings had ended about three thirty, and Danton, plus a few of the scientists, had nabbed Tess and headed out to his sailboat in the San Fran Bay. Dan, one of the development scientists that Tess often spoke with during project meetings, had prepared Tess ahead of time that they might get an opportunity to do a brief sailing stint on Danton's boat, so Tess had gladly made room for a windbreaker and sneakers in her luggage.

The five aspiring sailors met in the lower reception foyer at the TSK head office. Danton had changed into a dark blue turtleneck and beige casual pants complete with a blue windbreaker—and a matching dark blue captain's hat that he'd gotten across the bay in Berkeley. He looked very much the distinguished captain of a sailing yacht! Dan was standing directly in front of Danton with his arms crossed and a stern expression on his face. Danton and Dan were embroiled in the postmeeting lowdown on the executive level discussions, and from the snippet of Danton's voice giving advice to Dan of "switching to decaf before the next meeting"—Tess surmised that Dan was a little stressed about what he had heard about the future plans for biotech development, the department that he was currently heading.

Robert nudged Tess and motioned over his shoulder with his thumb, pointing behind him to the parking lot. Robert was a talented software developer, and he worked as a scientist with the team developing medical devices—and he had offered a ride to Tess. Tess caught Robert's eye, smiled back at him, and nodded, and they both turned toward the door.

"Hey, Danton, Dan, we'll meet you guys on the dock," called Robert as he and Tess headed through the glass doors out into the warm California air. Danton raised his arm and gave a short wave of his hand to acknowledge that he'd heard, but kept his focus on the conversation with Dan. The last of the five, Walter (he preferred to be called Wally), head of the analytical chemistry department, was standing on the steps with his eyes closed, soaking up the sun while waiting for Robert and Tess. Robert clapped his hand on Wally's shoulder as he and Tess whisked by, and Wally quickly started after them.

A short while later, after navigating the pre-rush-hour traffic through downtown, they all met at the entrance to one of San Francisco's many sailing clubs. There was a brisk wind as they walked along the wooden pier. Whitecaps dotted the surface of the bay. They walked along the docks, heading to the outermost layer of wooden walkways, their heads turning to look at the marvelous collection of sailboats of all sizes and colors. Sails were flapping in the wind, and some bells were chiming, and it seemed to Tess that the wind was actually picking up.

Finally they turned in toward the *Endeavour*. A fine forty-foot sailing yacht, it was composed of white fiberglass with dark marine mahogany wood trim, with a beautiful closed lower cabin and an open upper navigation cabin. The large white sails were neatly outlined with a crisp sea blue edging, and although they were flapping gallantly in the increasing gale, the mast was securely tethered. They all gingerly hopped onto the ladder and into the back of the boat and then turned and walked down the tiny stairway to a beautiful dark mahogany galley—which was complete with wall to wall seating and a round, dark oak kitchen table. The halogen lighting reflected off of the highly polished mahogany, creating a refined look to the interior of the *Endeavor*.

It is so small! thought Tess immediately. Five of them crammed into the tiny kitchen, a spot really meant for three or four, and Tess ended up sandwiched in the middle of the molded wooden seat between Dan and Wally. "Here you go!" and a small, plastic wine glass filled with an aromatic California cabernet sauvignon found its way into Tess's hand. She swirled the burgundy liquid and sniffed—a smile curled the corners of her lips, and she caught Danton's eye as he turned from the galley and placed the near empty bottle on the kitchen table, but he kept his hand on it, as the boat was rocking quite a bit from the strong winds. "Smells like black currents and nice cigars," said Tess, peering at Danton over the top of her glass.

"Ha ha-ha!" laughed Danton with his warm, gravelly voice. "Nice try, Tess. Now have a sip."

She swirled again and watched the liquid slowly drip down the sides of the glass. She took a sip. It was incredible! A robust raspberry and cedar flavor filled her mouth. She swallowed. It slid quickly down her throat and warmed her belly. She winked her approval to Danton.

"Let's sit upside," said Danton, and he slid past them and stepped lightly up the steps to the deck. The rest of the troop followed one by one, squeezing out from the tiny kitchen, each of them armed with their glass of sauvignon, and they marched up the galley stairway onto the deck of the *Endeavour*. The wind was now so strong that Tess could see what looked like two-foot whitecaps out on the bay.

Danton was standing with his hands on his hips staring out at the gale, and with a sigh turned back toward them, taking his captain's hat off with one hand and smoothing back his thick, dark hair with the other. "Oh, well, gang, you may as well sit back and relax," he sighed. "It's too windy to sail!" said Danton sadly, motioning to the seats along the sides of the boat, and he plunked down onto a sea-blue flowered cushion resting on dark wooden seats that were molded into the sides of the *Endeavor*.

"Damn," said Robert, with a smile on his face. "We'll just have to relax and sit back with a bottle or two of this lousy chardonnay," and he winked at Danton as he settled back into the cushioned seats in the lounge area. Robert and Danton were golfing partners and good friends outside of TSK. Danton pretended to be offended, turned up his nose, and quipped: "Hey, Rob, that's the Sav."

Robert flashed a smile back at him. "When did you bottle this batch, Dan?" he asked, twirling his glass and watching the wine as it swirled inside.

Well, that got Danton going, and he took great delight in describing the "viney patch" in his acre-sized backyard that he'd been cultivating for the last ten years. Tess watched the others listening to Danton's story, interested and eager to let go of the day's business and relax with another one of Danton's marvelous stories. As it turned out, Danton had actually been bottling the wine from his treasured viney patch—but only for the last six years, and Tess and the gang had been sipping on one of the very last bottles of the six-year-old batch. Tess was enchanted by Danton's graciousness in sharing his private reserve with them, and at the same time felt so fortunate to be included in this special outing.

They spent a relaxing evening with lively conversation, purposefully steered away from any talk of work, lubricated by the fine sauvignon and Danton's sharp wit. They munched on brie and crackers and watched the lights of Berkeley come on across the bay as the evening descended. It was a heady sight in every direction; downtown San Fran was directly behind them, Berkeley was shimmering out front and across the windswept bay, and the Golden Gate Bridge was boldly illuminated on their right. No one was out on the water except for large ferryboats, which seemed to easily cut through the choppy water. Tess dreamily thought that she'd have to return again someday for a chance to actually sail in the San Fran Bay. The intoxicating aroma of freshly roasted coffee came from the galley—Danton was brewing a pot for them. Tess couldn't believe that he had a coffeemaker stowed in that tiny galley, but a silver tray holding five steaming mugs of a dark Columbian brew appeared as Danton emerged from the galley, and the elegant Wedgewood mugs yielding the aromatic java were passed around at the end of the evening.

As they packed up for the night, the four of them left Danton on the *Endeavor*—he occasionally would stay on the boat overnight as his little getaway spot. He waved good-bye to each of them. Robert was holding out his hand to her as she stepped over the rim of the boat. Once safely on the dock, she turned back to say good-bye to Danton.

Have a good evening, Tess!

Tess blinked, and her heart skipped a beat. She stood staring dumbly back at him. He smiled and winked at her, then turned back and headed down the galley stairs. Robert tapped her on the shoulder. "Come on, Tess, it's getting late."

Tess turned around and walked beside Robert in a daze, the now chilly wind whipping her windbreaker and her hair flying around her head. Robert was saying something, but Tess did not hear him. She was absolutely certain that Danton had sent his good-bye message by thought! Holy smokes! How could that be? Tess gulped and realized that hearing thoughts sent by Spirit was one thing, but it was quite another thing to be hearing thoughts sent by a person …

As Tess and Robert walked back to the sailing club parking lot, Tess realized that as much as she enjoyed Danton's company, she was glad that he was her boss at a distance—this would give her a bit of time to adjust to this new way of communicating!

"Concentrate on your Tan Tien," said Jack, her Tai Chi sensei. Tess had been thinking about Danton and the magical evening on his boat during her recent trip instead of focusing on her Tai Chi forms—and quickly brought her thoughts back to the present moment and her Tai Chi class. Tess had started Tai Chi shortly after returning from San Fran. She looked over at Jack, and he motioned to his lower belly and looked at her. Jack's Chinese name was Jie Ki but Jack was easier for his students to say. Actually, most of the students called him Sensei Jack. He spoke mostly Mandarin, with a smattering of English, but most of the students were able to catch on to his teachings through his demonstrations. Although Sensei Jack was quite short, he was also very muscular and agile; he had such patience and a presence about him that somehow made his students feel that they were indeed being taught by a true guru.

On this particular night Sensei Jack was teaching them about the main power center of the body, the Tan Tien. This energy center in effect powered the whole body with chi, the life energy inside of everyone. Sensei Jack, through teaching the Tai Chi lessons, was helping Tess and her classmates learn how to tap into the Tan Tien through the slow, deliberate movements of the Tai Chi forms. Tess was thinking to herself that the Tan Tien seemed to be exactly in the same location as one of the chakras, the invisible spinning balls of energy that powered the human aura, or at least that is what she was learning in the Chios energy lessons. It seemed to Tess that Chakra two, the seat of desire, passion, and sexual energy, governing the female organs and lower intestine, was also the focus and source of power for Tai Chi.

When Tess had taken the introductory class, Sensei Jack and Tess had a very animated discussion—to Tess it was more like pantomime with a few words thrown in between, and Tess had relayed to Jack her reason for wanting to learn Tai Chi. Sensei Jack had gotten across to Tess that the Tai Chi was the best exercise to bring back her strength following her disease and surgery, that it would strengthen her lower abdomen and also strengthen her focus during meditation. And certainly Tess realized that she had to really focus on what she was doing during the elegant poses of the Tai Chi, otherwise she'd be falling over onto the floor!

They completed the practice on the five new forms that Sensei Jack had taught them, and the class broke up for the evening. Tess and the others in the class each bowed to Sensei Jack on their way out of the class, and once outside, Tess headed to her car. She shivered and felt a chill in the night air.

It's cold. Where's your coat?

Tess opened her car door. *That sounds like Mum,* she thought absently to herself.

That's because it is your mother, Missy!

"Huh?" Tess was sitting inside of the car and had just closed the door. She had just barely heard something, a voice that somehow sounded like her mother, Rose.

I am here, Tess.

Mum, is that you? sent Tess by thought. She didn't move or start the car; she had to be quiet and concentrate, to find out if she was really hearing this.

Yes!

Holy smokes! Tess was overwhelmed with this realization, and then the tears of sadness started—she really had missed her mother since her passing.

Mum, how can this be you? she sniffled. And then she realized she had broken the connection with Rose by getting emotional—strong negative emotions would block communication with the Spirit world. She grabbed a Kleenex and blew her nose. She started the car and pulled out of the parking lot. The radio was on, and Phil Collins was singing "You'll Be in My Heart." Tess couldn't believe it! This was their song, hers and Rose's! This song was playing all weekend when Tess went home to visit Rose upon first hearing of her illness. At the time Rose had thought it was quite significant, and had told Tess that she would always be (pointing to her heart) in her heart no matter what happened.

The tears really started flowing now, and Tess was having a hard time seeing the road as she was driving. *Mum, if you're still here, I have to get home before—uh, talking with you again, okay?* she sent by thought to Rose, grabbing another Kleenex and dabbing at her nose, steering with her left hand. *And, thanks for sending our song, Mum,* she added. Tess had read that spirits could do these things; somehow they could arrange these meaningful serendipities—coincidences that most people would think were random occurrences, but Tess knew otherwise!

Tess took some deep breaths and became a bit calmer, and by the time she arrived at home and parked the car in the garage, she was much more peaceful.

Stan was working evenings to meet a deadline, but The Mitz greeted Tess as she came in the front door. Tess bent down to bestow a couple of noogies and got a couple of rough licks on her hand in return. She headed to the bedroom and changed out of her tracksuit and into her pj's. Then she pulled out her flowered meditation cushion, sat down cross-legged, and took a couple of deep breaths, in—then out. And again, in—then out. When she felt that quiet stillness come over her, she thought about Rose. *Okay, Mum. Are you here?*

Yes, Missy.

It was very faint, but nevertheless, it certainly sounded and somehow felt like Rose was truly there.

I love you, Mum, sent Tess, bravely holding back her tears. She dearly wanted to hear her mother, and this was such an emotional moment—but Tess knew that strong emotions would block the "connection."

Mum, why are you here? asked Tess.

You need advice.

"Oh!" she said out loud in surprise, the impending tears quickly disappearing. Rose was absolutely right—Tess was stunned! Tess had been in a quandary with practicing and learning the Chios energy healing technique—she'd done all of the energetic practices that were at her current level, and had even read ahead in the manual at the next level up, but was unable to focus during the workbook meditation exercises that were a required part of the studies and could not move ahead without learning these particular exercises.

Tess eagerly formulated her next question. *Actually, I do need some advice, about the healing course I've been taking; I'm not sure why I can't do the mediation exercises. Can you tell me, Mum?* sent Tess, wondering how her mother would know anything about healing but at the same time understanding that Rose now might have a different perspective being on the other side.

You are afraid—of yourself. You need to ask Roger to do something.

"Oh!" said Tess, impressed that Rose would know that Roger was her healing teacher and also confused as to why she would be afraid of herself. Tess didn't really feel afraid. Hmmmmm, she pondered her next question.

Okay, Mum, what does Roger need to do? sent Tess.

Your fear comes from a past life issue, Missy. You know what to do.

Tess was both confused and stunned. A past life?! An issue from this past life? Just how could an issue from a past life be causing her problems in this life?

Mum, can you say that again? sent Tess, thinking that she just didn't hear Rose properly.

"…"

Tess couldn't hear Rose. She was certain that she had said something, though.

Mum, please say again? asked Tess.

"…"

Tess could feel, well, a certain something, but couldn't quite put her finger on it—as if a thought was on the tip of her tongue, but she couldn't quite hear what Rose was saying. Suddenly Tess realized that she was feeling extremely tired. Her eyes felt like sandpaper. Tess thought about this for a minute and then remembered a snippet of information that she had read recently from a book written by an incredible medium, George Anderson, who was well known for his grief counseling for people who had lost loved ones. When George first began to speak to spirits of the deceased persons, he became tired quite easily. It was extraordinarily draining to engage in this kind of session—it was almost like doing a workout at the gym except that it was kind of an energy field workout rather than a muscles workout.

Mum, I will talk to Roger as you suggested. Tess wasn't really sure what else to say—there was so much she wanted to talk to her mother about, but where to start? And Tess realized that it was time to stop the session for now.

Thank you for your advice, Mum. I love you. Bye!

Tess took a couple of deep breaths. Imagine, getting advice from Rose direct from the other side. *That's kinda cool!* she thought to herself. Tess was noticing another pattern in her life, first her voice or guide, then the visit from Rose, then the telepathic thought sent by Danton, and now actually speaking with Rose on the other side. Her clairvoyant abilities were expanding!

She got up and walked over to the computer in the TV room. It was hardly a TV room any more, as both she and Stan never watched television other than the occasional DVD. Tess moved aside a deck of archetype cards and an instruction book that were lying on the computer table. Tess had recently been doing quite a bit of research on personal archetypes and how to identify their patterns of behavior in one's own life. She had collected some books from Carl Jung, who really had done quite a lot of work on characterizing the familiar archetypes that are within all of us—and more recent professionals such as Carolyn Myss had expanded upon these to provide a system for identifying these patterns of behavior that are within everyone. The card for the healer archetype was on the top of the deck, and Tess had been most interested in the "wounded healer" aspect of this archetype because of her experiences with physical disease that had let her to discover the world of energy healing.

The familiar Windows theme chimed on her computer and Tess turned her attention to the blue computer screen, which promptly changed to a collection of photos from the digital photo collection of Tess and Stan, mostly pictures of their beloved Mitzi.

Tess wasn't quite sure what to ask Roger, but she fired up her e-mail program and then sat quietly. She remembered Rose's strange comment about Tess being afraid of herself, and something about … A sudden thought flashed into her mind, and she jumped off the chair and ran to her office in the basement. She rustled through her burgeoning bookshelf. Aha! She found it! She grabbed her Chios level four workbook and came back upstairs. Tess was still working on completing the meditation exercises in level three. She had skipped ahead in her reading to the level four workbook and was remembering a certain passage—here it was! This was the section that detailed how past lives were stored somehow in the aura, and the healer who had attained the "master" level of skill could detect and activate past life events that were traumatic, which were held in the aura and which were influencing the present life.

Tess had found it extraordinarily interesting that past lives were a reality, and not only that, but it was also so incredible to know that the information from the past life was actually sitting in the aura in the present life. And it's even more astounding still, Tess thought, that the emotion from a particular event or trauma from that past life could carry over somehow into the present. She wasn't quite sure why it had captured her interest and what exactly she was going to say, but she completed her e-mail to Roger.

"I hope you don't mind, but I have read ahead a bit into level four, and, well, I seem quite interested in the past life part, where you can use the Chios energy to heal traumas. Do you have any advice for me on this?" Tess typed. "Namasté" she added to close her e-mail. Namasté was a very quaint and respectful greeting or good-bye that honored the divine aspect of the person being greeted.

As she hit the Send button, she heard Stan's key in the front door. Tess paused and pondered the evening's events. She wasn't sure what to say to Stan about the visit and advice from Rose. He had gone along with her interest in learning energy healing but didn't seem particularly keen about it, and in fact had expressed the opinion that he didn't want her studies to interfere with her work at TSK. And a few years ago, when she had first told Stan about seeing Rose when she was passing to the other side, Stan was initially amazed—but didn't really say too much either, as if he really didn't believe that Tess had seen her mother and was just humoring her. So, as phenomenal as it was, she was reluctant to share Rose's visit with Stan. At least, not yet, thought Tess. She hit the Send button and then headed to the door to greet Stan.

"Hi, Stan," said Tess. Mitzi ducked between her legs and beat Tess to the doorway as Stan was just stepping inside.

"Mrrrowww!" said Mitz.

Stan and Tess laughed. "She's such a cutie," said Stan.

Tess agreed. Stan reached over and embraced Tess in a bear hug. Tess returned the hug, and they stayed embraced for two whole minutes. Both she and Stan didn't really want to let go and break the magical energy that seemed to flow between the two of them. *We're so different from each other and yet this unexplainable chemistry exists between the two of us,* Tess noticed.

"Mrrrowww!" said Mitz and nuzzled against their legs. "I think we're having a threesome," laughed Stan as he stepped away from their embrace.

Tess looked back at Stan. He had his green overalls with the words "Orion Landscaping" emblazoned on the front. Stan was a down-to-earth man who loved to be outside working with his hands, and also so practical—as he had to be with running his own business. And Tess was a businesswoman with interests so different from Stan's, most especially now that these mystical experiences seemed to be occurring around her. But somehow their relationship just seemed to click despite these differences.

"How'd it go today, Stan?" asked Tess, grabbing the lunch bucket that Stan had left on the porch.

"So-so. One of the guys didn't show up, though, so we were really slugging it today. But we got it done."

Stan's crew was working on landscaping the front and back yards of a newly built mansion just north of the city, and they had a two-week deadline to get the gardens dug and planted. The stone walkways had been installed during the first week and then there had been a two-day delay because of rain. They had a new contract beginning the following week, so there was a time pressure to get the current job done on time.

"I'm in the shower, Tess," called Stan. Tess unpacked his lunch remnants from the bucket and decided to do a quick check on her e-mails while Stan was in the shower. Sure enough, there was already a reply from Roger, a very short one.

"I will ponder it awhile and get back to you."

Hmmmm, thought Tess. Very mysterious indeed! Roger was an interesting character, and Tess was beginning to suspect that although his answers were seemingly very straightforward that perhaps there was something deeper and wiser going on. It felt as if something energetic and very deep were occurring, almost like Tess's readiness for certain lessons or teachings was being carefully considered before moving ahead.

A few days later, Tess was walking slowly up the stairs exiting from the subway on her way to work. Outside on the street it was a beautiful summer day, nice and warm, and a little breezy, which reminded Tess of the California breeze on the deck of the *Endeavour*. She shook her hair a bit in the wind, and as she walked amongst the commuters her mind went back to that magical evening, and she felt her body relax as if she were on the boat with that special group of people again. Then, she slowly became aware of a slight prickling of her scalp. She slowed her pace a bit and continued her saunter—the prickling was getting stronger. Then, she stopped completely—her entire scalp was prickling madly! She pretended to be looking at something in the tree next to her, but her focus was on the source of her mysterious prickling. Hmmmm, maybe it's a message, she thought and closed her eyes and quieted herself as much as she could on the street busy with commuters. And then she felt it … It wasn't so much of an audible message as it was a feeling—and not just a feeling either. It was like a chunk of knowledge had just been delivered to her all in one moment. She waited, and slowly it rose into her consciousness and then all at once she could identify it; it was past life information! Suddenly Tess knew the entire contents of the chunk of knowledge. It was almost like a shortcut to a database of information had been placed in her aura and had opened up! It was regarding traumatic events from a past life, and how this had affected her in this life. It was clear to Tess how the trauma had influenced the series of events that had led to where she was now with her health. Tess's eyes fluttered open, and staring at her with concern was a professional-looking woman dressed in a cream-colored skirt and jacket. "Are you okay?" she asked.

"Oh! Yes, I—I'm good," stammered Tess. "Thanks for asking," she added. The woman smiled and turned away. Tess, determined to find out more about this past life knowledge that had been opened up to her, continued her slow walking, and went back to delving through the information she had received.

Tess could somehow feel and hear that she was a woman in this past life. She waited and got a bit more—there was quite a bit of trauma; some of this trauma had been inflicted on other people by this woman. As she was absorbing that, Tess felt a little emotional, feeling guilty somehow that she would have been the cause of this trauma. Tess waited for a minute—it felt somehow like there was more information there—and then she got a last bit. Some of the trauma was also inflicted on this woman by others she knew in that life. Tess stopped—she was in front of the Mars building now. She waited for a few moments, knowing that these would be the last quiet moments of her workday—nothing else seemed to be there—she had "downloaded" the entire chunk of information. Well, that's pretty wild, thought Tess as she opened the entrance doors to the high-tech glass office tower. It must have been Roger who initiated the "thought" information—he must have used the Chios energy in a distance healing session to activate a past life memory, she deduced, remembering what she had read in the level four workbook. *Very cool!* thought Tess. *I wonder who I was and what that life was all about?* she puzzled, and stepped out of the elevator onto the tenth floor to begin her workday. Tess placed her hand on the scanner, and the door slid open. The noise from the lab enveloped her while stepping into the hallway of TSK, and Tess silently vowed to herself that she would most definitely be following up on this past life information to find out just what adventures she'd been having!

Back at home after a busy day at work, Tess once again was sitting in front of her computer typing another e-mail to Roger. As she was typing, Tess was appreciating this quiet time in the evenings with Stan working later hours—this really gave her a chance to do her metaphysical detective work!

Tess sat back and reviewed her draft e-mail to Roger which read: "I received some intuitive information this morning, about a past life. If you have initiated this—thank you! What do I do next, and how can I find out more about this past life?"

She hit the Send button. The Mitz was purring and head-butting her leg. Tess reached down and scratched the very top of the cat's head, giving her the pleasurable noogie that she was asking for. Tess settled back to review the stack of e-mails that had piled up in her home in-box.

Shortly a new message appeared. *It's from Roger!* noticed Tess eagerly, and opened it. Roger had given some instructions for Tess to do a meditation on the subject and to ask spirit to reveal the past life experience. During one of their previous conversations, Roger had said that "spirit" really was a collection of spirits that apparently everyone had around them, but of course most people were unaware of their presence except when they received the occasional insight or blessing.

Tess wasn't sure what else to do except to prepare for a meditation. She put the computer onto standby and headed for the bedroom, where her meditation cushion was, sat on it in the middle of the floor and took three deep breaths, inhaling deeply and exhaling each breath slowly. She felt her body relax with each breath, and she told herself to keep a clear and open mind. After the third breath she felt ready to address spirit.

Spirit, please reveal the past life experience that needs to be addressed now, she sent by thought, intending that her thought go to the spirit or spirits that were around her.

Tess relaxed and waited in her mindful state, that peaceful state where her mind was clear and calm. After a moment she felt and heard something; it was faint but might have been "1800s." And then she both heard and felt "female." Then slowly Tess could both feel and see in her mind's eye a woman, quite a buxom and shapely woman, and then Tess felt as if her own body had somehow merged together with this image in her mind's eye, and Tess was now the shapely body of this woman. Wow, I've got cleavage! Tess noticed and smiled to herself—she was in her present life small-busted. Tess could actually feel the heaviness of her bust, and the pressure of the bodice of the dress, which seemed to be stretched tight across her chest and down to her waist. The past life woman held her head high, and had long, dark-brown hair swept up into an elaborate figure eight bun. And she was wearing a gorgeous blue gray dress, a long dress or skirt suit perhaps, with a short jacket cut close to her body and open in the front to reveal a white blouse that felt smooth like silk, and a ruffled collar that kind of tickled her throat. The long skirt had many folds that would swish when she walked. She felt an air of sophistication and intelligence mixed with—what was it that she was feeling— importance and authority—that was it! Tess was thinking to herself that this woman must have been well educated and probably quite well off to be dressed so elegantly. And then she heard it, very clearly and so distinctly:

Penelope Lancaster.

~Chapter 11~

Ophelia and "O"

Tess was in the shower humming her favorite tune of the moment, "Blue Skies smiling at me ... nothing but blue skies do I see ..." The previous night's meditation had revealed some extraordinary information—that Penelope had been a female land developer! Tess wasn't sure exactly what country, but she seemed to be on a kind of a ranch with horses and native people and had assumed that it may have been the United States. She had felt that there was conflict going on around her and that a war was occurring. Perhaps that's where the trauma part comes in, Tess had thought.

Suddenly Tess felt something, a slight prickling of her skin—someone was near her. "Stan?" called Tess. No answer. *Hmph*, thought Tess, returning her attention to finish the shampooing of her hair. And then she felt it again; this time it was a more insistent feeling. Perhaps it was a spirit?

Hello? she sent by thought, and then paused and closed her eyes to help focus on her nonphysical senses. Wait a minute—the song! Tess addressed spirit: *Was it you that sent me that song that's in my head?*

Yes.

Thanks! sent Tess. *Who are you?* she asked curiously.

Ophelia. I am your guide.

Wow! thought Tess to herself. And then; *Ah, well you've caught me at an interesting moment,* sent Tess, looking at herself naked and soapy in the shower and wondering just how that might appear to a visiting Spirit.

I don't see you the same way you see yourself, said Ophelia. *Your energy field is what I see and feel.*

Tess thought about that for a moment and imagined what her energy field would look like to a spirit who was local, or visiting in the physical realm, which, according to her Rampa readings was about three feet up in the air from her. She knew that the aura extended about three feet out from her body and contained many colors, and changed depending on her physical, mental, and emotional state. She imagined an egg-shaped bubble around her with pastel patches of color floating on the surface of the bubble. Tess started rinsing the shampoo out of her hair while she was thinking about her next question.

If you would prefer privacy we can make an arrangement, said Ophelia.

What kind of an arrangement? sent Tess.

If you are in any room with the door closed, I will not visit unless you specifically request. And, other spirits will not visit. It will be kind of a "signal" to us.

Okay, sent Tess. Then she peeked out from behind the shower curtain—the door was closed. *But please continue for now,* she added quickly. Tess wanted to learn more about Ophelia.

There are three of us here with you right now, continued Ophelia.

As soon as her words registered with Tess, Tess could somehow feel the presence of the three spirits. Well, two of them anyways, there was someone—something else—that felt somehow slightly different, and also very divine.

Jacqueline. She is my helper, said Ophelia.

Hello, Tess, said Jacqueline.

Hello, Jacqueline, greeted Tess. Tess could feel Jacqueline respond, and also felt that Jacqueline was younger than Ophelia. Tess briefly wondered why Ophelia would need a helper. Ophelia felt older and wiser, and her "voice" was stronger than Jacqueline's.

And Caroline is here, said Ophelia.

This is the divine feeling one, thought Tess to herself. It felt like tiny gold sparkles were showering down around her, and she felt a peaceful, compassionate presence. *Hello, Caroline.*

She is your Angel, your Guardian Angel, said Ophelia.

Cool! thought Tess to herself. And then something occurred to Tess. *Why are the three of you here now?* Tess sent.

We are here to help you learn.

And then Tess began to feel herself as Penelope, the buxom body, the fancy blue dress-suit …

Suddenly there was a knock at the door.

"Tess, honey, where's the suitcase?" Tess and Stan were packing for their summer vacation.

"I put it on the bed in the spare room," replied Tess, and her thoughts of Penelope disappeared, replaced with thoughts of packing and vacation preparations.

"Okay, Tess," said Stan.

Later that morning, Tess stepped outside to wax the car. Her Saturn wagon was ten years old, still in great shape but in need of a wash and wax. Tess and Stan planned to leave in the early afternoon for their two-week jaunt through northern Ontario and Algonquin Park. They both loved the serene peacefulness of the natural wilderness. And they planned to do a combination of camping and bed and breakfast, depending on what was available. This was a spontaneous trip. The spring had been Stan's busy season, but now things had slowed a bit, and both Stan and Tess needed a vacation.

Tess got the bucket of car-waxing paraphernalia out of the garage and set it down beside the car, which by now had stopped dripping and had dried off from Stan's wash earlier in the morning. Stan was on the phone talking with Otto, arranging for him to come and look after The Mitz while he and Tess were away. Tess grabbed the waxing rag and opened the tin of wax, dabbing at the paste wax and then applying it on the body of the car in a circular motion. The sun was hot and warm, and Tess felt relaxed and happy that she and Stan had two whole weeks of vacation ahead of them.

A wealthy landowner.

Ophelia was back. And so was Penelope—Tess could feel Penelope's body again, as if it were her own. She stopped her waxing and waited.

Keep going.

Tess heeded the voice of her guide and went back to her waxing. It was kind of like a meditation, the repetitive motions. Ever since first receiving past life information while on her walk to work, Tess had begun to develop her meditation practice to include walking meditation, in that Tess could be slowly walking and at the same time have her mind in a mindful, or calm and peaceful, state. Tess realized that this was the state her mind needed to be in to clearly receive intuitive information, and thought that the Tai Chi was helping her be able to do this.

You had slaves, native slaves.

Oh! sent Tess by thought.

They were forced to do things. They were mistreated.

Somehow Tess could see in her mind's eye the outside of a homestead or ranch, and then the scene moved inside to the kitchen. There were staff inside, and they were white, and of British decent. They were busy making preparations for the day's meals. She saw the head cook; he was stirring a pot of stew and calling instructions to others around him, who were busy preparing the next ingredients. Tess knew him—she could somehow feel that! And she knew that in her present life, that soul was Christopher, her first beau from high school! Tess didn't understand how she could know this, but tried to keep open to more information about this past life.

Ophelia, is the cook my friend Christopher?

Yes.

How can that be? asked Tess by thought. She dabbed her rag into the tin of wax and began applying wax to the hood of the car.

You are soul mates. Part of the same soul group. Soul groups like to incarnate together. He was a part of that life.

Tess felt a little guilty. Penelope had been barking orders to the kitchen staff, and it felt like she had told off the cook about something—apparently she ran a strict household.

The scene in Tess's mind's eye changed, and Penelope was outside the kitchen door of the ranch-style homestead. A dense forest was off to the right, and what looked like a path was leading into it. And there was a fenced-off area like a paddock behind the house, and to Tess's delight there were horses, probably thoroughbreds! There were two dark-skinned men leading a couple of the horses to a nearby barn. Tess had always had a liking for horses, but never really knew why. As a child she'd collected statues of horses, and one of her favorite novels was *Black Beauty*. And Holy smokes! Stan was there ... he was white, and also working with the horses. *Perhaps he was the horse trainer,* she thought.

He looked a lot like Stan did now, except that he was quite pale, had longer, curlier hair, and was a bit stockier in build than Stan. And … Tess realized by how she was feeling at this moment that Penelope was in love with this man!

Suddenly the scene had changed, and Tess found herself in the middle of a forest; the trees were dense, and her long blue dress was catching on the branches—she was running and deathly afraid! Two assailants were after her, and one of them suddenly drew a sword and killed her with a stroke from behind, the sword going between her legs and coming out through her front, piercing her abdomen. Tess was shocked!

Traumatic events, both caused by you, and also done to you.

Tess had stopped waxing by now. *And these traumas have carried over into this life?* she asked Ophelia by thought.

Yes.

I want to know more! sent Tess and resumed her waxing. In the next hour waxing the car, Tess saw in her mind's eye snapshots of various significant events, and Ophelia would comment on certain people encountered, many of whom she seemed to know in her present life. These were members of her soul group, a group of very cosmically linked souls. Somehow Danton was involved, but it didn't feel like he was in this particular past life; it might have been another past life. But he was a part of the cosmic soul group! And oddly enough, even though Tess had been involved romantically with Stan in the past life she'd just seen, and now again in this life—he was not a member of her soul group. But, she was certain that she and Stan were meant to have a romantic relationship together in their current life! *So he must be a soul mate,* thought Tess. Tess was beginning to notice subtle differences between the energetic connection of soul group members and that of soul mates, or souls from differing soul groups that share life experiences together for a common purpose; in the case of Tess and Stan, that purpose was romance!

Tess had also been doing some reading from other metaphysical experts, such as Silvia Browne and Brian Weiss, who had similar insights about the nature of human consciousness and reincarnation. Tess had decided to keep this information to herself and not share it with Stan—for now.

The snapshots of her past life continued throughout the two weeks of her vacation with Stan. It seemed that whenever she was relaxed enough she would receive more information about her experiences. Tess figured that perhaps this was occurring, or that this could occur, because of her practice of walking meditation and Tai Chi exercises, which allowed her to keep her mind calm and relaxed. Tess wondered if Ophelia or her Angel were somehow facilitating the release of these memories by sending energy to certain spots in her energy field.

More and more snippets of information were being woven into the story of this past life, sometimes while relaxing in the car on the drive through Northern Ontario, and other times while hiking in the woods of Algonquin. Ophelia revealed to Tess that Jacqueline would run errands for her, doing research and bringing back information that would somehow help Ophelia communicate with Tess and provide teachings for her. One astounding event occurred while hiking on the Two Rivers Trail along the main highway running through Algonquin Park. It was a gorgeous, sunny day; the hiking path was covered in cedar chips, which made the air so fresh and "cedary." The path wound in and out of the woods, alongside rock cliffs overlooking the Madawaska River. Stan was hiking in front, and Tess was following along behind. Ophelia had just let her know that a native healer—Tess had assumed Native American—had been treating some of the slaves in her homestead ranch, and that native healer was none other than Ophelia herself! Tess stopped dead in her tracks. Stan, unaware that Tess was experiencing her past life lessons and that she had momentarily stopped hiking, was forging ahead.

You mean that in my past life you were also incarnated and that you were a part of this life, that you treated and healed native slaves that were mistreated at my direction, and now you are here as spirit, as my guide to teach and provide guidance to—me? asked Tess to Ophelia.

Yes.

Ophelia, I have the highest regard for you! Tess said immediately. Tess was amazed at her guide. What a very spiritual thing to be doing, helping someone who had previously caused so much trauma to others.

Jesus is here.

What? said Tess, incredulous.

He gives his blessing.

Tess didn't know what to say, do, or even think.

Uh—thank you! she sent finally, still in awe of these astounding events.

"Tess," she heard Stan call from the path ahead.

"Oh—coming Stan," called Tess, in a daze. Her head was whirling. What was the meaning of the visit from Jesus? Tess had no doubt that a significant series of events had just occurred, but she didn't quite know what to make of it all.

By the end of the two weeks Tess had a flavor for some of the significant events of her past life. It was as if she had been reviewing a film, in which certain parts could reach out and touch her as ringing true, parts that she could identify or resonate with. But she still didn't know where these events had taken place. Back at home, she and Stan were busy unpacking and doing laundry. Tess was running the events from her past life through her head, trying to understand and make sense of it all. She pondered about Ophelia.

Ophelia, what's your native name? she sent by thought.

"…"

What? Tess didn't hear what Ophelia had said.

"…"

I don't understand, sent Tess. *Can you spell it?*

That won't help. It is a word that you have not heard before.

Why should that make a difference? asked Tess.

Why don't we look together on the Internet sometime, said Ophelia.

Cool! sent Tess, and once she had a load of laundry in the washer Tess took a break and fired up her computer.

Tess googled Native American Indian names databases and scrolled through lists of names but didn't get any response from Ophelia.

Ophelia, could you please help me? Where should I be looking?

New Zealand.

"What!" exclaimed Tess out loud.

"Are you talking to me," called Stan from the kitchen, where he was preparing a cup of tea for them both.

"No, sorry, Stan," said Tess hurriedly. "Just looking up something on the computer."

Tess started googling New Zealand names databases, but still didn't find anything substantial. Finally she came across a link that took her to a historical site on native New Zealand Maori. Tess paused; this felt like it might be—something.

Check it out.

She clicked away and found herself at a native Maori names database. She scanned through starting with the As.

Page by page she worked her way through the alphabet, and then she got to the Ts.

Slow down.

Tess took her time scanning through the Ts. Hmmm, this one was looking interesting … *Ta-paro. Is that it?* sent Tess.

Yes.

Wow! How do you say it? Tap … Tapa—ro?

Slow it down.

Okay. Tay Pa Roo. Tayparoo, sent Tess. *How's that?*

That is it!

New Zealand, huh? thought Tess to herself. *Just how did she end up there?* She was hearing Stan clinking the mugs for their tea and rustling the bag of cookies.

You were a British in New Zealand. A land developer. You gave British names to the natives, and your name for me was Ophelia.

Tess was amazed. A female land developer, in the mid-eighteen hundreds, setting up and running a household and a horse ranch in New Zealand! How cool was that! *Hmmmm, I wonder what I could have done to cause someone to stab and kill me with a sword,* thought Tess to herself. Stan was calling her to come for her cup of tea. *Thank you, Tayparoo!* and she hustled off to the kitchen.

Back at TSK after her vacation, Tess was staring at the screen of her laptop, wondering what on earth was wrong with her computer, when the phone rang.

"Tess, can you come to my office, please." It was Carlos Anthony, the new Toronto site director. Just before Tess went on vacation, TSK had undergone reorganization, and three of its divisions had merged together. This resulted in a redundancy of administrative staff, and many upper-level directors and managers had been let go. Fortunately

Danton was still the head of the division, and Carlos was now managing the Toronto site.

"Sure, Carlos, I'll be right over." Tess put down the phone and looked over at her computer. She had not been able to log in, and after three tries she was now locked out. For some reason she wasn't entering her password correctly. Then something occurred to her. *Hmmmm.* A tingling feeling started at the back of her head. *Something's definitely up,* she thought, as she stood up and walked out toward Carlos's office. On the way Tess was reasoning it out. She was very likely laid off too. Although Tess's workload was quite high, her work could easily be divided up and divvied out to other project managers. She gingerly stepped into Carlos's office and found Lisa McKinnon, the site human resources manager, there also.

"Hello, Tess. Please sit down," said Carlos.

A few moments later they conferenced in Danton by phone, who delivered the news himself, and he sounded so businesslike until his voice cracked a bit. *Must be tough for him to do this,* Tess thought. Danton's words were melding into the background as Tess looked around the room at Carlos and Lisa. Both were studying their hands, and Tess felt that this kind of news was also tough for them to deliver.

Danton, don't worry, it's okay! Tess sent by thought to Danton. Tess thought this might just ease his stress about having to let her go, just in case he could actually hear her. If he was part of her soul group and so cosmically connected to her, he just might hear her! Tess knew that time and space were nonexistent in the metaphysical world. It didn't matter if Danton was right next to her or across the country, she could still send energy or thought to him just as if he were right beside her physically.

Afterwards Lisa led her to the spare office, and a friendly

older woman was inside. "Hi, Tess, I'm Margery. Please have a seat. I am a career councilor, and I'm here to help you." Tess smiled back at her. Another tree trunk had fallen in front of her, creating another change in her life path. To Tess it was beginning to feel more like a life adventure!

The time off had been a blessing. TSK had provided quite a substantial package, and Tess had about six months to find another job. In the meantime, she could continue her energy healing studies. Tess was finding that the more she learned about the metaphysical world, the less she really knew, and the more her desire to learn grew—this was now her passion, her purpose!

Stan had mixed feelings about her layoff. He was sorry, of course, that she was no longer employed and was forced now to look for another job. That was never easy to do. But the package really gave a bit of breathing room so that she did not have to rush out and take just any job that came along.

Tess had decided that it was time to figure out how to validate all of the experiences that had been revealed to her. But how? How could someone confirm that she really had lived a past life in New Zealand, that Stan had been a part of it, that the voices she was hearing really were a guide and not some mischievous spirit trying to lead her astray somehow, or that Tess was simply going batty, perhaps even schizophrenic? And just what was the real meaning of these past life experiences? Why were they coming to her now? Tess was bouncing back and forth between the intensely real flavor, the feel, the impact of each experience—and the notion that most people would indeed think that she and her experiences were psychotic.

The answer came while she was at her regular massage session with Liam. A number of years previous, Tess had gotten whiplash from a skydiving stint with her ex, Frank, when she was about twenty-five. Tess had found that regular massage kept her neck from seizing up. Liam was a very spiritual man, not spiritual in that he was a churchgoer—to Tess being spiritual meant that a person was open to being guided by spiritual forces higher than themselves. You could call these forces God or Jesus or whomever you liked, but in their most positive form these were forces that were recognized as being divine. Liam and Tess talked about mystical events that had occurred, sometimes with Tess and sometimes with Liam. It was comforting to share these experiences with someone who understood. At what felt like the right moment, Tess shared information with Liam about her recent past life. Tess revealed to Liam the quandary that she was in as to whether these past life events were real or whether Tess going a little psychotic.

"You have to go and see my friend O," said Liam. "He's clairvoyant, and he does readings, and—he's good."

"O?" said Tess.

"His name is Ben O'Rian, but he goes by O."

Tess wasn't sure. There were so many charlatans out there. How could you know who to trust?

"I'm sensing that you're a little hesitant," said Liam as he found another knot in her upper shoulder. Tess gasped as he pushed hard on it, forcing the muscle to unlock out of its spasm.

"I was too," continued Liam. "But, he's fantastic. Everything that he read for me I found later to be dead on. He's quite incredible, Tess! But I'll leave it with you to decide."

Tess was thinking about it. Well, what could she lose? She didn't have to tell this "O" who she was or why she was there—let him tell her. Let's see what he comes up with. There—she'd decided!

However, Stan was hesitant about her plans to visit O.

Stan had actually agreed to come with Tess to her first Reiki class. And, Tess thought that it was so fantastic of him—he really wasn't into energy healing or the metaphysical world. He really agreed to come just because it had meant so much to Tess. Roger had recommended another Reiki master to Tess, as he was not currently teaching Reiki himself. And he wholeheartedly felt that Tess could easily be learning a few energy modalities as once. Tess was worried. "Can I mix these energies, or do I use one first and then another?" But Roger assured her that she would learn the best way to handle the different energies. Michael Grandstone was his name, and he was apparently a fantastic teacher. Tess was especially happy that Stan would come with her to experience the Reiki himself.

"This is your decision, Tess," said Stan, referring to her appointment with O. "I can't tell you not to go. Just know that I'm worried about your safety. Keep your cell phone on, and promise that you'll call me as soon as you are done, okay?" he asked Tess.

Tess knew that Stan was worried about Tess's safety, going into the downtown area at night to visit a person she'd never met before, and so she agreed to call him as soon as her session with O was over and she was on her way home, so that Stan would know she was safe and sound.

O had a loft-type office that was located over top of a busy cafe. She walked up to the top of the stairs and knocked on the door. She heard him call from inside. "Come in." The office was open concept, wooden floors with a beautiful Persian rug in various shades of blue. There was a small, lacquered pine table with a set of cards and a photo of the Mona Lisa on top. The photo made Tess smile.

How appropriate, an enigmatic smile for those seeking enlightenment from their own enigmas! Two pine chairs were around the table. Tess sniffed—lavender incense with a dash of rosemary. Tess relaxed a bit. The lavender-rosemary fragrance was so exotic smelling and made Tess want to take deep breaths. There was a small sofa to the right of the table, and a wingbacked chair was adjacent to it. There were several plain chairs stacked in the other corner of the room. It was all in all a very cozy office.

Tess was just pulling out a chair from under the table.

"Have a seat at the table; I'll be right there," called O from an adjoining room. Tess smiled to herself. His voice sounded very friendly, and he had an accent that she couldn't quite identify, but it certainly didn't sound Irish.

"Hello—Tess is it? I'm O." A tall and handsome young man came out of the adjoining room. He looked at Tess—he had blond hair and sparkling blue eyes that had a hint of mystery about them. He smiled and held out his hand, and Tess shook it. "Have a seat," and O motioned to the chair that Tess had pulled out. They both sat down, and O looked over quizzically at Tess.

"You know, before we get started, there's something, well, I don't know. Something … well, it's about you, Tess. Something a little magical. Yes, I'd have to say that—magical. Your aura—it's such a high vibration!"

She looked at O, and his eyes looked a little teary. He seemed genuine, but Tess wasn't sure about the "magical" stuff and hoped that wasn't a line that psychics used when meeting new people.

"There's something else going on too," he said, and he kind of looked over Tess's left shoulder. "I haven't even started looking at the tarot cards yet! I see a woman, long hair blowing in the wind, and a beautiful shawl wrapped over her shoulders. She's standing on the shoreline looking

154

out over the ocean. I'm not exactly sure where this is, but it might be—New Zealand."

Tess's mouth dropped open in surprise, and she just about fell off of her chair.

~Chapter 12~

Stan and Penelope

@#$*!

What the heck was that? thought Tess.

&%#@$ @#$*!

Who is there? Tess sent by thought. No answer.

Tess stood up and, using her thoughts, turned on the flow of her Chios energy and then swept her arms slowly though the bedroom, where she had been meditating, clearing away any negative energies that might have been lingering. Tess had heard these rude words quite often lately, and she was starting to become alarmed, wondering if there was a negative energy that was somehow attaching to her. Then she sat back down on her meditation cushion.

Tess was practicing the meditation techniques from the Chios masters level workbook but had been interrupted by the rude words. Tess was close to completing the Chios courses and had one case study left to complete. Tess had recently bumped into a good friend that she hadn't seen in about twenty years—and she had cancer. It was aggressive and terminal, and she'd already started chemo. But Katrina was an indomitable soul. She had agreed to let Tess practice her Chios energy healing on her once a week to gather data for her case study. Tess was more than happy to actually be putting all of her energy healing lessons to good use!

They'd been having a grand time together. Monday afternoons at one o'clock Katrina would come, and Tess would have her massage table set up in the basement; the lavender aromatherapy was warming in the burner, and the heating pad would be warming the fluffy white towels on the massage table. Tess became familiar with the condition of Katrina's chakras and aura, and initially, while she was still on the chemo, her chakras seemed quite robust although definitely out of balance. The chakras in the area of the cancer were definitely overactive. Although Katrina never told Tess where the tumors were located, Tess did know that it was lung cancer—the same cancer that had claimed Rose's life. At one point Tess had Katrina lying on her back, and Tess was scanning her right lung, near the bottom toward the spine, and something was coming into her vision. Tess used her "glancing" technique, where she would focus at an area that she wanted information from and then look away toward an area of light color, like the wall beside the massage table. She could see what looked like the outline of Katrina's lung on the wall! She could see all of the blood vessels and the shape of the lung, and—she could see a mass, the tumor, on the bottom of the lung near Katrina's spine.

Tess was able to gather quite a bit of data for her case study, and Katrina found the sessions quite relaxing, and she often fell asleep during them. Tess was glad to be able to provide at least some comfort for her friend.

And afterwards they would go together to the local café for coffee and a treat, and chat for a few hours together. Usually they never talked about Katrina's condition, but instead chose to keep the conversation positive. Tess could feel that this was really beneficial for Katrina, to have a bit of time to just forget about her situation for a while. Tess did try chatting with Katrina a bit about what could happen if she did succumb to the cancer and pass over—that her Spirit alive inside of her would go back to another life, the life in the nonphysical, and then perhaps incarnate again. But Katrina was not interested in any of this information, so Tess did not raise the subject again. Tess remembered how she had felt before Rose had become ill with her cancer—she never would have listened to someone try to tell her about the other side either. *If she hadn't experienced it first hand with Rose's visits, it still might be tough to convince herself,* Tess thought.

During later visits, when Katrina's chemo had finished (she had reached her maximum lifetime dosage for the drug), Tess could clearly notice the energy coming from the residual cancer, which was now free to grow unhindered by the chemo—it caused an angry redness in Katrina's aura. And it was quite distinct, almost like a signature to Tess. Tess noticed that her chakra seven was very overactive, and it felt likely the cancer had spread to her brain. And then— Katrina had stopped coming, and would not answer her e-mails or her phone. Tess was learning lots of life lessons on many levels—lessons about respecting the wishes of the person, the ego, in this case—not to know about "the other side." And also on a soul level—if healing of a disease was not desired by the soul, it would not occur. Tess also understood from some of her reading that some souls would incarnate in order to experience a disease and the life lessons that would accompany such a process.

Tess had found out through a mutual friend that Katrina simply wanted to be alone before passing. Tess could respect that but at the same time was so sad for her. Even though all of what she had learned until now told her that these were life events, however sad, however much suffering was involved, that we chose to go through before incarnating. As tough as it was to believe that we would actually choose to be ravaged by an aggressive cancer, to take drugs that were so toxic and had such horrid side effects to try and stave off the cancer, and then slowly and painfully succumb to the ravages of this disease. It sure didn't make sense to Tess, but then again she knew that she still had a lot to learn. There must be another perspective, a higher perspective, on coming to this Earth just to suffer and die a painful death, simply to learn a couple of lessons.

Tess could hear the rattle of Stan's key in the front door, and she realized that she had not been meditating at all—she'd been remembering and reflecting on her time with Katrina. She could hear The Mitz meowing as Stan stepped inside, and Tess stood up and headed to the front door to greet him. Her spirits lifted a bit as she realized it was a Friday night—and tomorrow morning she and Stan would be going to their first Reiki level I class!

"Hey, Stan! How was your day?" Tess asked. Mitzi was head-butting both of their legs, and Stan wrapped Tess in a bear hug. Tess felt grateful that she had such a loving partner and that both of them had reasonable health. Tess's previous issues seemed quiescent of late, although Tess realized that it was because she was doing self-healing treatments at least once per week and going to Tai Chi classes. The problem was perhaps not gone, but more likely was kept under control by the healing treatments and the subtle Tai Chi postures. Tess was wondering about all of the past life information she'd received from her New Zealand life, and wondered if the traumas from that life had anything to do with her health issue.

"Tess, why don't we get out of town this weekend? How's our schedule look? Do we have anything planned?" asked Stan as he picked up his lunch bucket and headed for the kitchen. Tess just looked at him, dumbfounded and unable to speak, an angry retort about his forgetfulness on the tip of her tongue.

Stan turned around and smiled back at Tess. "Just fooling, Tess. I know, it's the Reiki class this weekend, right?" He put his lunch bucket on the kitchen counter.

Tess relaxed and smiled back, realizing that Stan was just teasing her, and she was a little annoyed at herself for getting all in a huff so quickly. Stan sure liked to push her buttons. But she also knew that she could push his just as easily. "Hey, Stan, you don't have to go, you know. I think you'd rather go to the casino with your friend Rob." She smiled back at him and bent down to bestow a noogie on Mitz-cat (Mitzi now had a number of affectionate pet names). Stan looked over from the freezer, where he was storing his freezer packs from his lunch bucket.

"Touchè," said Stan. "Tess, do you feel like a *Star Trek*?" Stan and Tess were confirmed Trekkers, and found that unwinding after a long, stressful week by watching a *Star Trek* episode with a little popcorn was a good, positive tonic for both of them.

Soon they were snuggled on the couch, a big bowl of popcorn between them, butter on Stan's half of the bowl and salt on Tess's half. They became immersed in one of Tess's favorite episodes from the *Next Generation* series, "The Inner Light." The captain of the starship *Enterprise* finds himself in the midst of a beam from a strange probe that causes him to live an entire lifetime on a planet called Katan, which had gone extinct. Before the planet died, the inhabitants created this probe that could teach someone what life on that planet was all about by emitting a beam that would allow the person to holographically relive the life experiences on the planet as if he or she were one of the inhabitants.

Tess thought it was an ingenious way to express the

concept of feeling as if you could live a whole lifetime of experiences within a very short period of time. Tess's favorite character in this episode was Batai, who guided the captain in his "new" life and became the captain's best friend during this lifetime on the now-extinct planet. Tess soaked up every minute of the episode—and Stan had fallen asleep with the Mitz-cat curled up in his lap. Tess smiled and turned off the DVD player and TV and gently shook them both awake so that she could chase them both to bed.

The next morning Stan and Tess arrived just before nine o'clock. Tess could feel the energy in Michael's studio. It felt almost divine, like a horde of Angels was inside sprinkling gold sparkles everywhere. What was it that O had said to her during his reading? That she was clairsentient, that was it! In other words, she could "feel" stuff, psychic or metaphysical stuff. In this case, Tess could definitely feel the divine energy in the room. She made a comment to Michael complementing him on the wonderful energy.

"Thanks, Tess. I did my best to create a high vibration inside the studio today, and I'm certain there are a few spirits contributing as well!" He smiled and motioned to the chairs in the middle of the room. "Please, have a seat. We'll get started when everyone has arrived." They were in a medium-size room that had chairs set up in the middle, each with a white workbook on top. A whiteboard was set up, and—Tess sniffed. Bergamot—a lovely aromatherapy essence! Tess relaxed into her chair and basked in the energy and the aroma. Stan sat next to her, calmly flipping through his workbook. Tess couldn't resist, and she nudged Stan's elbow. He looked over with one eyebrow raised.

"Bet you never ever thought you'd find yourself in a place like this when you married me, did you?" she asked Stan with a smirk on her face. Stan just rolled his eyes at her and went back to studying his workbook. They were in a back seminar room of a holistic therapy store, and Tess caught the occasional bit of conversation from those browsing in the shop. The shop was filled to the brim with different crystals, stones, aromatherapy, spiritual books, Tibetan chimes and bowls, and a plethora of other holistic items. There weren't too many places that you could find these items all together in one spot. Tess looked over at the bulletin board for upcoming events and saw the Reiki I flyer advertising this weekend's course.

Michael began the class with five out of the ten students who had registered. It seemed to Tess that with many of these classes, often the people would just not show up or even call to say that they couldn't come.

Michael began with an overview and history of Reiki and then dived into the details of Reiki I. Next came the attunement for the Reiki I energy, which was sort of like opening to 220 volts from a 12-volt system, Michael had said.

The attunement was done in such a way that each person could not see exactly what was being done for each attunement. Tess could feel somehow that the energy level in the room had increased in vibration; the quality of the energy was quite high and pure. She almost felt as if there were purple clouds of this pure and rare energy circling around her. Then, Michael was behind her. At the right moment she would raise her hands as he had instructed everyone earlier. Tess had her eyes shut, and could now see the purplish clouds of energy. Then—something was coalescing in front of her—symbols! They were gold and surrounded by a purple mist. And they were moving; slowly they moved past her. Tess couldn't quite make them out or determine exactly how many symbols there were. Then the swirling energy changed hue, and now there were red swirling energies around her. And another set of symbols, different from the first; somehow they seemed to have an Egyptian flavor to them—Tess was pretty sure she saw an ankh—and the symbols were a deep red in color. Then the symbols were slowly engulfed by the red clouds of energy. And next she heard a voice addressing her.

You chose it.

Who is here? sent Tess by thought.

Dr Usui is here, with Jason, Ra, and Jesus.

Tess was astounded, and her eyes filled with tears. She was struggling to understand why they were all here with her.

You chose it, Tess. It is your thorn. And your gift. It was sent with love.

With a jolt Tess realized they were referring to her recent encounter with the rude words. Why on earth would she choose to have rude words spoken by thought to herself? She totally understood the thorn part—what if she was with someone like her cosmic soul group that could at times hear her thoughts—and the rude words came up? How nasty could that be! But a gift?! Tess simply did not understand. *Unless,* Tess thought, *perhaps their purpose was to warn me when something negative was around or approaching me.* But what she did truly understand right at this moment was that she was privileged to be in the company of some pretty incredible spirits.

Namastè, divine ones, sent Tess to the spirits, as she felt the session closing. She continued to struggle with her whirling thoughts and many questions. Another load of questions for her I'll-understand-that-later box.

Michael had wisely scheduled a break following the attunement for everyone, and Tess had some time to collect herself before diving back into the learning. It seemed logical that the spirit of Dr Usui—the original Reiki master, would be present at an attunement to Reiki energy. And spirit

Jason, a being of light that Tess had already been meeting with, also seemed logical to attend. But to find Ra, who Tess remembered as an Egyptian sun god, and also, incredibly, Jesus to be present with the others was a bit overwhelming. By the end of the weekend both Tess and Stan were energized and exhausted!

On Monday, Tess was back on the Internet scouting for biotech jobs. For some reason Tess had been drawn to job advertisements in the HIV field, hoping to apply her biotech experience toward a job in this growing area of research. She couldn't quite pin it down to any specific interest other than perhaps it might prove to be personally rewarding to be able to contribute to the research efforts. Her six months was drawing to a close, and she'd have to go on unemployment if she didn't find a job soon. It seemed like every move she made went absolutely nowhere. She had no leads and had no interviews—despite having had some really excellent career counseling and sending her revamped résumé to what seemed like hundreds of job advertisements.

Stretching, Tess took a break from the computer and headed to the kitchen to make a cup of tea. She was into Rooibos tea now—it had a unique flavor that at first Tess didn't like, but now she'd developed a taste for it. It was a hearty kind of tea, a tea for spiritual adventurers! She didn't know where that idea came from, but it seemed to fit. Tess returned to the computer but couldn't seem to focus on the job hunting activities and instead got up and went downstairs to her desk, which was sprawled with various items, all having to do with her archetypes research, including a special deck of cards. Each card captured the essence of a particular archetype, which really was a personality or pattern of behavior that produced a character trait. These character traits were known to influence human behavior. Some well-known archetypes that Jung had characterized would be mother (nurturer) and father (mentor), etc. Other archetypes were characterized by other experts in the field like Carolyn Myss. Using this deck of archetype cards you could determine which archetypes were currently influencing your own behavior by following certain techniques to activate your creative or intuitive brain, followed by sending your personal energy into the cards and then picking the cards that were intuitively resonating with you.

Through the research that Tess was doing, she had learned how integral our chi is to each of us, that it was part of who we are. We could use it for energy healing, exercise like Tai Chi, and for doing detective work into our true nature! Tarot and other methods of divination are essentially energy-based methods of obtaining clues to who we are and what it is that we are doing here on Earth. Tess had set aside the archetype cards that she had already picked out during a previous session, and as she went through the descriptions she had been astounded to see how accurately they described her current situation. One of the cards was the wounded healer, and most certainly Tess was wounded by her bout with peritonitis and endometriosis, and then healed by Ximon's herbs and then by her own energy healing—and these events had most certainly influenced her life path over the past few years, leading her to study the world of energy. Tess sat pondering the other cards, a few of which were "student" (Tess loved to learn) and "rebel" (for some reason Tess always felt a little at odds with authority figures). Then she stopped for a moment, getting a feeling that someone was gently tapping her on the shoulder.

Hello, Tess.

By now Tess was accustomed to new spirits dropping in, and she felt a good feeling from this one.

Hello, she sent by thought. *Who are you?*

I am Btai. I am your new guide.

Tess could feel straight away that Btai was not his real name, and at the same time was really delighted by her new guide's use of the name Btai—a name of a similar guide to the captain of the *Enterprise* in one of her favorite *Star Trek* episodes. She stood still for a moment and focused on her guide, and just about fell over when she realized his real identity. *No,* she said to herself, *it cannot be him.*

You could call me Btai-Paul if that helps. I am here as a good friend, and as a guide.

Tess liked this approach. She could feel a genuineness coming from him. Btai was the good friend part. Paul of Tarsus was the spiritual guide part.

~

Just before Btai Paul arrived, Tess had been in between guides for a few months. Ophelia and Jacquelyn had left one day while she was driving home from work. Usually Tess had the radio turned up or a CD playing (she alternated between classical, usually Bach, or relaxation music). Tess had felt their presence and switched off the radio, and then tuned in to them.

We are leaving.

Huh? exclaimed Tess, keeping one eye on the traffic but also trying to focus a bit more on what Ophelia had just said.

It is time for us to go.

Why? asked Tess. But there was no answer. They were gone.

Good-bye … sent Tess, sadly. *And, thanks for all your insights!* And that was that.

Tess was quite surprised. This was not exactly what she had expected. Tess remembered Rampa's experiences with his guide Mingyar Dondup—he had remained with Rampa throughout his life.

Btai Paul did not reappear to Tess for a few days. Tess

presumed that this was to give her a few days to absorb this information; after all it wasn't every day that an incredible Saint would appear and offer to be your guide! A few days after Btai Paul had introduced himself, Tess was in the middle of a deep meditation, and this was only unusual because she was sitting on her meditation cushion and not lying on the bed. So far she hadn't fallen over, which was her worry with such a deep meditation, but somehow her back stayed straight, and she had remained sitting even while deeply focusing inward to that very quiet and peaceful place in her consciousness.

Also unusual was the day, it was Saturday, and usually Tess spent Saturdays with Stan, since they didn't get so much time together during the week. But today Stan and Otto were out together somewhere; they didn't say where they were going, but Tess had suspected that it was a casino day for them.

Today's meditation had a subject—her cosmic soul group. She remembered from Rampa's teachings that we were each connected to about nine other souls that shared the same oversoul. Tess was trying to put all the pieces of her metaphysical puzzle together, all the information that she'd been receiving this past while, to form a bigger picture of where all of these experiences were going, what their purpose was. Tess was reviewing her connection with each person, and realized that she had met seven of the nine of them in this life! This cosmic connection between soul group members was a really special kind of feeling, the feeling that there was something deep about the other person with whom the connection was shared—often some really unique life experiences had been shared between each person. It was hard to put a finger on it, but Tess could feel without doubt that each of these persons was indeed sharing this cosmic connection.

There was Christopher Thomas, her beau from high school who, it seemed, had also shared the New Zealand life with her as the cook in the kitchen of the ranch home. Tess had been visited on a few occasions by Christopher's spirit—he had apparently died from AIDS a number of years ago (much to Tess's sorrow), and first "dropped by" to tell her about some kind of a project, when Tess had been listening to her Cat Stevens music (popular music of the time when Christopher and Tess were dating). Then there was Liam, her massage therapist—he had also been a part of the New Zealand life, one of the Maori ranchers working with the horses. Then there was Danton—he was definitely a part of her soul group, but Tess didn't know if they'd shared a past life together. Also Rose's mother—Tess's grandmother, who was still alive at ninety-five but quite stricken with Alzheimer's. Tessa (Tess was named after her) would always show a sign that she recognized Tess, usually by taking her hand and squeezing it and giving it a kiss (Tess always thought this was so endearing). Tess's uncle also shared Tess's soul group connection. Then there was Caroline, the Angel that was connected to Tess and also a part of this soul group (Tess didn't yet understand how an Angel that had never incarnated could be a part of an oversoul, and so this connection was in her I'll-understand-that-later box), and lastly there was a friend she hadn't seen in quite a while, Reiner, who ran an art gallery on Manitoulin Island (Tess had a couple of beautiful watercolors from his gallery hanging in the house).

She wondered briefly about the other two soul group members that she had not met, but finally she brought her focus back to her mindful state, so that her spirit, her soul, could bring forth the issues she needed to be reflecting on. There seemed to be a name there, just on the edge of her awareness … Tess took a few slow, deep breaths to deepen her state of relaxation and strengthen her focus.

Rick.

She had heard it clearly. *Who is Rick?* she sent by thought.

A part of you.

How could that be? she wondered to herself. But it certainly fit with what she was asking in her meditation. It was starting to dawn on her that perhaps the purpose of all her experiences was to learn just who she really was, to connect to her soul, and to see and understand the range of experiences she had undergone in her lifetimes on Earth! Just at that moment she heard some noise from the front door. Stan and Otto were back from their day's escapades, and her soul meditation had ended for now.

Tess slowly stood up and put her flowered meditation cushion in the corner of the bedroom and headed to the front door. Mitzi dashed between her legs with a short "Rrrr," heading for cover. She always headed for higher ground when someone other than Tess or Stan came into the house.

"Honey, are you home? Dad and I are back," called Stan. "Oh, here you are, Tess!" he said as Tess stepped through the kitchen toward the front hallway. Stan and Otto were putting a large rectangular parcel down and leaning it against the wall while taking off their coats.

"Tess, I found a really lovely painting. I really hope you'll like it because I have fallen in love with it," exclaimed Stan. Tess hadn't seen Stan so excited about a painting before. She looked quizzically at Stan. "That's nice, Stan," she said, very curious as to what had captured his interest so deeply.

"Wait until you see," said Otto with a smile. "You're gonna love it!"

"Yeah, the detail is incredible; that's what drew me to it!" said Stan.

Tess was curious all right. "So, you weren't at the casino today?" she asked with a smile as Stan gingerly picked up the package and laid it on the dining room table to open it.

"Ha-ha!" laughed Otto. "Not today. It was so nice out we decided to take a drive out to Niagara-on-the-Lake."

Wow! Tess thought to herself, secretly glad that Stan and his Dad were able to spend a whole day together having their own adventure.

Stan and Otto ripped open the brown paper packaging and then started to work on the layers of bubble wrap.

"So, what shop did you find this in?" said Tess, looking at the mysterious painting that was just about unwrapped.

"A little hole-in-the-wall place right in the middle of town," said Stan. There were a lot of really quaint things in it and piles of these paintings, and there is no artist's name on any of them. Quite unusual. The owner said that students painted them. There we go," and Stan lifted up the painting and turned it around so that she could see it.

Tess could not believe her eyes. It was a beautiful woman, voluptuous, in a blue grey jacket, white ruffled blouse, and long blue grey skirt with many folds. There was a sash around the waist. She was reclined on a red velvet sofa and was waving a flower, teasing two white Persian cats on the sofa beside her.

It was Penelope!

~Chapter 13~

Vasari

"My God, Stan!" exclaimed Tess. "What on earth made you pick this picture," she cried.

Stan and Otto stared back at Tess with their mouths open.

"Don't you like it?" asked Stan, disappointment clearly in his voice.

"Isn't she beautiful?" said Otto with encouragement, winking at Tess.

"Well, of course she is!" exclaimed Tess. "But, well, I don't know what to say …" Tess had not revealed any of her past life information to Stan. There was no way he could consciously know about Penelope. A million things were running through her head at the moment.

"Then you don't mind if Dad and I hang it up, then," said Stan, looking over at his piano. Stan had Royal Conservatory training and played wonderfully, and he always picked the most beautiful, romantic pieces to practice on. The piano was against the east wall of the living room, and Stan was eyeing a spot on the wall just above the piano. Essentially it would be the very centerpiece of the room.

"Yep, that's the spot" said Otto in agreement. "Don't you think so, Tess?" He glanced over at Tess and gestured with his hand, as if trying to signal to Tess to agree with the two of them.

"Well, I, uh …" Tess didn't know what to say. She just let them go to it, and shortly Penelope Lancaster was on display in the very center of her living room!

Tess's mind was whirling. She was busy fixing dinner for Stan and Otto, and this was giving her a chance to sort out the myriad of thoughts running through her head. Talk about validating her past life information! Tess was running through all of the steps that would have had to take place for Stan to come home with that picture—let alone the picture having even been painted in the first place! It was mind boggling—and exciting, all at the same time. Tess was beside herself, and she had come to a decision. It was time to tell Stan about Penelope and the past life experiences.

After dinner, Otto had left for the evening, and Tess poured her and Stan each a glass of wine from what was left in the bottle they'd had for dinner.

Stan had put some beautiful music on the stereo, and they sat in the living room and dimmed the lights.

"Cheers, Tess," said Stan, and they clinked glasses, as was their routine whenever they were having wine.

"So, what's up, Tess? You look kind of freaked out about my painting. I didn't want to say anything because you were being so nice about letting me put it right there," he said pointing to the spot over the piano. "But I can sense that there's something going on with you."

Tess knew that Stan was very much in tune with her. She suspected that Stan was a little clairvoyant himself, although he had denied this vehemently whenever Tess had brought up the subject.

"Well, Stan …" and she started with her first visit from

Rose, then moved on to the visits from Ophelia and the past life information given during their vacation. By the time she had finished, the music had long stopped, and the wine bottle was empty. Stan hadn't said too much, but Tess could tell that he was listening intently. He nodded his head here and there and asked a question or two to clarify what she was saying, so Tess knew that he was engaged in her experiences and not just humoring her.

Afterwards they both sat silently for a bit, each of them absorbing the day's events.

Then Stan broke the silence first. "You know, Tess, I just bought this painting because I loved the detail in the dress. That's all! I didn't have any ulterior motives. At least, none that I'm aware of."

Tess paused and looked him straight in the eye. "I know, Stan. It's lovely, really. I'm glad you brought it home," she said reassuringly. Inside, Tess knew that there was a lot more going on than Stan was probably aware of. Tess was just hoping that she hadn't freaked Stan out with recounting her experiences.

The next day was a housecleaning day, and both Stan and Tess were embroiled in vacuuming and laundry. Mitzi usually was hiding from the purple monster (the vacuum) on a dining room chair. Then, Tess got a call from Margery, her career councilor. Margery was away at a conference in California, and had run into someone from a consulting company that was looking for a person with good coordination and speaking skills that had a biotech background, and immediately she had thought of Tess. Twelve Point Consulting was their name, and they had an office in Toronto! Tess immediately agreed to an interview. Although it wasn't really up her alley, it sounded quite interesting.

The next day Tess was back into downtown Toronto,

this time in the ritzy Yorkville area. The office building was a newly built older-style building with red brick and yellow accent in a kind of a contemporary Victorian style. An upscale coffee shop was on the lower level. *Another plus!* thought Tess, and she made a mental note to drop by to pick up a Tall Bold after her interview. She walked into the marble and etched glass lobby and headed to the elevators. Once on the fourth floor, she saw the entrance to Twelve Point Consulting just to the right of the elevators. She stepped inside and introduced herself to the well-dressed receptionist sitting behind a high oak desk.

"Oh, yes, Richard is expecting you. Have a seat, and he will be right out," she said, smiling at Tess. Tess was admiring her beautiful makeup, it looked professionally done, and her lipstick was the most amazing shade of frosted plum. Her beautiful appearance made Tess want to learn how to apply makeup like that herself!

Tess shot a smile back to her. "Thanks."

Tess sat in the small waiting area and admired the fresh-cut flowers in a large crystal vase. There were stargazer lilies and huge pink roses with baby's breath in between. She thought those flowers looked a little familiar somehow. Tess inhaled the fragrant air around the flowers, and this seemed to have a calming effect on her. She relaxed back in the chair.

"Hello, Tess." Tess looked up at the well-dressed young man approaching her and stood to shake his hand.

"I'm Richard," he said warmly, shaking her hand.

"Nice to meet you," replied Tess, immediately feeling a good vibration from his energy.

"Let's go into this meeting room over here," and he motioned to the open door to Tess's right.

They settled in, and Richard gave a brief overview outlining what Twelve Point Consulting was about and what role they were looking to fill. He looked directly into Tess's eyes when speaking, and this was a trait that Tess associated with a balanced personality. Tess was listening with one ear but also trying to get a feel for the energy that was around Richard. So far his energy felt light to Tess. He was definitely comfortable to be with. Even though he was much younger than Tess, Tess felt she would enjoy working with him.

Twelve Point provided facilitation services to companies, in that they would provide consultants to help run meetings, usually brainstorming or negotiating meetings in which certain deliverables had to be yielded by a diverse group of people. They had a number of biotech clients that needed facilitation in moving their processes from development to manufacturing, and also in dealing with health authorities. Richard thought that Tess's experience in biotech combined with her project management skills would fit the bill exactly. The only proviso was—the schedule was erratic. She may be working two weeks straight on one project, and the next may only be needed for one or two days a week.

Tess was secretly ecstatic—this suited her just perfectly! She could handle having an intense schedule temporarily if it meant that she would have a relaxed schedule once in a while so she could continue to pursue her energy-related studies.

At the end of the interview Richard thanked her for her time and said that he would follow up by the end of the week. They shook hands, and Richard led her out to the reception area and walked her to the elevators.

"Thanks for coming by, Tess. Talk to you soon," he called, and then he turned back and headed inside the Twelve Point entrance.

Tess had a good feeling about him.

The next day Twelve Point human resources had called

with a job offer, which Tess promptly accepted. Stan was ecstatic when he got home. He enveloped her in one of his famous bear hugs and swung her around the living room! This made The Mitz jealous, and she started her "murring"—a series of loud meows in which she really sounded like she was giving them both a blasting! "Murraow murraow murr*rrr*!" Stan and Tess laughed and gave Mitzi a good noogying as well.

Her first few weeks at Twelve Point had flown by, and Tess was now embroiled in a reading with O. Since Tess was working downtown, it was convenient to drop by his studio occasionally after work.

Tess had never had any psychotherapy before. But this is what O was advising for her. Tess implicitly trusted her new friend O. Their initial meeting had been quite an experience for both of them, and O's reading had overwhelmed Tess. Not only had he described Penelope and her situation and where some traumatic events had taken place, but he had made connections from Penelope to Tess in her present life and how this past life would affect her going forward. Incredibly he predicted that Tess would do some kind of healing that would affect the Earth! Tess didn't know what to make of that (and filed it away in her I'll-figure-that-out-later box), but she was shaken by how accurately O had "read" her past. O also saw children in Tess's life, which was a mystery to Tess, as Michael, Tess's Reiki master teacher, had also mentioned this to her. Tess was quite in awe of O, and O seemed also to be quite taken by Tess. Tess felt that this was a spiritual kind of link that O and Tess now had. Tess knew instinctively that O was gay, but O did tell her later in his reading. Later, Tess was reassuring Stan about the new friendship that she and O had, so that Stan did not have to worry about O getting too friendly with Tess.

And now O was advising her to see a spiritual psychotherapist. "Tess, read up on them; it's not traditional psychotherapy. I'll send you the link to the TAC curriculum— they have a good description of their training." TAC was an innovative healing arts college located in Toronto. O looked at Tess, who was still frowning. "It will really help you put your experiences into perspective, Tess. They totally believe in the holistic approach, that spirit and spiritual experience are a natural and normal part of our lives." This seemed to resonate with Tess, and she agreed to see O's friend (but maybe in a month or two, she thought to herself).

Tess's first few weeks at Twelve Point were quite busy. She was given two medium-size assignments. The first one was to prepare a training slideshow for a company that needed to transfer a research process for their new biochip—a microchip with a biological process embedded inside of it. The biochip was part of a small handheld medical device. When a drop of blood from a finger prick was placed on a small paper strip embedded with one of these chips and then placed into a slot, it would provide a reading on that person's LDL, the "bad" cholesterol. It was Tess's job to design the training program so that all concerned parties, research, development, and manufacturing, would have a good understanding of each other's requirements and the main tasks that each department needed to do to achieve the transfer.

Her second project was to mediate a brainstorming meeting that had already been set up—but the appointed mediator, who had already met with both parties, was out sick, and Tess had to step in cold.

It was the end of the week, and Tess had spent a good part of Friday finessing her training slideshow and had just printed a copy for her new boss, Richard, to review. She had the pages spread out over the meeting room table as she gave it one last look see before Richard came in, and was peering at one slide that to Tess looked like a bit of a mess, with too many spreadsheets overlapping to really get the message for that particular slide.

"Hey, Tess," said Richard's friendly voice from just behind her.

Tess turned around and smiled. "Hi, Richard. You're a little early." She looked at him curiously.

"Yes, well my last meeting finished up quickly, so I thought I'd just drop by to see how you are making out with the presentation for Lakeland Biotech." He took a sip from his steaming mug, and Tess could smell that it was a cup of freshly made coffee. This made her feel a bit hungry, and she realized that she'd worked straight through lunch. Her stomach growled a bit, as if in agreement with her thoughts.

"Tess, why don't you go and grab a sandwich, and I'll sit with your outline for a bit," he offered.

"Great. Will do. I'll be right back!" said Tess, standing and glad to stretch her muscles a bit.

A short while later Tess was back with a sandwich and a mug of the freshly brewed coffee. Soon Tess and Richard were embroiled in conversation, with Richard providing feedback on how to clarify some of Tess's concepts. They'd both gotten stuck on the "ohmigod" slide with all of the complex spreadsheets on it, and now both of them were silently pondering it, trying to determine how to simplify it a bit. Tess was standing at the end of the table, sideways to the slide, and Richard was standing just beside her but at the side of the table, facing the slide. Suddenly it came to Tess—rather than using spreadsheets to portray the validation process, they could use a standard vee diagram.

Tess could see the vee diagram in her mind's eye. She looked over at Richard, ready to say this when suddenly she felt the thought leave her body and go to Richard! Richard looked up at her strangely.

Then he said simply "Yes. A vee diagram would work."

They were both silent for a moment. Then Richard broke the strained silence. "You know, Tess, I think the training presentation is just right. We don't need any further tweaks—you are good to go! I'll touch base with you Monday morning just before the meeting."

And with that, he picked up his mug and headed out. Tess was still collecting her thoughts. *Did I say that … or did I think that?!* she was wondering to herself. Tess was pretty sure that she had sent it by thought. And not just the thought itself, but the whole concept of presenting it as a picture or diagram, and the image of the diagram itself was sent all together in one chunk—almost like when she herself had received the very first past life information while walking into TSK that one morning.

And not only had she sent that message by thought, by telepathy, but—Tess knew from Richard's reaction that he had received and understood it! Tess started mulling this over, thinking about how she could "speak" with Spirits, her guides, and also Rose—essentially souls who were on the other side or other plane. That is definitely telepathy, and definitely a very spiritual, almost a divine, form of communication. But, being able to speak to other people in the physical by thought … that was a whole other kettle of fish. And why hadn't this happened before? If Tess was indeed telepathic, how come this wasn't happening with everyone? Why just Richard? And, thought Tess with a surge of fear, what if it happened again while she was thinking her own personal thoughts, thoughts that she wouldn't want just anyone to hear? Or, God forbid, thought Tess, while those rude words were making an appearance? She shuddered.

And then it occurred to Tess. She was quite good at mindfulness meditation, even outside the usual meditative process—her walking meditations, for example. Hmmm, perhaps all she needed to do was be mindful in everything she did. She needed to keep her focus on the moment and not get carried away with distracting thoughts. That felt like the right solution to Tess. She smiled to herself and gathered up the slides that were sprawled out all over the meeting room table. She would start being mindful right now!

"Were you in a battle? said O in amazement. Tess and O were embroiled in another of O's readings for Tess, this time specifically about her recent telepathic experience with her boss. "I see you being, well, it looks like you are being stabbed with a sword, and then dying!" exclaimed O.

Tess had met O in a coffee shop after work. O had often done readings in a cafe before, and he was doing a short one for Tess at the moment.

"That's exactly what happened," said Tess, nodding her head.

"But I thought you were female in that life," he said quizzically. Actually there are two of you. I see twins!"

"Huh?" said Tess. "Ah, yes, definitely I was female. I even had cleavage!" said Tess, and Tess and O both laughed heartily. "So—the twins?" prompted Tess.

"Oh, right," said O, looking back at the cards on the table and turned over the top card. "Oh, look, Tess …" O had turned over a card that had twin Angels on it! O had a set of very cosmic-looking tarot cards. Actually, he called this particular deck Oracle cards because they did not contain the traditional archetypes and symbols seen in the tarot but instead had varying themes usually centering on positive thought, sometimes with combined astrological images and highly spiritual forms like Angels. O was looking at a card showing two identical Angels holding hands and gazing down at the Earth from a lofty height in the cosmos.

"Yes, and since our intent today was to discuss your situation with your boss, I'd say it's more than likely that he was your twin sister in the New Zealand past life," said O. "And you know what else? You have this hugely cosmic connection; I'd say that he is also your twin soul!"

"Holy smokes!" said Tess. "How wild is that? Hmmm, if we were twins, I've heard that they can be telepathic. That would explain it, O!"

O just laughed as he collected his Oracle cards and put them back into their deck. Tess filed that bit of information away in the cosmic connections section of her brain, and at the same time felt a kind of a nagging feeling that there was something she already knew about this particular connection, but it was eluding her at the moment.

~

Tess had spent the weekend practicing her being-mindful-in-the-moment technique, keeping her mind focused on the events of the here and now, and trying not to allow her thoughts to wander. It certainly wasn't easy, and Tess was certain that it would take quite a lot of practice. After all she'd spent forty odd years allowing her mind to roam like a wild mustang, pursuing one thought after another without realizing that she could actually control her thoughts if she did the right exercises. It had only been recently that Tess had started meditating, and only after a couple of years of practice that she could do the walking meditation. It might take a bit of time to achieve the be-in-the-moment kind of mindfulness that she would need to be in the company of a person that could hear her thoughts.

This realization was really making Tess think about the

spirits that were guiding her and dropping in to give advice; how difficult a job that must be, first of all to navigate around any negativity that was being experienced (as negative thought and emotion could block communication from spirit). And then, the spirit would have to communicate in a way that would resonate with that person—something that Tess had learned from O to be absolutely different for each individual.

But then, once all of these conditions had been met, to then find a time when the person was also being mindful or calm and in-the-moment to actually get a word in would be a rare moment indeed. A golden moment!

By the time Monday morning rolled around, Tess felt a slight bit more confident about her new state of mind, that she could at least be aware when she wasn't in-the-moment, so that she could remember to focus her mind to actually be in-the-moment.

The boardroom at Twelve Point was nearly full; twelve chairs were around the table, and eleven were now filled. Tess and Richard had strategized on where they should be seated, Tess at one end of the table and Richard at the other, so that they were in the "control" positions, as this would be their first session with Lakeland Biotech. However, one of the attendees, Gerrard Anderson, the chief director of manufacturing, was not being cooperative and, despite Tess's polite urgings for him to sit beside Richard, he had filled the chair at the end of the table across from Richard. Tess caught a barely perceptible nod from Richard, and Tess had relented, allowing Gerrard to sit where he desired, realizing that although the positions had shifted, the intentions of herself and Richard still remained, to facilitate understanding of the situation by all parties. She took her seat beside Richard, and the meeting began.

They were on time, about halfway through Tess's

training slideshow, when they got the signal (the meeting room door opened slightly and a head appeared) from Adriana, Twelve Point's pretty receptionist, that lunch had arrived, and it was time to break for a bit. It had been a lively morning with plenty of discussion from all sides, and the dynamic of this group seemed to be quite good—Richard and Tess simply needed to reign in Gerrard occasionally so that his views didn't overwhelm the group, so that each party, each concern, could be heard and examined by the group. Tess had found that sitting beside Richard seemed to have allowed the existing group dynamic to flow and that Richard and Tess could contribute to this flow rather than trying to control it.

Tess had been quite pleased with her ability to keep her focus on the meeting activity and dynamic, and not have her thoughts roaming all over the place. There had been one interesting moment for Tess, when she had summarized the recent discussions centering on plans for a series of pilot manufacturing runs—what milestones and time frame for each milestone was agreed upon by the morning's discussions. She verbalized this summary for the group to reiterate what they had agreed upon, and right after she completed her summary Gerrard had started to speak. He at first disagreed with what Tess had presented, and then launched his own summary. Tess's mouth dropped, as Gerrard essentially rhymed off almost exactly what Tess had said moments before.

Isn't that exactly what I just said! thought Tess heatedly to herself. And then, at that moment, Tess could feel a silent agreement on that point—from Richard! It was not sent by thought, but somehow Tess could feel a certain resonation from him ... they were on the same wavelength! This realization brought a comforting wave of peacefulness over Tess, and this allowed her to listen to what Gerrard was saying without getting emotional about his seeming disregard of her efforts.

During the lunch break, Richard had briefly conferred with her regarding the morning's progress, and he let Tess know that he was quite happy with how things were going. Then, he disappeared for the rest of the break, and Tess presumed he was back in his office catching up on the morning's e-mails and phone messages.

However, the afternoon did not go smoothly. Gerrard had essentially reverted from the morning's decisions and instead was now insistent upon a very rigid pilot phase followed by a second, more extensive process validation phase, essentially doubling the workload and time line that had been laid out in the morning's discussions. This had resulted in heated debate between the development and manufacturing groups, and by the day's end, despite both Richard's and Tess's efforts, there was now a brick wall between the two groups.

Richard had conferred with Tess afterwards and had reassured her that this type of situation was in fact quite common, and that is what Twelve Point's specialty was. They could help each side or each point of view begin to build a common ground between them, to bridge the gaps and identify a path forward. But first, the sides needed to air their grievances, and that is exactly what had happened today.

Tess was comforted to know that this was normal, and she realized that it was going to take some time and a fair amount of work to get this group to all be on the same side!

Tess arrived home around 8:00 p.m., exhausted by the day's efforts. The Mitz greeted her at the door, anxious to give her hell, from a cat's point of view, for being away from her for so long! Stan was late too; Tess realized the house felt empty. Mitzi was head-butting her legs as if to reminder her that it wasn't exactly empty!

After a good amount of head noogies, Tess decided that the best tonic for a tough day was a nice, hot, bubble bath. She filled the tub and poured in a scoop of soapy lavender bath salts; soon the whole bathroom was warm and filled with the relaxing fragrant essence. She turned off the water and dipped her big toe in the water—ahhh, just right! She slipped into the steamy tub and felt waves of stress being released from her whole body. The day's thoughts just melted away from her. After a few moments she felt something tugging at her thoughts. Her mind flew to Btai Paul, her guide—is he here?! Her eyes flew to the door of the bathroom—it was closed, her signal that she didn't want any spiritual visitors. Hmm, she could still feel that someone was there.

Who is here? she sent.

Katrina.

Tess was astounded! *Katrina! It's so nice that you came to visit!* sent Tess, feeling happy and a little shocked to find that her friend could actually visit her this way.

I see that you are right about the other side!

Tess's eyes filled with tears. She took a deep breath, trying to regain control of her emotions—she didn't want to break the contact with Katrina.

Thank you, sent Tess, feeling such gratitude for her friend's thoughtfulness in confirming what Tess had tried to tell her before she "left" and passed over.

I can't stay. It's not easy for me to be here, said Katrina.

Katrina, thank you, it is great of you to contact me, sent Tess. And she was gone.

Tess sank a bit deeper into the bubble bath, smiling to herself. It was really quite amazing being able to keep in touch with friends on the other side!

Yes.

Btai Paul! sent Tess eagerly.

I allowed her in to visit.

Thank you! I so enjoyed hearing her, sent Tess.

Newly arrived spirits don't find it so easy to come into your atmosphere when they don't have a strong connection, said Btai Paul.

Why is that? asked Tess, and at the same time realizing that Katrina wasn't one of her soul group or a family member, so perhaps it was indeed harder for her to "find" Tess from the other side.

They have to remember what to do, said Btai Paul.

Tess sat up, and then remembered she was in a tub of soapy water and eased back down into the bubbles.

Don't worry, Tess, we don't see you the same way that physical people do, reassured Btai Paul.

Okay, said Tess, still only partially convinced. She'd stay under the bubbles for now.

You have homework, said Btai Paul.

Huh? Tess's thoughts were wildly trying to sort through her recent meditations, trying to remember what homework she had been given.

Paperwork, said Btai Paul.

Oh! You mean from today, from Twelve Point? asked Tess.

There was no answer.

Btai Paul? He was gone. Indeed, she had brought home all her notes taken from today's meeting to review in preparation for tomorrow, plus some notes taken by Richard.

She hopped out of the tub, pulled the plug, and dried off. With the towel wrapped around her she opened the bathroom door to find Mitzi curled up on the rug outside of the door.

"Ah, Mitz, thank you for guarding the hallway for me!" she said as she gingerly stepped over her sleek grey form. She slipped into her pj's and housecoat and then went to the kitchen to put on the kettle for some tea. Stan should be home soon, and Tess would get a snack ready for both of them.

Tess got the tea steeping and picked up her bag with the day's notes inside and placed it on the dining room table. She pulled out the notes, and Richard's were on top. She sat down just for a moment—the tea would be ready shortly, and Stan was likely to be home any minute. She picked up Richard's notes and flipped through them quickly. On the last page Tess stopped—stunned! There was a short note to Tess here about the strategy they should employ for the next day's meeting. Underneath was Richard's signature—Ric. He called himself Ric! Rick—Ric, was the name that she had heard during that really deep meditation just before she got the job at Twelve Point. He's a part of you—is what she had received during that meditation.

Suddenly Tess felt a very strong connection to her higher self, almost like a really powerful magnet had been placed over her head, and she could also feel that there was a vastness of information, almost like she had just been plugged into the bandwidth of the universe.

He is your Twin Soul. Your soul was split into two, each identical to the other, just prior to your New Zealand life. There was a disagreement about this incarnation. You were stubborn and wished to follow your own plan and not take the advice given to you. Your soul was split to explore each choice; you following your own plan, and the soul of Ric following the plan of the advisors. Twin souls and twin sisters, each following a different plan.

Tess received this chunk of information all at once. She

sat absolutely still at the dining room table, the steeping tea forgotten for now.

Where is this information coming from? asked Tess.

It is your higher self, Tess, said Btai Paul. *It was the right moment for you to understand this situation.*

That's phenomenal! exclaimed Tess, staggered to learn of the strategy that her soul had followed just prior to incarnating for the New Zealand life experience, and also ecstatic to have another piece to the ever-growing puzzle of her soul.

You are quite right, said Btai Paul.

It took two weeks of tough meetings to bring the two sides to an agreement. Tess had only one day off during that time, and it wasn't really a day off; she was facilitating a brainstorming session for another one of Twelve Point's clients, and although it was an intense day, it was a good break from the previous meetings. Now that both projects were complete, she was able to really reflect back at her interactions with Richard, which of course were all very business focused—but Tess couldn't help but wonder what kind of a life the two of them had shared as twin sisters, and twin souls—essentially the same spirit in two different bodies, each having different experiences and at the same time sharing this most cosmic connection. And, of course, Richard would have no idea of this incredible connection that the two of them shared—other than the sharing of a thought, a telepathic event which could easily be dismissed by a skeptical mind. But, not by Tess. Tess also realized that now almost all of the members of her soul group were accounted for; just one more to meet—according to Rampa's teachings. She was really beginning to have a whole new view on the events taking place around her.

Stan had recommended a three-day getaway to Ottawa.

He had heard about a quaint bed and breakfast there, and Tess knew that the National Art Gallery was having a rare exhibition of Renaissance art—something that Tess had always been fascinated by. The Renaissance was such a creative era, as if the universe had decided the time was ripe on Earth to be enriched by art, especially religious art, which was the subject of many Renaissance artists like Da Vinci, Michelangelo, and others. Tess had always been fascinated by Da Vinci and had read numerous books about and by him. She even had his self-portrait hanging by her desk—such a fascinating and talented man! Even Rampa had written about Da Vinci in one of his books—if Tess was remembering correctly Rampa believed Da Vinci to be one of the engineers of life, studying life in all its forms, and he had incarnated on Earth just to get a bird's eye view of this creation!

Tess was quite excited to get away with Stan to spend some R and R time together and also to have a chance to see some of the paintings from the Renaissance masters live rather than from a picture in a book.

Ottawa was a beautiful city, with a busy downtown core surrounded by peaceful and lush countryside that was just minutes from the center of the city. The Parliament buildings were picturesquely positioned at the edge of the Ottawa River. The Peace Tower was situated in the middle of the stone buildings. (Tess thought it was kind of ironic, as she'd seen some of the parliamentary proceedings on one of the B and B's TV channels, and they were hardly peaceful.)

A number of markets were in the downtown area, and Tess and Stan spent their first afternoon poking their heads into numerous interesting shops and scouting for a nice restaurant for dinner. Tess had wandered into an exotic gift shop that had one wall filled with shelves of various crystals.

Tess was drawn to them but was not sure why. She knew that crystals had metaphysical properties and could be used for healing and channeling energy, but she had not really studied them in any detail. She scanned each basket and felt drawn to pick up a perfectly round one with green swirls—it kind of reminded her of the planet Saturn, with its rings. She picked it up and held it in her hand—it felt right somehow. *That's a keeper, I guess*, thought Tess. Next there was a basket of heart-shaped crystals of many colors—an orange one sparkled when the sun hit it. Another keeper!

"So there you are."

Tess whirled around to find Stan behind her. She stepped on her toes and planted a kiss on his cheek. "Sorry, Stan, I peeked inside and before I knew it …"

"It's okay, Tess," said Stan with a smile. "What have you got there?" Tess showed him the shelves full of crystals, and Stan started poking through them as well. Tess explored the other side of the shop and found a small table with large quartz crystals, some clear and some with bubbles and frosted patterns inside. Tess realized these were master crystals. She had heard about these crystals being used to strengthen one's connection to the universe. One of them seemed to stand apart from the others, and Tess picked it up—it felt warm in her hand. It had seven sides and was longish, flat on one end and sort of pointed on the other end, with one very flat surface at the pointed end, almost as if one side of the original point had been cleaved away. Tess stared inside of the clear crystal—there were white and clear flecks inside, almost like looking out in space at a collection of galaxies. Tess continued to focus on the inside of the crystal and was just starting to feel the beginnings of a story—it felt like the story of the origin of this crystal. As if the crystal had not really originated on Earth, but came from another galaxy somewhere!

"Hey, Tess, I'm starving. What's say you and I head over to that Greek place we saw two streets back and get some dinner?"

"Sure, Stan—I'd just like to pay for these first, though," said Tess, opening her hand to show Stan her fistful of crystals. He rolled his eyes. "If it makes you happy, Tess," he said and smiled back at her. "In that case maybe you can pay for this one too." He placed a small amber pyramid into her handful of crystals.

"Sure, Stan," said Tess looking at the pyramid. Tess knew that pyramids had special properties, but to truly utilize them properly the pyramid had to be precise, and you really had to know what you were doing. She could see that the sides of this pyramid were not symmetrical. What the hell, guess it can't really hurt anything, she decided, and headed to the cashier to pay for her collection.

The next day Tess and Stan were at the entrance to the National Art Gallery when the doors opened at 10:00 a.m. They'd had a lovely night's stay at the B and B, which was within walking distance of downtown Ottawa and the gallery, and were both looking forward to a day of beautiful art. The very first room had a work from both Da Vinci and Michelangelo, and a collection of information regarding the written works of Da Vinci. Tess was amazed to find that Da Vinci created all of his written works back to front—the same way that Tess liked to write in her journals!

For both of them, being surrounded by incredible works of art was quite intoxicating, room after room of really divine art—these masters were so exquisitely able to portray their interpretations of some of life's most extraordinary people and events, such as Mother Mary and baby Jesus, and the crucifixion. Tess was just entranced by one artist's interpretation of the events around the tomb of Jesus. Franciabigo (Tess hadn't heard of many of these artists before) had an interesting depiction of the events around the opening of this tomb in his fresco *Noli me tangere*, in which the foreground is Mary Magdalene on her knees imploring a resurrected Jesus to stay and speak with her. Jesus, holding a hoe and at a quick glance appearing as if he is a gardener, is gently signifying no with his outstretched palm, and in the background the two other Marys, Jesus's Mother Mary and another Mary who was allegedly an aunt of Jesus, are in front of the tomb conversing with an Angel, who has informed them of Jesus's departure. Tess noted the halos just visible above the heads of Jesus and Mary Magdalene. Tess could feel the emotion captured around these spiritual events. What incredible vision and passion these artists had!

In the next room were some works from Verdi, an artist that Tess had actually heard of. She was drawn to one in particular, *The Conversion of St Paul*. Tess had always thought that Saint Paul was the most interesting saint, even before being introduced to him as her guide—what better evangelist could there be than Paul, who was converted by the spirit of Jesus. There was a lot going on in this painting; they were literally on the warpath, a team of warriors including Paul of Tarsus, and in this depiction he was actually still on his horse, with the horse kneeling in reverence. Paul's helmet is on the ground, and he is looking up at his vision of Jesus and the twelve disciples, who are busy enlightening Paul to their presence and their purpose. Tess was secretly wondering what it must have been like for Paul to have experienced such a divine and spiritual event.

Please don't ponder it.

But ... Tess really wanted to know more about Btai Paul.

That is not why I am here with you. Please don't study it.

But Btai, implored Tess. *You can't blame me for being curious, can you?*

I implore you to let go of needing to know, replied Btai Paul.

I will, said Tess somewhat reluctantly. But deep inside she was busy trying to figure it out. He really did not want Tess to know him as that Paul, as Saint Paul—even though she could feel his identity. Hmmm, perhaps he didn't want Tess to associate his presence with a religious context? This was making sense to Tess, because she had firmly stepped outside the box of current Christianity and straight into the world of the metaphysical. And while the metaphysical was quite divine, it was definitely not religious or dogmatic. Tess was still pondering this while slowly walking through the room full of beautiful art. She came to a standstill in front of *The Annunciation*, by Serumido, which depicts an Angel who visits Mother Mary to inform her of the divine plan—above them in the sky is an opening of sorts in which golden rays illuminate a dove. Tess found it to be rather a cosmic kind of painting. *That's it!* thought Tess suddenly. Btai Paul is really a very "cosmic" Paul, really much more than Saint Paul or Btai Paul. If Paul had other incarnations on Earth then this spirit was certainly much more than Saint Paul.

Tess felt a warm, comforting feeling, as if she were just being embraced—a cosmic embrace by Btai Paul. She smiled and enjoyed this spiritual hug.

She felt a touch on her shoulder and turned quickly around—it was Stan. He smiled and pointed to the next room. "I'll meet you in there, okay, Tess?" He turned and headed into the next room.

"I'm coming, Stan," she said, and followed him into the adjoining room.

This room had the largest paintings Tess had ever seen. The room must have been about twelve or fifteen feet high, and some of the paintings hanging on the walls filled the entire height. There were some statues in the middle of the room as well, but Tess was really entranced by the paintings. She walked slowly past the beautiful works and then stopped suddenly in front of a truly magnificent piece depicting the baptism of Jesus. Suddenly her entire energy field began to tingle! All at once she got a message—that she had been the artist who painted this and, incredibly, that this painting was a favorite! *A favorite?! A favorite of whom*—Tess began to ask, and at the same time came her answer. *A favorite of Jesus!* Tess was overwhelmed with emotion, and her eyes filled with tears. *How was this possible?* But she could feel it, like the information of the knowledge that she had just felt was absolutely cemented inside of her, that it was indeed a part of her.

She blinked away her tears of amazement and stepped closer to the painting to see the artist—Giorgio Vasari. Tess had never heard of him before. She stepped back again and took a few deep breaths. She was shaking now. She glanced to her left—Stan was way ahead, now in the next adjoining room. She looked back at the immense work in front of her. It really was extraordinarily beautiful. Jesus was standing in the river in a very humbling position, his head bowed, hands crossed in front of his chest. St John the Baptist and three Angels were reverently standing beside as St John poured a handful of water over the head of Jesus. Two Cherubim were over top of their heads, and a dove with divine light coming from the clouds was at the very top. Tess stepped a little closer, noticing something curious—they were both smiling! Jesus and St John each had a very slight smile, almost as if—well, to Tess anyways—they were really happy about carrying out their plan together! Like it was their little secret. She stepped back again, soaking it all in.

"Tess." Stan was standing at the entrance to the next room.

"Coming," said Tess, smiling to herself, mentally vowing to do some research about Vasari as soon as she and Stan returned home, and also secretly ecstatic to know about another past life!

The rest of the day flew by as they reveled in the marvelous art of the Renaissance, and the weekend was over before they knew it. Stan and Tess had a marvelous minigetaway in Ottawa. Tess had found that she could somehow feel the energy of the city—and it was quite interesting, almost as if the original settlers, those who had founded Canada, were still there somehow creating an air of new dominion and harmony in the city. Too bad the current government didn't seem to notice these energies of harmony surrounding the city, Tess had thought. When Stan and Tess arrived back at home, Tess had immediately gone onto the Internet to do some research on Vasari. He seemed to be a well-known Renaissance artist, and quite a good one at that. Tess recalled the artwork she had created when a teenager—she had loved to draw. Tess thought she might have even saved a few of her drawings, and made a mental note to go through her old boxes to find them. Through a few more Google searches Tess found references to architecture and writings of Vasari.

It seemed he had a special interest in art history, and, interestingly, his focus was on Da Vinci. Scanning through many of the links, it seemed to Tess that Vasari had likely met Da Vinci while in Florence. Interestingly, Tess had always been fascinated by Da Vinci, and even had a couple of prints—his self-portrait (he certainly looked like a wise old soul) and a stylized version of the *Last Supper*. It was starting to dawn on Tess that all the information that she was receiving—and somehow understanding, was a rare occurrence. She was gaining a new insight on her life, and starting to understand the bigger picture of her true self, the soul who clearly had a strategy for each incarnation, and the soul who slowly but surely was allowing her access to this privileged information. While this was extraordinary, and Tess was actually quite humbled to be the recipient of this information, she wondered if this knowledge would help her to find her purpose, that special something that she had always felt she came here to do.

~Chapter 14~

Multiverses

"What do you mean by, 'You are afraid of yourself?'" asked Sam.

"Well, I'm not quite sure," said Tess. She was in the midst of her very first spiritual psychotherapy session and was finding that it wasn't so easy to talk about her feelings. She had taken O's advice and booked an appointment with Sam. O felt that because of the intensely spiritual or metaphysical nature of Tess's experiences, spiritual psychotherapy was absolutely suited to help Tess understand and deal with these experiences.

"Perhaps I could vocalize for you, and you can see if that fits," said Sam.

"Sure, go for it," encouraged Tess, happy that the pressure of figuring out what she was feeling was now in Sam's hands.

"Perhaps you would really like to honor yourself as a woman, to honor your femininity, maybe by dressing up in fine clothes, fine makeup, do your hair, just be the fine and elegant woman that you are! But you are afraid perhaps of all the attention that you'll get or perhaps afraid that you don't really deserve to look so fine." Sam paused and then added, "When in fact you so totally deserve it."

Hmmm, Tess thought about that. "Well, that feels good," said Tess, not really knowing how to proceed.

"Okay," said Sam. "Let's try this angle then. How about your mother. How did she dress?"

"Well, she had really lovely outfits and had a passion for beautiful clothes. And she was absolutely gorgeous in her outfits. When I was a small girl I just loved to go into her bedroom and open up her closet and try on all of her dresses and skirts, I'd even put on her shoes!" Tess laughed, and so did Sam. Then Tess remembered something. "You know, I've just remembered something I haven't thought about in such a long time. My mum had a couple of books hidden inside of a shoebox in her closet. I found them one day thinking there was another pair of shoes I hadn't tried on yet. I'm pretty sure the books were about psychic stuff; they might've been called 'Psi' or something like that."

"Wow, that's huge Tess!" exclaimed Sam. "Psi or psionics is the ability to use extrasensory perception, or psychic abilities. Considering that you've told me about some of your psychic experiences, I'd say that your Mom might have had this gift as well. And maybe she was afraid of it—you said that she had those books hidden away in a box inside of a cupboard. Did she ever talk with you about psychic stuff?"

"No, never," said Tess, wondering to herself why she did not.

"Okay," said Sam. "Well I think this all fits together nicely with what we were discussing earlier about you being afraid of yourself. Perhaps you are really afraid of your psychic abilities, just like your mother may have been."

Sam's words seemed to ring true with Tess. She sat silently absorbing this information, and then looked back at

Sam, who seemed also to be pondering and scratching the side of his cheek with his fingers.

"Yeah, I think that fits," said Sam. "And also, by the way, perhaps that's why you dress so casually now," he said.

Tess thought about this. She was always at her most comfortable self when in her jean jacket, stretch jeans, and white cotton T-shirt. She really only dressed up when she had meetings with clients at Twelve Point, and then wasn't very comfortable in those clothes.

"Wow, Sam! I think you are on to something," she said. "You know, you have quite a gift," Tess continued in earnest. "Somehow you can take all the bits and pieces of my life and fit them together like a jigsaw puzzle so that it all makes sense."

Sam laughed. "Thank you, Tess, that's so sweet," he said. "It looks like our time is up. I've really enjoyed our session," he said, and stood up with his hand out.

Tess stood and shook his hand. "Likewise, Sam, this has really been great!" said Tess earnestly. Tess could feel something resonating in her energy field when they were shaking hands. She couldn't quite put her finger on it, but it was significant enough to get her attention.

"Can I come back in two weeks?" asked Tess.

"Ah, let me look," and Sam went looking for his appointment book. He found it under a journal on his desk and started flipping through the pages. "Yes, Friday the twenty-fifth, same time?"

"Great!" said Tess, feeling quite happy to have a few answers to her many questions about herself and her experiences.

⁓

Tess arrived home to find a message from Harold on the answering machine. She pushed the message button on the machine while Mitzi head-butted her legs and purred.

"Tess. Call me. Bye." Harold's messages were always short and to the point. She checked the time—it was 4:00 p.m. Too early. She'd call him tonight.

She pulled some veggie burgers out of the freezer and looked in the fridge for salad bins—yes, there was still some salad, and it looked fresh enough. She and Stan were currently trying a vegetarian-only diet—Stan was a real health nut and from some of the information he'd been reading about the modern diet, felt that it would be good for both of them to stay away from meat for a while. She put the frozen patties on a plate to thaw for a bit and headed into the TV room, where her computer was, and fired it up. A short time later, Tess was embroiled in reading and answering her e-mail. One item had captured Tess's interest—an e-mail from David, one of Tess's new colleagues at Twelve Point. Tess had seen this e-mail while at work the day previous and had forwarded it to her home e-mail. She opened it. It seemed to be about joining a network that could connect you to your high school mates. *Hmph!* Tess normally didn't pursue these e-mails. But it had come from David, someone she knew and trusted. And it wasn't really spam, or at least it didn't feel that way to Tess.

She clicked on the link, and it took her to a page that essentially said the same thing as the e-mail, and that she had to click another link if she was interested in connecting to her old school chums. Upon clicking this link Tess was taken to another page that prompted her to enter the e-mail addresses of three other friends. *Holy smokes!* she exclaimed to herself. I just want to find out what the network is about! She hotly debated with herself as to whether it was going to be worth the effort of giving away e-mail addresses of three friends to go further. Dammit! She entered the names of three friends who might not mind too much if they got spam from a high school networking site.

"Now what?" exclaimed Tess when she got to another page that didn't reveal anything about high school networking. She was being prompted to pay twelve dollars using a credit card in order to proceed further.

Tess sat back and wondered again why she was doing this. She didn't like giving away her credit card number to just any old website. Although she had a special credit card just for web purchases that had a very low limit on it, she still didn't like to use it much.

She took a deep breath. *Okay, let's do it!* She went and got the card and entered the information into the page, and then double checked it and hit the Okay button.

Finally! She was at the high school networking page. She filled out her high school information and years she attended and hit Enter. A few seconds later, she appeared at a page that listed some of the members of the network from her years at high school. She recognized the first name, Susan Wildwood. Tess dimly remembered Susie from her days in track and field. Tess had loved to run when she was younger. She scanned down the list; none of the rest seemed familiar. And then she found it.

Christopher Thomas.

Holy smokes! Tess sat back in her chair, astounded. *He's alive!* Tess didn't know what to make of this. The date on his membership indicated that he had joined only last month. So ... on the one hand she had heard that her high school beau had died from AIDS twenty years ago, and that his spirit was visiting her on occasion, and that he was here to help Tess with a future project. And on the other hand she now had evidence in front of her that he was indeed alive and well in the physical world. Tess's thoughts were in turmoil. *Okay! That has to go into the I'll-learn-what-that-is-later box*, thought Tess, and started to compose an e-mail to her dear old friend. After a few moments she felt a familiar spiritual tap on the shoulder.

Multiverses.

Huh? Tess had just sent her e-mail off. *Btai Paul is that you?*

Yes.

Multiverses? asked Tess.

Don't you remember?

Tess thought deeply. *Hmmm, I seem to remember reading something a while ago about that. Yes!* She remembered Stan giving her a magazine while she had been in the hospital a few years ago. She jumped up from the computer, ran downstairs to her office, and scanned the crammed bookshelves. *No, that's not where they are!* She strode over to her desk and bent down and looked underneath. There were four plastic bins filled with assorted magazines and paperbacks. She tugged on the bin on the left-hand side and pulled on it. Once it was out from under the desk, she lifted the lid and started sifting through the magazines. Tess was a voracious reader, and she loved to keep everything that she read, and as a result had bins and bookshelves overflowing with all her books. In this particular bin were various science magazines and a few natural health magazines. She kept digging. *Aha!* She'd found it. *Scientific American*, "Multiverses" it said on the front cover. This was it! She sat down on the floor and started poring through the article. It was starting to come back to her now. A fairly complex topic, the physicists and cosmologists were working together and had mathematically determined that there must be an infinite number of universes in existence! Tess remembered thinking about how wild a concept this was, but it seemed to be making sense to her now. Tess imagined herself reading this article through to the end just now, and then, somewhere else, another Tess just like her decides to put the magazine down and go to the kitchen to start making dinner. And in yet another place another Tess puts the magazine into the recycling bin and picks up a romance novel.

Tess read on. Although it was initially overwhelming to consider that there were an infinite number of Tesses living an infinite number of different lives—all apparently at the same time, it seemed that the mathematics was telling the physicists that there were five universes that were local. Tess put the magazine down. This was starting to sound very familiar—she'd read something recently about five local dimensions that sounded as if it might have been the same thing! She rustled through her burgeoning bookshelf—*aha!* Here it was, a book on learning how to astral travel. Tess had been interested in learning this metaphysical technique where one portion of your energy field, your "astral" field, would leave your body, usually at night while you were asleep, and it would have learning experiences that would be embedded in your subconscious. But some could consciously travel in their astral bodies and remember their learning experiences once they awoke from their night's sleep. She flipped through the book—here it was. *Yes!* This fellow Dr Goldburg was writing that he had extensively astral traveled and had found that he could astral travel to five dimensions. And, he had learned how to actually move his physical body from the current dimension to what he called his most optimal dimension. Tess was thinking that perhaps the five local universes and the five dimensions we could astral travel to were the same thing.

And, Tess thought, *there might be some bleed through from universe to universe.* Perhaps even enough to allow for a Christopher from one of his other four universes to have died and come to visit Tess, to talk about a project?

Pretty wild stuff, but it made sense. Tess decided to put that one aside for now.

She headed back upstairs to find the phone ringing.

"Hello."

"Tess, its Harold."

Tess slapped her hand to her head—she'd totally forgotten to return his call. "Harold I meant to phone you earlier. How are you?"

"I'm good, Tess. I'm going to be in town tomorrow night and flying out again the next morning. Can I bunk in with you and Stan? A good chance for us to catch up, I think," he said.

"Great, Harold, it'll be good to see you!" Tess was excited to be seeing him. "Ah, Harold, can I ask you something?"

"Sure, Tess."

"It's about Rose."

"Okay, Tess."

"Was she psychic?"

"Actually, yes, Tess," he said in a curious tone of voice. "She did read tarot cards and was quite good at it. But, she was afraid of it, really. Why do you ask?"

"Well it seems that I am developing some psychic abilities myself, and got curious about Rose."

"Hmm, okay, Tess. We can chat more about this tomorrow night. I think I know where Rose kept her tarot cards, and actually she has a couple of books about the tarot too. I'll bring them along. See you, Tess."

Smiling, she said her good-byes to Harold and hung up the phone. Tess was tickled pink!

~

Tess and O were in their usual coffee shop the following week. They often met in the evening after work for a coffee and chat, and this often led to spiritual insights for both of them. Both O and Tess were always trying to make sense out of their experiences, to try and put all the pieces together to find their path in life. Tess had told O about Rose's abilities and her beautiful tarot deck that Harold had left with Tess.

"Yes—I have a workshop on the tarot" said O. "I think you'd find it quite interesting and a good way to start learning how to do readings yourself," said O.

"Wow, O, that would be fantastic! I've been doing a bit of studying on archetypes and stuff, but I don't know too much about the tarot symbology. Actually I'm a little afraid of doing readings because I don't really know what I'm doing," confessed Tess.

"Oh, Tess, you're so into the whole energetic nature of things, and that's what the tarot is all about—reading the energies around people. I think you'd be an excellent tarot reader; you just need a little direction and a bit of experience, that's all," said O with a wink at Tess.

"Well, I think I understand that spirit and soul energies so totally will guide the flow of events—if you allow them to, and if you are open to it."

"Absolutely, Tess. The key is to allow yourself and the other person to just relax, and then focus on the main theme or question at hand. The rest, knowing the meaning of the cards and how to apply this to a particular reading, will come with experience."

"Okay, O, please let me know when the …" Tess was cut off.

"Uh, who's that behind you, Tess" asked O.

She followed his glance over her left shoulder and then looked back at him. "Is it a spirit?" asked Tess. O nodded. "It's probably my guide, Btai Paul."

"He's nodding" said O.

"What's he look like," asked Tess excitedly. Tess had never mentioned Btai Paul to O before and was curious to see how O saw him.

"He's quite big, I mean big-boned, like he's strong. And he's got dark hair and a dark beard. He seems very protective of you."

"Yeah, I can feel that," said Tess truthfully. She knew that Btai Paul protected her as if she were his own child.

"You have a connection with him," continued O. "In fact you may have had a past life with him—perhaps you were his daughter. Oh, he's nodding again," said O. "He calls you—his little "Bit," whatever that means."

"Wow, O, thanks!"

"This is really interesting Tess. I never get past life stuff like this with anyone else, just you!"

"I'm totally amazed at how well you can see spirits," said Tess. "I'm envious!"

"Oh, well, I just wish that I could hear them like you," said O, and they both laughed.

"How's your tea?" asked O. "I'm getting another one, can I get you one?"

"Sure!" said Tess, and she started rustling around in her bag for her purse.

"No, Tess, this is on me."

Tess stopped rustling for her purse and instead pulled out her journal. She'd been keeping a number of journals for some time, and this one was her "serendipity" journal. All her coincidences were recorded here, and whenever she found the meaning behind certain events she would jot that down as well. She had bookmarked a spot well forward in the journal, but she flipped past it to a blank page to create a new entry.

O arrived with two steaming cups of chamomile tea for them both. "How's your friend Katrina?" asked O as he sat back down.

Tess realized that it had been quite a while since she had talked about Katrina with O. A while back, when Tess was giving Katrina healing sessions, she was hoping to find a way to bring some comfort to Katrina and asked O for advice.

"She passed on about six months ago, O."

"I'm so sorry, Tess."

"That's okay, O. Actually she came to visit me a little while ago, so I know she's on the other side."

"Tess, is she short, very pretty, short dark hair, wears a grey, tight sweater and short grey skirt?" She's pointing at you … no, at your bag there."

"Another spirit? Oh you mean Katrina—she's here?" asked Tess.

"Behind you on your right," said O.

Tess took a sip of tea and tried to relax. It wasn't easy for Tess to tune in, being in a busy cafe and a little excited about having another contact with spirit, but she took a deep breath and let it out slowly.

Who is here? sent Tess.

It is Katrina. Your friend can see me. Why can't you hear me? she asked Tess.

Sorry, Katrina, I have to focus quite hard to hear your voice in here, she sent. *Why are you here?* Tess asked.

You called me.

I didn't call you.

I'm talking to him. Your attractive friend.

Tess smiled and so did O. "I can hear her too," he said. But only when you hear her. It's like I can tap in somehow," he said.

"You must have called her when you asked me about how she was doing," said Tess. That brought her here."

"She's still pointing at your bag—no, wait, she's pointing at your book. Maybe you have something important written in there," he said excitedly.

Tess flipped the pages. *Is it here? What is it that you want me to see?* she sent to Katrina.

You almost have it. Keep going.

Tess flipped back to her bookmark, and then she realized what it was!

Katrina, it's your bookmark! You gave this to me after you came back from Paris!

You've got it, Tess. I didn't come to give you any special information. Just to tell you to use my bookmark!

Both Tess and O laughed heartily, and when they were done Katrina was gone. It was always an adventure being with O, Tess thought to herself.

"How was your appointment with Sam?" asked O.

"Well, O, Sam is really fantastic. I'm going back on Friday," exclaimed Tess. "It's not so easy, but I'm learning a lot about myself. I think that he can really help me to learn and grow," said Tess.

"Exactly," said O. "Do you know that he does hypnotherapy?

"No, I didn't." Tess had always been apprehensive about hypnotherapy, worrying that somehow it would damage her subconscious.

"Well you might give some thought to having a past life regression. It's a powerful technique to delve into past life issues. And don't worry, Tess, if you are having it done by a reputable professional it is quite safe."

It was almost like O was reading her mind! "Thanks, O, that makes me feel a bit better about—what'd you call it? Past life …"

"Regression. The therapist basically helps you to relax, just like a deep meditation. Then your subconscious comes to the forefront—you won't be asleep, you'll still be aware of what's going on. And then the therapist will ask questions to help stimulate past life memories. Your soul will determine what memories need to be brought forward and released."

"Cool, O. Thanks!" And Tess made a mental note to ask Sam about hypnotherapy on Friday.

It had been a frantic morning at Twelve Point. Tess had been working with a client that was seeking a partner to manufacture their specialty biotech drug. Richard had worked directly with their vice president, Nicholas Grandby, to create their request for proposal, and they had contacted three different contract manufacturers with it. They had had two positive responses that very morning, and now Tess was involved to help set up and coordinate the negotiation process.

Richard, Tess, and Nicholas had been locked in Twelve Point's boardroom all morning poring over the two offers and making inquiries to clarify certain points. Richard had quite a gift with negotiating; he knew just when to push beyond the boundaries of a situation, and then when to reign it back in. This had always been a tough line for Tess to walk. She just didn't have the vision to go outside the rules once in a while to open opportunities that may not have been apparent if keeping to the rules of the game. On the other hand, Tess was certainly able to go beyond the laws of physicality when having metaphysical experiences! She was indeed learning how to balance these two patterns in her life.

They had taken a break from the meeting to grab a bite to eat, and Tess had left Richard and Nicholas in the boardroom chatting and tucking into the tray of sandwiches while she stepped out to check her messages. Tess had been scribbling down a message from a new client when Richard popped his head into her cubicle.

"Tess, could you help me out?" She looked up and

nodded, then finished jotting down the rest of her message and put down the receiver. "Sure, Richard, what's up?"

"I'm sure that I've had a previous client with a situation similar to Nicholas's; would you mind having a look through my files for me? I have to get back for a conference call in five minutes."

"Definitely!" said Tess and she followed Richard around to the back of the office where the archive room was. This room was full of floor to ceiling bookshelves that were packed with binders of case information. Each binder was labeled with the client name and date.

"I'm not sure; I think it was about four years ago …" said Richard, heading down the second row of bookshelves. Tess followed behind. He stopped midway down and pulled out a particularly fat binder and laid it on top of a nearby cart. Tess stepped beside Richard to look at the information.

"We're looking for Melander Morroway—I think that's the name of the contract," said Richard, flipping to the table of contents of the binder.

Tess watched Richard focus intently on the table of contents, admiring his ability to remember the name of the contract from a number of years ago, when suddenly she started to feel—something, she wasn't quite sure of it at first. Richard flipped the binder closed and took out the one next to it and flipped it open on the cart, muttering something under his breath. Tess stepped back a bit and looked at Richard. He was almost exactly the same height as Tess, but a little heavier. His mannerisms while searching through the binder and quietly focusing on his task were reminding Tess of her own mannerisms—and suddenly Tess could feel something truly incredible—she could feel herself as if she were inside Richard's body! She was still feeling herself inside of her own body but at the same time feeling what it was like to be Richard, a man, standing and flipping pages, focused intently on his search. It was just a little too wild for Tess.

"Ah, Richard, I'll start looking over here," said Tess stepping quickly away and moving to the next set of binders further down the row. She was about four or five feet away from Richard and now out of close range of his aura, and the feeling that she was inside of Richard's body subsided. Tess began to nonchalantly scan the binders, but her thoughts were running wildly through her head. *What the hell was that all about?* she thought to herself. It must be the twin soul connection! Our energies must be the same frequency or vibration—that must be how I can feel what it's like to be him, Tess realized. Richard looked up at her.

"I have to get back, Tess—would you mind scanning these binders?" and he pointed to the binders on the cart in front of him. "It should be in this set of binders, I'm quite sure."

"Sure, Richard," said Tess, and Richard gave her a smile as he turned to head back to the boardroom.

"Thanks, Tess" he called back on his way out.

It was slowly dawning on Tess that although it was incredible to be experiencing these remarkable and very spiritual situations, but … if she could feel these things, then very likely so could Richard. Tess was debating whether to bring up the topic of things metaphysical with Richard to see how open he was to them. It was a tough one because he was her boss. He could easily think that she was off her rocker and find an excuse to let her go before she potentially started scaring clients with her weird experiences. So perhaps it was best to not say anything for now. But still—how often did you get to meet your twin soul in a lifetime, or even a lifetime of lifetimes? Wouldn't you feel kind of obligated somehow to let the other twin know what was going on?

Tess sighed and turned back to the tall bookshelf full of binders and pulled one out and set it on the cart. A fine pickle!

~Chapter 15~

Two Swords

A few weeks later Tess was down in her basement where she and Stan had her exercise equipment. Stan liked to use the cardio machine that made you feel like you were cross-country skiing. Tess liked to do her yoga, and she was on her purple flowered mat, in the middle of doing her warm-up stretches. She'd recently switched from Tai Chi to yoga and enjoyed it immensely. It was amazing how the stretches and postures could release muscle tension that could build up after a long day at the office or after sitting at the computer for a long time. Tess was a bit stressed because the day previous she'd gone on a job interview on a whim, and was hoping the yoga would allow her to relax again.

One of the résumés that she had sent out while unemployed after the layoff from TSK Inc. went to a well-respected HIV clinical research organization, and it must have actually been kept on file. The HTRG, or HIV Treatment Research Group, had called her a few days previous about a project management position that had opened up, and although Tess was happy with Twelve Point and her varied schedule, something told her to just go and see what they had to say. Although initially excited at the prospect of pursuing work in the HIV field, Tess was feeling quite guilty because she had to take an afternoon off of work, and somehow she had the feeling that Richard knew very well that she was not really off to a doctor's appointment. As she was leaving his office on that day, she distinctly heard him say, "Remember, Tess, I need you here. Okay?"

However, the interview was quite extraordinary. Tess knew from a former colleague who was working there that all of the key people were scientists, and good ones at that. Tess wondered about their motives in wanting to interview a project manager who had no scientific credentials, and so had re-reviewed all of her project management courses materials thoroughly before the interview.

Although she had spoken with Dale Stewart, the director of HTRG, over the phone—meeting him in person was altogether amazing. As soon as she had shaken his hand she realized instantly that he was the remaining member of her soul group! He had shaken her hand firmly and looked directly into her eyes, and had hesitated for just a moment. She could feel the connection—Tess was now familiar with the sensation (to Tess it almost felt like the entire universe had come and tapped each of them on their shoulders, as much to say, "Get with it, you two; you have been best buddies, and you know it"), and she knew that Dale Stewart could feel something as well.

The interview was one of the most challenging experiences of Tess's life. Six of HTRG's key people were gathered around the boardroom table, and Tess was shown a seat at the head of the table. Tess was introduced to each section head, and then Dale briefly outlined to Tess how the interview process would run. Each person would briefly describe his or her role at HTRG and then have ten minutes to ask her pertinent questions about her credentials and experience. At the end of the session Tess would be asked to present how she felt that she could contribute to their team.

As Tess was in the midst of answering questions from each person, all of whom were highly credentialed scientists, Tess could at the same time feel Dale's impressions of how well Tess was handling each situation, almost like Dale could read the mind of each of his team members and know how they were feeling about Tess's answers—and this was more than a little unnerving to her! The impressions were of frustration from most of the interviewers, that she was not a scientist, and that this interview was a waste of time. And at the same time she could feel from Dale that he was hell-bent on pursuing a project manager for this position. It was a highly stressful situation for Tess. A bit of a break came from one interviewer, the head of the software group, who seemed to resonate with Tess's responses to his questions, and this positive few moments allowed Tess to gather her wits and at least look calm through the rest of the interview process.

At the end, when it was Dale's turn to ask questions, the only question he asked was, "And so, Tess, what is it that you feel that you could contribute to our team?"

Tess decided that she should be direct. "Well, I think that HTRG should first decide whether they need a project manager to run their new initiative, or a scientist. If it is a project manager that is being sought, then I offer to HTRG project management skills and experience to run this new project. But if you are seeking a scientist, then I wish you well in your search."

Instantly Tess could feel disappointment coming from Dale, even though he maintained a calm demeanor. That was definitely not the answer he was looking for. And the interview was over. As Dale escorted her back to the main entrance to HTRG, she again could feel that amazing soul group connection. As he shook hands with her and said good-bye, Tess could feel the magic of that cosmic connection and was so pleased to have had an opportunity to meet Dale; and thought that perhaps that was all that the universe had in mind for her that day—just to meet her remaining soul group member!

It had been a tense and overwhelming experience, and Tess was now determined to release all of that stress with her yoga stretches. She'd done her deep breathing and was now doing her touching-the-opposite-toe limbering-up routine when a particular book caught her eye on her ever-burgeoning bookshelf. *Dianetics.* She hadn't read this book but remembered picking it up at a garage sale about twenty years ago.

She shook away the thought and tried to empty her mind while continuing her stretches, now touching her palms to the floor while keeping her legs straight.

This type of yoga was apparently quite unusual in that it was an energy-based yoga that was designed to open all the energy meridians in the body. These were lines of energy just like the acupuncture meridians (Tess thought they were the very same meridians), and the various stretches, movements, and body tapping were all designed to release stagnant energy so that new, fresh energy could begin to flow throughout the body. Tess always felt like a new person after doing these stretches, and the energy that the instructors brought into the yoga center was so beneficial.

After twenty minutes Tess had finished her "in-between class" set of stretches. She checked the clock—it was 11:11 a.m. She had about forty-five minutes to get downtown to her appointment with Sam. Tess had a few days off between projects at Twelve Point and was excited to be on a mini learning adventure for a few days.

She arrived five minutes late and knocked on the door to his Yorkville office.

"Come in, Tess," called Sam.

She opened the door and walked into the small, cozy office and found Sam already sitting in one of the two chairs set up beside a small table in the center of the room. Sam put down the book that he had been reading, and Tess wasn't quick enough to catch the title, but she'd caught a glimpse, and it seemed familiar somehow.

"Have a seat, Tess." Tess settled into the comfortable chair.

"So, what's been happening, Tess?" asked Sam.

"Uh …" Tess never knew where to start.

"Well, Tess, from what we chatted about during our last session I'm sure that you always have some interesting experiences to share." Sam smiled warmly at her.

Tess started to relax. It was so comforting to be able to share her weird experiences with someone who not only understood but could actually help her make some sense out of them. To Tess it felt like one mystery after another.

Tess shared her recent experiences with Richard, and the information received from her higher self. Sam had interrupted to find out how Tess knew that the information about "Ric" came from her higher self, and so Tess told Sam about her guide, Btai Paul, who had helped her identify where that information had come from. Sam was initially taken aback by the identity of her guide, so Tess quickly mentioned her experience in the Renaissance art exhibit that had helped Tess to see her Btai Paul in a more cosmic context, and she suggested that perhaps Sam could see his identity in this way. This seemed to resonate with Sam.

Finally Tess asked Sam about hypnotherapy and past life regression, and if he would be willing to use this technique to help Tess release the issues around her New Zealand life.

"Definitely we could have a past life regression session, Tess," he said eagerly. Then pausing, he scratched the side of his face, pondering his next thought. "You know, Tess, I was just reading this interesting book." He picked his book up off the table, and this time Tess caught the title.

Dianetics.

"Holy smokes, Sam!"

"Do you recognize this book? Have you read it already?" he asked quickly.

"No, I haven't, but I just looked at it this morning before coming to our session. The book has been on my bookshelf for ages, and I just noticed it, or, well, noticed it again, this morning."

"Okay, Tess, well, that feels quite significant. I think you should read this book. The auditing technique is what I'm thinking is the part that is important for you to know about. It seems to be quite a fantastic way to resolve issues, including past life issues, without using hypnosis."

"I'll definitely start reading it today!" said Tess excitedly. She looked at Sam—he had paused again and was scratching the side of his face. "What's up, Sam?" she asked.

"Well, I'm not sure. I seem to be somehow picking up something. I'm not sure what," he said slowly. Then he sat up straight. "Okay, here's what I'm thinking," he said quickly. "If you decide to do the auditing you need to use discernment."

"What do you mean exactly?" asked Tess.

"I'm not sure, but I think Dianetics and Scientology are linked together. You need to be discerning and to remember whose path you are on, your path or their path. In other words, stay on your path, Tess. Actually this might apply to any organization that you approach for learning as well.

You know, why not talk to Btai Paul and get his opinion?" said Sam with a smile. "Do you mind doing that together just now?

"Sure, Sam. Just give me a minute to relax my mind a bit," said Tess, and she settled back into her chair and took a few deep breaths.

Btai Paul are you there? she sent.

Yes.

"He's here, Sam."

"Great. Keep going."

"What should I say?"

"Ask him if it is significant that we both were looking at the Dianetics book today."

Did you hear that Btai Paul?

Of course. And yes.

"He says yes."

"That's it?"

"Just yes. That's all he said."

"Okay, ask him if this is something you should explore."

Btai Paul, should I be exploring the Dianetics techniques?

Can you be more specific?

"He's asking me to be more specific, Sam."

"Ask him if you should try the Dianetics auditing."

Did you hear that Btai Paul?

Yes.

Should I try it?

What do you think?

"He's asking me what I think."

"Well, what do you think?" said Sam with a smile.

"I think that I need to read the book first!" said Tess.

They both laughed. And then Sam was quiet for a few moments. Tess looked at him—he was staring at her face—well not quite at her face, his eyes seemed to be focusing just in front of her.

"Sorry I'm so quiet, but something really unusual is happening," said Sam in a hushed voice. "I can feel my scalp prickling like mad, and there's something like a fog around me."

"Wow," said Tess in a low voice. "What else is going on?"

"Ah, well, there's an image of a woman, the head of a woman over top of your head. She looks like a woman from the Roman era. Man, my head is just prickling like mad!" he exclaimed.

Tess kept as still as she could, not wanting to interfere in whatever was occurring for Sam. She could sense that Sam was having a metaphysical experience of some kind; and it seemed to be a vision.

"It's calming down now. The woman is gone. That was kind of wild!" he said, and took a deep breath. "Whew!"

"So what happened? asked Tess.

"Well, as I said, I kind of got all prickly, and that has happened to me before. When I was in the TAC, one of my courses involved channeling, and a classmate was channeling her guide, who was telling her about my guide. At that moment I got the same prickly feeling in my aura, and she got some information about my guide."

"So it seems to happen at significant moments," said Tess.

"Yes. And so I saw this image of a woman; it looked like a Roman woman, dark hair shorter than yours; her face was a bit heavier, larger nose. And that's it!" He paused, thinking. "Maybe you can ask Btai Paul who it was."

Btai Paul, who was visiting just now?

That's for Sam to figure out.

"Oh!" exclaimed Tess.

"What, what, tell me!" said Sam anxiously.

"It's for you to figure out."

"He's so vague, isn't he!" commented Sam.

"Yes, and it kind of makes me a bit crazy sometimes; he almost always throws the ball back in my court," exclaimed Tess.

"That's actually a very good sign, Tess" said Sam seriously.

"How's that?!" exclaimed Tess indignantly. "I thought guides were supposed to tell you stuff!"

"Wrong, Tess," said Sam gently. "They are here to guide you, not to give you all the answers."

"Oh! Hmm, well, actually, that does make sense," Tess acknowledged. "Otherwise we'd be just like little robots, wouldn't we, just following the whims of spirits rather than doing what we came here to do, or learn what we came here to learn, I guess."

"Absolutely," retorted Sam.

There you go.

"It sounds like Btai Paul agrees," said Tess.

"Okay. So, Tess, for our next session we can chat more about auditing and whatever else is going on for you. Let's leave the PLR for a bit, okay?"

"Okay," said Tess. "Sounds like a plan."

Sam smiled. "Great. See you in two weeks."

Tess thanked him and headed out. As she walked to the subway she noticed that she was feeling so light somehow. Her burdens had been lifted. She really seemed to resonate with Sam, almost like they had a cosmic connection somehow. But what kind of a connection? She knew all of her soul group. Perhaps a past life? Maybe that's what he was seeing during the session, part of a life they'd shared together. A myriad of questions were whirling around in Tess's mind as she stepped onto the subway to head home.

Tess spent the next two days reading voraciously. It was tough reading, Tess found that she didn't really resonate with the writer, somehow, and she had to keep putting the book down for a bit. Tess usually had four or five books on the go, and so she would pick up where she left off in one of her other books for a bit and then go back to the *Dianetics*.

Tess was picking up a flavor for the auditing, though, and was beginning to think that this technique was really quite brilliant! It seemed to fit with other readings that she had been into recently. The audit technique was a way to have someone guide you through the memory of a traumatic experience but in a very impartial way in that the person doing the auditing would not place any bias or judgment on the experience itself. They would only provide input on whether to move forward or to back up and move through a portion of an experience again. In essence you would walk through the traumatic experience multiple times; each time it seemed that you would release your emotions regarding the trauma. Once you had released all your emotions around the event, so that you could walk through the experience and not feel emotional about it, then you had cleared an energy blockage around that particular trauma.

Tess was noticing that the removal of energy blockages was becoming a theme with much of her energy-related studies of late. Including her yoga! This really seemed to be a key element to regaining health, not just physical health but mental, emotional, and spiritual health as well.

Tess was so impressed with her readings about the auditing technique that she'd gone in person to the Dianetics center to book an appointment. It hadn't been easy, because she was keen on stressing that she wasn't there to join the Scientology institution, but that she only wanted to book one block of auditing sessions. She had practiced a bit with Stan, who was not at all keen on Tess going through with this but relented when Tess made it clear that she only wanted to experience the audit and did not want to join their organization.

After going through the necessary introductions at the Dianetics center, watching a video about the auditing process and filling out some paperwork, Tess had gotten a series of appointments with an experienced auditor. One block of sessions was about twelve hours, with each session being one to two hours, and the sessions being held within a few days of each other.

The first session had been quite interesting. She was asked various questions about her life, and notes were made around events that seemed significant. Then each significant event was examined one by one. The first event was the death of Rose, and Tess was surprised at how much emotion she was still holding around her death, even though she felt happy that Rose's spirit was still alive and that she could still speak to her spirit on occasion from the other side. The auditor was experienced and knew how to guide Tess to relax enough to recall the events around Rose's last hours in the hospital, and to walk through Tess's visit with Rose again and again until Tess was able to visualize being with Rose in the hospital during her last hours alive, without getting emotional. Next was the visit from Rose's spirit, and the very same process was used to allow Tess to reexperience this visit again and again until Tess could walk through it calmly. Tess had found it extraordinary that the auditor would calmly accept that Tess had actually seen Rose's spirit on her way to the other side, and had felt her first session to be quite remarkable. She felt a little apprehensive about how the auditor would feel about walking through past life traumatic events, and felt that his ease in dealing with her experience with Rose's spirit to be a good indication that he might be open-minded enough to pursue them as valid experiences to be resolved.

In Tess's next session, two days later, they walked through a number of other significant experiences, including her claustrophobia and a fear of dark, enclosed spaces that was revealed during her camping days with her ex, Frank. She could not sleep with the flaps on the tent closed; some light had to be coming into the tent, otherwise she'd panic and run right out of the tent. And they'd also walked through the recent experience in the hospital with peritonitis. Toward the end of the session it seemed that they'd touched upon all of Tess's significant life experiences. Then the auditor asked Tess to go back to the peritonitis experience. He was specifically pointing her to the fear that she experienced when awakening from her operation, her irrational behavior that caused the nurses to call the doctor to reassure her. Although Tess had walked through that experience calmly enough, it was the irrational fear, a fear that did not seem to have any obvious origin, that brought the auditor back to that experience. He asked Tess to take a few deep breaths and just reflect back on what might have caused her to act in such a manner. At first Tess didn't know what to do, so she relaxed in a mindful state and just allowed her soul to bring thoughts in front of her.

Then, slowly, Tess could feel Penelope! She voiced this out loud to the auditor. He asked her to visualize the events around her. She was deathly afraid and running for her life! Someone was behind her, someone that wanted to kill her! Tess/Penelope could feel the intense fear of being chased by an assailant! She was in a thick forest; it was dark, and the branches were catching her dress, causing her to stumble and

allowing her assailants to catch up with her. Assailants—
there were two of them—and Penelope could hear them
calling each other as they chased her. Suddenly she was
stopped dead in her tracks.

"I got you!" said a female voice that Penelope knew, and
her assailant had indeed caught up with her and stepped on
the back of her long dress, stopping her dead in her tracks.
Penelope knew that the voice of her assailant was that of a
Maori native woman that she had mistreated—and she also
knew that the Maori woman had a connection to Tess in
her present life—it was her Chios master teacher, Roger! He
must have had a previous life in New Zealand as a Maori
woman. Suddenly Penelope could feel the piercing pain of
a sword that went up between her legs and out through her
lower abdomen—she could feel a gush of blood rush out as
she collapsed on her side onto the forest floor. It was dark,
so dark, and she was in pain from the sword through her
abdomen; her eyes were screwed shut, and she could hear
the second assailant's footsteps behind her, and then at her
shoulders. Penelope knew this person; she could hear his
voice from behind when she was being chased. He was
David/Stan's "second," who also looked after the horses.
This person was also connected to Tess in her present life—
and Tess realized that it was Dale Stewart, the scientist from
her interview at HGTN! Somehow Penelope knew what was
coming next, and a second blow—also with a sword, took
her head right off! As it was happening Penelope had the
deep and clear knowledge that she had somehow deserved
it!

The auditor stopped the session for that day, and they
discussed the events of the chase and the two sword blows,
and together they were able to connect each blow to events
in Tess's life now. The sword through the abdomen was
linked to Tess's irrational fear right after her operation (the

fear that she was exploding), and the sword that cut off her head was linked to her fear of dark, enclosed spaces. Tess was amazed at these revelations and was totally impressed with the process. The next session would allow Tess to walk though these events until she had released all the emotion around them. The auditor seemed quite unaffected by the fact that these events were from a past life and even mentioned that many people did experience or reexperience past life traumas during the auditing process.

Tess was so curious about Penelope's feeling that she deserved to be killed, and wondered just what she had done to deserve being chased by two assailants bearing swords—only to be stabbed and then beheaded!

~Chapter 16~

Rebecca

Tess had scheduled the rest of her Dianetics audit sessions for the evenings, as she was now on another big project at Twelve Point. She was anxious to find out more details about this past life, and at the same time wondered just how many past lives she had had. So far she was aware of four past lives: the life in New Zealand as Penelope, the life in Tarsus as Btai Paul's daughter, the life in the Renaissance period as Giorgio Vasari, and the life in Rome as Sam's wife. Tess toyed with the notion of someday actually going to visit the places where she had experienced these lives. And now, remarkably, she even had some clues as to the strategy followed in between lives prior to incarnating to the New Zealand life, with the information revealed to her by her higher self and the splitting of her soul to create the twin souls of herself and Ric.

Wildly interesting, but leading to a plethora of new questions, thought Tess. If Ric had been her twin sister in the New Zealand life, and they were indeed souls who had been twinned or, in essence, were exact duplicates of each other, then the only difference between them at the start of the New Zealand life would have been the advice given prior to incarnating, according to what she had heard from her higher self. And how did Penelope get to New Zealand? And where was her twin sister—did she go to New Zealand with her? If not, then what kind of life did her sister have? How was it different or the same as her life? What changes did each life make to each of their souls?

And now, meeting Ric, Tess could see many similarities between them, particularly how connected their energies were, but also many differences, most notably how each of them reacted in a situation where a set of rules was in play—Tess always went by the rules, but Ric could see when it was right to go outside of the rules. This seemed to be quite significant to Tess, and raised even more questions. Did they each have another life in between the New Zealand life and this one? Why did they meet now in this life? Should Tess raise this topic with Ric now? So many questions to solve!

Tess was also beginning to understand that there was an underlying strategy behind certain serendipitous events; that somehow a higher power was at work helping to navigate Tess through a complex series of events that seemed to be heading toward a certain purpose. Tess had done quite a lot of reading lately from many authors who seemed to be either looking for their "path" or "purpose," or who were providing help to others who were seeking their path, by relating their experiences in finding their own path. Tess had been torn between mentioning the topic of reincarnation to Ric just to see what his thoughts were—whether he was open to this concept or not, and simply not saying anything at all. Tess had thought long and hard about this. She put herself in Ric's shoes and thought about being a manager and supervising an employee, having to work together on large projects with clients, and one day having this employee ask her about reincarnation out of the blue. How would she feel about that? Had Tess been a manager at the same age as Ric (he looked about ten years younger than Tess), Tess would not have entertained the idea of reincarnation at all and would have instantly dismissed the topic as nonsense. And so Tess had decided that if the topic should be discussed between the two of them, that one of those serendipitous events would just have to happen to cause the topic to come up between them, and that it would just be best to wait until the time was right.

Tess's next two audit sessions were very revealing, and quite a lot of information about her New Zealand life circumstances was coming out. By asking Tess to move back in time from the scene where her assailants were chasing her, they were able to trace the entire day's events plus even go back a few days earlier to gain perspective on why Tess had felt she deserved to be killed.

Penelope was in charge of a British household and horse ranch, and had undergone some training back in Britain that provided various strategies for keeping native peoples from getting "out of hand." It seemed that all those working in the household and ranch required a firm hand and strict adherence to rules. If any of the native Maori didn't follow the rules, they were whipped. But not by Penelope; she had the quartermaster, David/Stan, perform this. David was initially not so willing to use his horsewhip on people, especially the Maori, but Penelope was apparently quite persuasive. So persuasive, in fact, that she had begun an affair with David!

And so the memory of Penelope's last few days in New Zealand began with a trip out to the barn. Penelope was anxious to find David and tell him the news, news that Penelope was pregnant with David's child! After ensuring that everything was running perfectly in the household, she had then gone outside to the barn to find David. A side entrance was closer to the house, and Penelope opened the large wooden door. As it swung open, Penelope walked inside and could smell the mix of hay and horses. There was a short walkway between two stalls that opened out into a larger area where the horses were groomed and shoed, and Penelope walked out into this area—only to find to her great dismay that David had hanged himself from the rafters of the barn! Penelope was stunned and overcome with the realization that it was her fault; she had manipulated David not only into a love affair but also into whipping some of the natives who Penelope had thought were getting out of hand. Penelope stood looking in disbelief at David, dressed in his coveralls and blue shirt, hanging in the center of the barn. After recovering from the initial shock, Penelope had run out of the barn back to the house and had barked orders to the staff to find David's second, to look after David's body in the barn.

Two days later Penelope was arriving back at the household in a black horse-drawn carriage. It was a circular drive in front of a large homestead; the ranch portion seemed to be behind the house. She had been to David's funeral and was arriving back at the house alone, very somber and sad. The homestead was quite large and was usually bustling with activity. But at the moment there was no one to be seen, and this seemed unusual.

Penelope got out of the carriage and dismissed the driver, who immediately moved the carriage away from the house. Penelope walked up the steps of the front porch and opened the front door into a large foyer. No one! This didn't feel right to Penelope; the house should be bustling with activity. She walked through the large living room, past the large floor-to-ceiling fireplace toward the kitchen, feeling angry that the staff would be slacking off like this, leaving the house unattended. She opened the swinging door to the kitchen area and walked inside and stood unbelieving, with her hands on her hips. No one! She glanced over to the side, where another doorway to a side porch was. The screened door was closed, but the outer wooden door was open, and Tess did not see anyone on the porch either. She was getting angrier by the minute, and then suddenly she heard a slight noise to her left. Whirling around, she found a small girl of nine or ten, blonde hair and big blue eyes, peeking through the door to the pantry. Marta! Penelope smiled and called to her.

"Marta, please come in. Where is everyone?" she asked. Marta slowly opened the pantry door and stepped inside, never taking her eyes off of Penelope.

"They've gone, ma'am," said Marta slowly.

Penelope looked quizzically at the girl. She trusted this girl; Marta provided Penelope with secret information on occasion.

"Marta, has everyone gone? And where did they go?"

"Ma'am, you have to leave right away," she said in a fearful voice, keeping her eyes carefully on Penelope's. "They are coming!"

"Who is coming?" she asked in a stern voice.

"The warriors. They are coming to kill you. You have to go, ma'am" said Marta firmly, still looking directly at Penelope. She pointed to the side door. "You have to hurry, ma'am!"

Penelope was at once afraid. She knew that there had been native uprisings against the British and that there had been fighting nearby but hadn't believed that they'd attack her homestead—until now. She stood firm, unwilling to believe it.

"Marta, are you certain of this?"

"Ma'am, you are in danger. You have to go now,"

she repeated and pointed again to the side door. "Hurry, ma'am!"

Penelope hesitated for a moment.

"I'll just quickly go upstairs and get my things ..." she started.

"They are coming *now*," she yelled, and then disappeared back through the pantry door.

Penelope made up her mind and dashed through the screen door on the side and ran out through the porch and headed to the path through the forest to her secret path. She ran into the cool forest along the path that she and David had walked on many times during their short romance. The main path broke off onto a secret one, leading to her safe place by the sea, a small cabin that was built on the shore near the dock where the British ship that had originally brought them from England, complete with all of their supplies, had landed.

She slowed a bit where the main path curved to the left. It should be here somewhere, and she stopped and pushed back a branch from the thick brush on the side of the path. A smaller, less-worn path showed behind the branch. That was it!

She pushed her way through and tried to hurry as fast as she could, but her long dress was hindering her progress.

After a few minutes she heard a noise behind her. A voice—she recognized that voice! No, wait—there were two of them! The Maori woman that Penelope had sent for punishment (David had given her ten lashes at Penelope's insistence) and David's second, who was also a quartermaster but not a veterinarian like David. They were running behind her, and as Penelope ran for her life she was certain that she had been set up by both of them. These two had been waiting for her! She tried to run faster but kept stumbling. She could hear the voices stronger now; they were catching up! Penelope was terrified and slipped again on a tree root. She jumped up and was running wildly though the narrow path, tree branches whipping through her hair and across her face. Suddenly, her whole body jerked back—the Maori woman had stepped on her dress from behind.

"Aha, I got you!" came her triumphant voice. And then Penelope could feel the sharp blade of the sword pierce through her body, and she saw it emerge, unbelievably, from her abdomen. Overcome with pain, she grabbed the sword as if to stop it from penetrating any farther and fell over on her side. She could feel blood pouring out of her body. It was so dark, and the pain was unbelievable … Now she could hear someone breathing heavily behind her—and then she could feel heavier footsteps by her shoulders. It was David's second!

She squeezed her eyes even more tightly shut. She felt wretched and knew that he was raising a sword, intending to cut off her head. *Why, oh, why did she have to be so strict, to follow the rules so exactly, to have to hurt them to keep them from getting out of hand; to manipulate David into hurting them? And now David was dead, and his dear friend was about to avenge his death!* And amidst her anguished thoughts she felt the heavy thud of the sword upon her neck, and knew at once that she was totally deserving of it before blackness descended upon her.

The auditor was satisfied after walking through this series of events a number of times that Tess had released all her emotions around it. Tess could recount all of the events and did not get emotional, and even was able to reflect back on the series of experiences with the auditor. A few of the twelve hours were still left in the block of sessions, and the auditor felt there was still an issue in her present life experience that had not been examined—her fear of her boss, Richard. Tess had mentioned this in passing to the auditor during their first session. If Tess was willing, they would pursue this during their remaining sessions.

Tess was a little afraid of Richard, and she couldn't really pin it down to anything concrete. It didn't make any sense; Richard was a terrific boss, very talented, and excellent to work with. In fact, Tess was learning a lot from their work together. She was thinking perhaps it was the psychic experiences she had occasionally with him—the telepathic experience, being able to feel what it was like to be Richard. And also, in a way she found him quite attractive; it was not as if she would ever pursue a relationship with Richard, or anyone else for that matter, as she was quite happy with Stan. But she did feel a certain *je na sais quoi* when she was with him, and was assuming this was due to how similar their energies were. So, all of this had been causing Tess to keep her distance a bit from him.

And so two days later she was back for her last audit session. She relaxed, as prompted by the auditor, and then he asked her to think about her boss. As she relaxed into the vision, she felt Penelope, but this time a younger version of her. She was about twelve or thirteen. She was in a beautiful bedroom brushing her hair—it was long and dark brown—and she had on an elegant violet dress. Then she felt something, uncertain at first of what it was. Then she realized it was her sister, her twin sister, and that her name was Rebecca, and she was crying! Penelope could feel her before hearing her voice in the hallway. They were both quite psychic! She put down the brush and went to the door. She could hear her name being called through tears, and Rebecca rushed into her room. She looked remarkably like Penelope, and she rushed into Penelope's arms sobbing. Apparently their mother was planning a trip to the country for herself and Rebecca but was not planning on taking

Penelope with them. The two of them were inseparable, and Rebecca was quite upset that Penelope would not accompany them. And, remarkably, somehow Tess knew that their mother, the mother of Penelope and Rebecca, was connected to Tess's present life—she was Rose!

Then the scene changed. It was about five years later, and both Rebecca and Penelope were in the large drawing room of a mansion owned by a teacher. This teacher was a special person, a land developer. He was teaching those who had been specially appointed by the British government to go overseas and develop lands that were now British colonies. Penelope and Rebecca had been appointed, and quite unusually so, as it was uncommon for a woman to be a land developer. However, they each had a gift; their psychic gift combined with a strong business sense had made both of them quite influential in dealing with people. In addition, both seemed to be very strong women, both in temperament and character.

Their father had brought them by carriage each week for their lesson, and today was the last lesson. Each of them was due to depart in a week's time, Penelope for New Zealand and Rebecca for South Africa! Both of them were distraught. They did not want to be separated from each other. However, this enterprise would be very beneficial for their family. As part of this, Penelope had entered into an agreement with a family friend, an arranged marriage with the son of the Lancasters. Their son Duncan was in his mid-forties and had some kind of mental disorder that caused him to be a recluse. The Lancasters wanted to contribute to Britain's land developer project, and so Penelope and Rebecca's father had made this arrangement, which Penelope had agreed to. The Lancasters would provide the needed financing for the lessons for Rebecca and their new daughter-in-law, Penelope. This arrangement had severely disappointed

Rebecca, because a few years earlier Penelope and Rebecca had agreed that neither of them would ever marry, and that they would always stick together. And now here they were, Penelope was married, and they were both heading to new countries, separately!

The morning had been full of the practicalities of life on a sailing vessel completely filled with necessary supplies, crew, and horses—thoroughbreds. They had sat around a great table discussing the details and examining maps, and they were fortified with tea and crumpets.

After lunch, the afternoon was spent in the middle of the room, with their teacher drawing on a large chalkboard and explaining how to manage native peoples, and the importance of correcting aberrant behavior. It was stressed that they had to maintain control of their house, ranch, and land at all times and that they had to rule with a strong hand, especially so since they were women. Penelope was not keen at all on the methods of correcting aberrant behavior, particularly using a whip on any person, regardless of whether he or she was a native; however, she did understand why it was important to maintain control—otherwise they would lose their foothold in the newly developing British colony. When their last lesson was complete, both Rebecca and Penelope hugged the teacher and turned together to walk out to the front foyer. Rebecca moved slightly ahead of Penelope and then turned back to her and whispered, "You're not going to do that, are you?" and then ran ahead out the front door to their father and the waiting carriage. Penelope understood Rebecca's comment but did not answer her.

The auditor had walked Tess through these experiences a number of times, and now Tess could reexperience them without the sadness of parting from her beloved twin sister. They briefly discussed Tess's fear, and both thought that it may be due to the fact that Penelope indeed had followed the strict correcting methods for native peoples as taught, even though she had found the practice to be distasteful; whereas it seemed likely that Rebecca/Richard had not!

~Chapter 17~

Memhotep

"That is pretty wild, Tess" said Sam, as Tess finished explaining the details from her auditing sessions. "Good work; you really kept with it! I'm sure it wasn't easy having twelve hours of walking through your traumatic experiences. So, what do you think the higher meaning of all this is," Sam asked Tess, smiling.

"Ah," she stopped. "Well, I've sure learned a lot about myself and others that I'm connected to in this life."

"And what else," prompted Sam.

"Well, I released all of my emotions around these events," said Tess firmly.

"And how does that serve you?"

"Hmmm." Tess thought about this. "Well, it explains some of my irrational fear and behaviors in this life. My irrational behavior right after my surgery was because I was kind of reexperiencing the sword wound to my abdomen. And my fear of the dark and my anxiety attacks while in a closed tent while camping happens because I am reexperiencing the fear of having my head chopped off while trapped in the forest; it was dark, because my eyes were shut tight."

"I think you've got it, Tess" said Sam, smiling back at her. "But I think there's still more going on."

"Hmmm. I dunno."

"Let's ask Btai Paul."

"Okay." Tess relaxed and took a few deep breaths.

"Okay, Tess ask him if we have covered everything or not."

Did you hear that, Btai Paul?

Yes.

Have we figured everything out, or is there more going on?

How do you feel?

"He's asking me how I feel."

"Well, how have you been feeling lately?" asked Sam.

"You mean my pelvic infections?"

"Yes."

"I keep them away by doing my healing sessions once a week. And I've been doing quite a lot of exercises. I think that's been helping."

They will not return.

"What?!" exclaimed Tess, hardly believing her ears. "Oh, Sam, he said they won't return! Wow!"

"Ask him why not."

Did you hear that, Btai Paul?

You know the answer.

And suddenly she did know. "Because I released the emotions from the sword stabbing and gained an understanding of the situation. That has released a blockage in my second chakra that had caused a weakness," she said out loud.

"Right on," said both Sam and Btai Paul.

And so I'd continue to have problems there until I could release that trapped emotion about this past life trauma? asked Tess by thought to Btai Paul.

Right!

"That's pretty powerful!" exclaimed Tess. "Hmmm … I wonder if having my head chopped off gave me a predisposition to whiplash?"

"Huh? Explain, please," said Sam.

Tess explained about her skydiving stint with Frank and how she'd been keeping her neck from seizing up by regular massage therapy and now by practicing yoga as well.

"Well, that would make sense, but you know what to do," said Sam.

"Okay." *Btai Paul, how about my neck?*

Yes and no.

"He says yes and no."

"Ask him to explain."

Btai Paul, can you explain or be more specific?

There is more going on with your neck. This is for you to discover.

"He says there is more going on with my neck, and it is for me to discover."

"How exciting!" said Sam and laughed.

Tess smiled. "Only you would laugh at that," she said, smiling back at him.

"By the way, I went to my friend Rina for a reading to find out more about that vision of the Roman woman I had during our last session."

"Cool—what happened?" asked Tess curiously.

"Well, it was definitely a past life that you and I have shared. It was in Roman times, and you were my wife!"

"Wow, Sam, that's wild. I wonder if you and I have had other lives together?"

"Let's ask Paul! Paul, have Tess and I had other lives together?" asked Sam.

Btai Paul, did you hear Sam's question?

Yes.

Have we had other lives where we've met each other?
Yes.
"He says yes, Sam!"
"Wow. How many, Paul?"
Tess smiled at Sam's enthusiasm.
How many Btai Paul?
"… … …"
I can't get the number, Btai Paul.
Between forty and fifty.
"Between forty and fifty, Sam."
"Tess—ask him how many lives in total we each have had, not just the Earth lives," said Sam anxiously.
Did you hear him, Btai Paul?
Thousands.
"Holy smokes, Sam. He says thousands!"

"Whew!" That was a lot to absorb. Sam put down his notepad and sat back into his chair. After a few moments he said, "Well, you know, Tess, there's more from Rina. She thinks that you and I are soul mates."

Tess could feel that this was true but didn't know what to make of it. She already knew her ten soul group members. How could she have more than ten? Was it even possible to have eleven? But Tess could feel that something deeper was going on. It sure felt like a cosmic connection that she and Sam shared, and a pretty strong one at that. Tess was absolutely certain, however, that between Sam and herself they would get to the bottom of it!

It had been such a delight to catch up with her dear friend Christopher Thomas from high school. They had been e-mailing each other quite a bit since reconnecting through the high school database. It was quite amazing; they were both so into reading spiritual books, with Christopher having

241

read books with more of a Buddhist flavor than Tess, who seemed to be leaning toward those with themes around that of cosmic consciousness. Tess was so amazed at her friend, who she had been calling the bionic man recently because he'd had a serious car accident about the same time that Tess was in the hospital. He'd had massive injuries to his brain during the accident, in which a young fellow in his thirties had run a red light. Christopher had been the first to move into the intersection, as the light had been green his way for a few moments, when he was T-boned by the fellow who was driving a sport utility vehicle. Christopher, in his ten-year-old compact car, was no match, and the car had flipped over onto its roof, pinning him inside. The firemen had to use the jaws-of-life to pry him out of his crushed vehicle, and he had massive head trauma. Internal hemorrhaging inside of his brain had caused swelling in the center of his brain, so much so that his brain was compressed to about two centimeters in width against his skull. Christopher's neurosurgeon had saved the MRI scans to show him because he'd never seen anyone survive this type of injury before.

It had really seemed to be therapeutic both for Tess and Christopher, corresponding by e-mail to catch up on the last twenty-five years of their lives. And Christopher could recall the minutest detail of their high school days, including all the names of Tess's family and girlfriends. Tess had been quite impressed by his incredible recall and felt bad that she couldn't remember the names of his brothers and sisters. Tess hadn't spent much time thinking back on her younger days, and it had been extraordinary to reflect back on the experiences they'd shared together so long ago.

And so Tess had followed up on three of Christopher's book recommendations and had gone to the local library in Richmond Hill, quite a huge library. But none of the three books that Christopher had recommended were available—they'd been checked out already. Rather than wasting a trip, Tess had on a whim decided to do some further reading on Edgar Cayce. She had recently read a book called *Edgar Cayce on Channeling Your Higher Self*, written by Henry Reed and Charles Cayce. This book was what Tess considered to be a pivotal work for those like herself who had experienced what she was calling mystical experiences and were looking for an explanation of what was behind these mystical or metaphysical events. She thought that she'd see what else Edgar Cayce himself had written, and was taken aback to find search results displaying four pages, each with about thirty records per page! Some listings were other authors writing about Edgar Cayce, and one in particular caught Tess's eye: *The Reincarnation of Edgar Cayce*, written by David Wilcock and Wynn Free. *That looks interesting,* she thought and began wondering how extraordinary that would be to meet someone who had discovered that they had previously incarnated as this famous mystic and healer!

She found the record number and then wove her way through the many bookshelves to the section that contained paranormal material. Tess had always loved libraries, especially large ones that were packed to brimming with books. Walking around all of the books somehow made Tess feel kind of magical, to be surrounded by so many stories, so much information, so much to learn about. One of her most favorite spots was in the stacks of the science library at the University of Toronto, which housed an archive of scientific journals. The five floors of this archive were glass, and at night it was kind of eerie walking about with luminous floors and stacks of books from floor to ceiling, but somehow Tess always felt at home being surrounded by books. Perhaps she had been a librarian in another one of her past lives! There was a special kind of ventilation in the stacks, and the air was always moving. It did have a funny kind of musty book smell that Tess had always associated with books that she considered to be treasures from the past. She'd spent many an hour down in that spot retrieving journal articles at her various biotech jobs, before they were available electronically.

She scanned the books on her target bookshelf in the Richmond Hill Library by record number and finally saw the "Free/Wilcock" author and pulled out the book *The Reincarnation of Edgar Cayce*. There was an unusual subtitle: *Interdimensional Communication & Global Transformation*. The book cover was the color of that special indigo that creeps into the night sky just as the sun is setting, and in the middle was what looked like a cosmic opening in the night sky, into which a photo of the young Edgar Cayce appears. Tess could feel that this book was quite unusual and eagerly started flipping through the pages, finally settled on reviewing the table of contents. The contents ranged from the "History of David Wilcock" (who Tess assumed was the reincarnated Cayce); the "Great Pyramid," through to a "Scientific Blueprint for Ascension," and "The Energetic Engine of Evolution." Tess thought that all of these themes would make for a fascinating read! She checked her cell phone—holy smokes! It was nearly noon, and she had her first hypnotherapy appointment scheduled with Sam at 2:00 p.m. She tucked the book under her arm and hurried off to the checkout.

Sometime later, Tess and Sam were seated in Sam's small, cozy office. Sam had given Tess a briefing on the hypnotherapy technique and had reassured her that she would not in fact lose consciousness but that she would consciously remember her past life information while in a deeply relaxed state called a trance state. Then Sam said that he would prompt her with various questions, and he had found in his experience that usually the soul of the person would bring memories forward that were most in need of being addressed while at the same time recognizing what the person was capable of handling at that particular time.

And so Tess closed her eyes and allowed herself to relax deeply as she listened to Sam's instructions. As he instructed her to more deeply relax, she felt her head droop forward slightly. She could still hear Sam's voice but was very deeply relaxed, and Tess felt as if she were in a very deep meditative state. Sam's voice paused, and then he asked, "Where are you now?"

Tess wasn't sure. "I don't know," she said.

"Look down at your feet. Tell me what you see."

Tess could see bare feet and what seemed to be tan-colored clay tiles beneath them, and her feet felt warm. No, that wasn't quite right, it was becoming clearer now. The tiles were hot, and her feet felt warm on the hot tiles. "I see my feet. They are bare," she said. "My feet feel good. I like the feeling of the stone, the warmness, on my feet."

"Good. What are you wearing?"

She scanned up her legs. Her legs were a tanned color, and she had on a long, white, linen skirt. Now she was starting to feel something about this person … she was tall. She was sitting on a stone chair; her arms, also tanned, were resting on stone armrests. "I see a skirt, white, cotton or, no, linen, I think; it seems quite stiff," she said. But the words felt like they were coming out so slowly compared to what she was seeing.

"What else do you see?"

Tess could feel her thighs, her bottom, and her back resting against the warm stone chair, and now her arms resting on the warm stone armrests. "I see a chair. A stone chair. It's warm."

"Good, Tess. What else?"

Tess looked back at her feet. "There's a ring on one of my toes. No, wait, it's a snake, a silver snake." She felt her arms. "And bracelets, metallic, maybe silver, on my arms."

"What color is your hair?"

Tess now felt as if she were outside of her body, a short distance away. She could see herself! Well, it's black, and long. And I have a band, a headband. There's a stone, no, it's a crystal—yes, there's a crystal on the headband." Tess felt herself go back inside her body. "It feels like a wooden headband." And my hair, it's back, off of my face. I like it like that, away from my face."

"Now, Tess, I want you to look around and tell me where you are."

Tess looked ahead. There was a doorway, but it wasn't a square doorway. "There's a door," she said. The doorway was on an angle. She was inside of a small room made of tan-colored clay tiles or bricks. It was warm, and Tess felt a serene kind of peacefulness.

"What else do you see, Tess?"

Tess looked beside her. A man was sitting in another chair beside her, who felt like her husband. Like her, he was tan in color, dark hair, wearing a white linen robe. But she couldn't make out any details, almost like she needed glasses or something to see him more clearly. "My husband, he's there with me. We are waiting in a chamber for our day to begin."

"Where are you?"

Tess looked to the right, and there was another room. Then she somehow knew what it was and where they were. "We are inside of a pyramid. We are getting ready for our day. We heal people, the people that are building this pyramid, and others, the higher ones. We heal all levels of people, the workers and the more evolved ones."

"Tess, what country are you in?"

"Egypt."

"Do you know when? What year is it?"

"Uh, I'm not sure. Twenty … no, twenty-seven … uh wait, its twenty seven sixty. It's 2760 BCE."

"And does the pyramid still exist today?" asked Sam.

"Yes. It is under water."

"Oh! Okay, Tess. Now, what is your name?"

"Mem … Memho … Memho-tep. Memhotep." *That was it!* felt Tess.

"Good. And you said you are getting ready for your day?" prompted Sam.

"Yes," said Tess. "We are healers. We heal people, and we are preparing our healing room—with our thoughts. We use our thoughts to prepare the room!"

"Good, Tess, that's good. Now, Tess, where do you live? Can you describe your house?"

Suddenly Tess was in a very large room. It seemed to be part of a larger building, but they lived in this one huge room. There was a large pillared balcony, with long curtains separating the room portion from the balcony portion. The curtains were billowing gently in the breeze. "We live with the higher ones, but in our own place, a beautiful place," and Tess described the room.

"How old are you and your husband."

"Uh …" Tess could not hear the age exactly. "In our forties, but not yet fifty."

"And what is your husband's name?"

"Cha … Ron. Cha, something, Ron. Cha-ga-ron, yes—it sounds like Chagaron." Tess was feeling something else about the name. "It has a meaning; a meaning like 'one who is guided by animals.'"

"And what does Mem, ah," Sam rustled through his notes. "What does Memhotep mean?"

This was clearer to Tess. "It means wisdom-bringer.

I help bring information to those that need to hear it. I bring this information to them in an unbiased way, to the lower ones and also to the higher ones. This is part of the healing."

"That's good, Tess! Now, do you have children?"

"Yes. Six."

"Oh, my!" said Sam. "Boys or girls?"

"Uh, five; yes, there are five boys. And one girl."

"Tess, do you know any of your family now, in your present life?

"Yes." Tess could feel a strong connection from her husband. "Chagaron. He was a boss in my previous job." Tess could feel that Chagaron was the same soul as Danton!

"That's good, Tess. Anyone else?"

"The son. The number one son."

"Yes, Tess."

"He's Liam, my massage therapist."

"Good, Tess. Anyone else?"

"I'm not sure."

"Okay Tess. Now, do you all live there together?" asked Sam.

"No. Our son, the number one son, is a consort to one of the higher ones. Ra."

"Who?!" said Sam.

"Ra. We are working on a project of his."

"Okay, Tess" he continued. "What do you eat there? How do you cook?"

"There are others, lower ones. They bring us our food. They serve us. They like to serve."

"What do they bring you?"

"It's a kind of paste, or rice. On a large leaf. It's sweet; it tastes good."

"Great, Tess. And what is going on outside of your home? Can you go to the balcony and look out?"

"Yes. It's large, and we are high up." Tess/Memhotep could see down to a village that was bustling with activity, and nearby was a large pyramid! "We are above a village. The villagers, they are here to work on a project. A project of Ra's. We have to finish this pyramid. It has to be finished soon. We have to do it quickly." Memhotep could feel that there was urgency in the air as she looked out at the pyramid.

"Okay, Tess, now let's move ahead a bit toward a significant event. Move to a significant event in this life," said Sam.

"The water is coming. We are running." Tess could see villagers running toward her and Chagaron.

"Where are you running to?"

"We are running in the opposite direction to all of the villagers. We are running toward the water."

"Who is running, Tess."

"Me and Chagaron. Not the children."

"Why not?"

"They were taken away before, to another village. Ahead of time. We knew the water would come."

"Where are you running to?"

"To the pyramid. We go inside the pyramid. It is sealed. The water cannot get in. The water comes up over top of the pyramid."

"What happens inside the pyramid?"

"We lose the air. We thought that we would go to another place, the place where the others went. We thought that the transformation chamber would transport us out. To another planet." Tess/Memhotep could feel the confusion and now apprehension experienced by her and Chagaron.

"Where did you go instead?"

"We went to the afterlife."

"Tess, can you describe what happens when you go to the afterlife?" asked Sam.

"We realize that we will go to the afterlife, and that we will not be transported out. So we lie down in our healing chamber. We embrace. We lose the air." Suddenly she felt the air get thin, so thin, it was tough to breathe! She started gasping, and her heart was pounding.

"Tess, keep calm. You are okay," said Sam reassuringly. "Keep moving, Tess. What happens now?"

"Oh!" exclaimed Tess. She was outside of her body, and so was Chagaron! She felt calmer again. There was a bright light, so bright she could not see the top of the room. "I can't see the ceiling. It's so bright. I can see Chagaron; we are both outside of our bodies at the same time!" Tess could feel how excited Memhotep was about this.

"Keep going, Tess."

"We go to the afterlife," and suddenly she felt sadness, and tears started running down her face. She couldn't talk.

"It's okay, Tess," said Sam, slowly and calmly. "You are okay, Tess."

"I'm finding it a little troubling," said Tess.

"What is troubling you?"

"All of my lives on Earth. They've all been quite traumatic. Except for this one."

It is why you came here. To experience all of the trauma. All of the drama.

"Why not this one?" asked Sam.

"It was my model life," said Tess.

"Okay, Tess, now I want you to ask your higher self if there is anything you need to resolve about this life in Egypt."

Tess felt calmness come over her.

There is nothing to resolve.

"There isn't anything to resolve."

"Good. And are there any lessons for you regarding this life in Egypt?" asked Sam.

Relax. And, allow.

"Yes. I should learn how to relax and allow."

"Explain, Tess" said Sam.

"Memhotep can help me. I should learn how to relax enough so that I can allow Memhotep to come in. Memhotep will teach me things that will help me in this life. She, or rather her personality, is like a filter, a filter that I can add to my consciousness, so that I can access her teachings."

"Okay, Tess, very good! Now we are going to come back to the here and now. And together we send thanks to your higher self for sharing these experiences. Now, slowly Tess, come back to this room, to our session together; feel yourself sitting in a chair talking with me, with Sam, and then open your eyes when you are ready."

Tess thanked her higher self and then felt herself in the room with Sam, and opened her eyes. Sam smiled at her.

"How do you feel, Tess?" he asked.

"Great!" She did feel quite peaceful. "That was pretty wild," said Tess.

"You said it," said Sam.

Tess was busy thinking about the significance of having a past life in a part of Egypt that was now under water. She'd secretly been hoping to some day visit all of the sites of her past lives. Just how was she going to visit a pyramid that was under water?

~Chapter 18~

Wanderers

"Do you think that you are a wanderer?" Tess asked Stan. It wasn't often that Stan would read one of Tess's rather cosmic books, but he was in the midst of the David Wilcock story of self-discovery and his connection to LL Research. LL Research was a not-for-profit organization dedicated to researching and supporting "wanderers," or highly evolved souls from other parts of the universe. Tess had read that wanderers were souls who have apparently incarnated on Earth to help with a coming transition, or evolution of humanity, that is seemingly linked also to the evolution of Earth itself. It seemed that wanderers from other parts of the universe who have chosen to incarnate on Earth at this time are quite different from those souls who are undergoing the Earth evolutionary experience, and that their purpose is to bring light to humanity and the Earth, which will help with the coming transition or evolution.

"Whew, Tess I don't know. What do you think? Are you a wanderer?" Stan threw the ball back in Tess's court.

"Hmmm. Well I don't know, Stan. I'm not sure I like the connotation of just wandering around the universe; it sounds so haphazard. I kind of feel like there is a greater purpose to being here than just wandering and stumbling upon Earth." Tess puzzled over this a bit more. "But then again, I do admit that my experiences certainly haven't been … normal. It's quite possible that I am a little different—or perhaps it might be more accurate to say that my soul is a little different."

"Well isn't that the same thing, Tess," asked Stan with a wink.

Tess gave Stan a really hard look. Stan smiled back at her and raised his right eyebrow, and this made Tess smile.

"Well, okay, Stan. It's quite possible that I'm a wanderer. It fits the profile on LL Research's website. And …" Tess smiled back at Stan but couldn't mimic his eyebrow-raising trait. "So do you Stan?"

"But I'm not like you, Tess. I can't talk to spirits and relatives that have died. But, yeah, I do feel kind of like I somehow don't belong here," he said mysteriously and went back to his book reading.

"Well, give it a bit of time, Stan."

"Hmph," he replied, his attention now back in the book.

Tess was thinking that simply the fact that both she and Stan were actually reading and understanding both the David Wilcock story and the LL Research information for wanderers was quite significant. It was apparent from the information presented that the mere presence of the souls of wanderers on Earth was helping to bring light to Earth itself and all of humanity during a transition of sorts, a very cosmic transition! And if she and Stan were indeed wanderers, they must be a part of this transition too—and perhaps this was their role or path!

Tess was aware of a plethora of information written about the time period that was approaching. She had been researching 2012, and "the end times" was the catch-phrase that was being tossed around lately. But this had never resonated with Tess. Tess was slowly building a vision that modeled life on Earth as a means for souls to awaken and evolve through trials and tribulations. The trials and tribulations themselves seemed to be opportunities to grow, to let go of negative patterns and embrace positive ones, and for the most part the norm was to resist change and avoid suffering as much as possible. But to Tess, anyways, the change and suffering seemed to just happen anyways, so why not look at the trials or challenges of life in a different, more cosmic way? The way of the wanderer! Tess understood from her research that the more we embrace change and personal growth, the higher our personal vibration would become, and this is how so many of the wanderers were helping humanity and the planet—by simply being here on the planet and increasing the total vibration. Creating momentum for evolution!

In essence, thought Tess, our souls are choosing to come to Earth to incarnate and become a part of this planet's unusual way to evolve; and at the same time these souls get to learn what life is like in this corner of the universe. It seemed that by becoming a part of the life process on Earth, wanderers were helping lighten the load of negativity that was currently swamping Earth. The souls of wanderers were incredibly light, or of energy that had a high vibration. With the thousands of wanderers on Earth right now, and many more apparently incarnating in increasing numbers, Tess suspected that there indeed was a more cosmic event in the making for the Earth and all who had incarnated upon it, kind of a convergence of synchronicities. And more than likely it might look like end times to those who had not yet opened their awareness to the incredible reality of their inner nature, that indeed we were more than an elegant collection of chemicals and enzymes in a body that rots in the earth after our life is done. Tess understood that our true nature is rather that of a highly evolved, intelligent, and conscious energy, extending one very small portion of themselves into a physical body to experience the necessary trials and tribulations that would evolve their soul and the soul of Earth all at the same time!

The staff at Twelve Point had grown, and as a result Tess had been booking less hours with them. This had suited her just fine, as it gave her more time for her cosmic pursuits. Stan, always the pragmatist, was less than thrilled at the prospect of fewer dollars with which to run their household, but Tess had held firm with the situation. She couldn't help but feel once again that there was something more to the relationship with her and Stan, and that there was something special that Tess needed to do. But, she just couldn't put her finger on it! Tess had completed her healing certifications and was doing occasional sessions for family and friends. She'd even put together a website and put an ad in a local holistic magazine. But she was certainly not earning an income from healing, and although Tess felt an intense desire to pursue her holistic endeavors further, the healing sessions certainly weren't presenting an opportunity for a new career or even a supplemental income.

Tess knew quite well that she had to continue to move forward, to learn more about her own cosmic nature, and at the same time about the cosmic nature of all humanity. But why did she have this burning desire? Tess couldn't fathom it. And she could see that her continued pursuits seemed to Stan to be an obsession of sorts, with no tangible result and no end in sight.

All of O's guidance had given Tess (and O) the

impression that healing was in Tess's future, and in a big way. And certainly now from Sam's past life regression, having a previous life not only as an Egyptian but as an Egyptian healer, gave more weight to this end. The fact that her own soul had provided information about Memhotep (or the energy of Memhotep) being able to help Tess in this life, quite remarkable information, made it obvious to Tess that she should indeed keep at it. But still, there didn't seem to be a firm direction—the "why." What was it that Tess came here to do? She needed more answers.

Sam had given her the phone number of Rina, a friend of his who was a spiritual advisor. She had an incredible gift that allowed her, through her spirit guides, to speak directly to another person's spirit guides, and relay information back to the person that would help answer his or her questions about their life's events, information that would meet his or her soul's highest needs. In other words, she could provide detailed and specific guidance for those that came to her seeking this, and that was exactly what Tess was looking for!

Rina opened the door, and immediately Tess could feel that the energy in Rina's studio was very serene and peaceful. Rina welcomed her inside, and Tess could smell the sweet, smoky fragrance of the smudge that she had used to clear the room of any residual energies, making it a clear space for a new session. She showed Tess to a smaller room where she did her readings and asked her to relax in a very modern curved chair, and Rina settled into a duplicate chair right across from Tess.

Rina was a beautiful young woman, very exotic in appearance and very warm in her manner, making Tess feel right at home. Rina had both a tape recorder and a pad of paper, and she explained that she would tape the entire session and that she also would take notes of the information that her guides would provide to her. She started writing immediately, and Tess looked over quizzically, not wanting to disturb her but at the same time wondering what was going on.

"Yes, they're telling me a bit about you; please just relax for a few minutes 'till we're done," she said to Tess with a reassuring smile.

Tess did relax and while Rina was filling her pad of paper with writings, Tess glanced over to a picture on the wall that had caught her eye. It was a Native Indian, in warrior dress, but surrounded by a colorful mist—as if he were in the process of materializing right out of the mist. Although he had one hand held high, there was no weapon other than a fistful of beautiful feathers. Maybe they are eagle feathers, thought Tess. And the expression on his face was so mysterious, peaceful and yet strong, as if he were bringing some ancient and powerful wisdom into the room.

"So, Tess, a little about who you are," said Rina, looking up from her notes. "They're telling me that you are a wonderfully quiet person, a quiet energy, with a lot of animal and natural energies around you. You are a nature-balanced person, you are at peace and in balance when in the garden and around nature. You are rejuvenated there."

Tess nodded. She loved gardening but had not spent much time recently there because she'd been so caught up with learning energy healing and the job responsibilities at Twelve Point.

"But you are fragile as well," Rina continued. "You are wary of human beings. You've been taken advantage of frequently by energies who seek power. They are using this word—steamrolled."

Tess was aghast. Steamrolled? Had she really allowed that to happen?

"You are influenced in all your decisions not to create

conflict," Rina continued. "Human energy is so out of balance that it bombards you and puts you out of balance."

As Tess soaked this all in, it began to resonate with her. During her past life regression with Sam she had felt this, because all of her lives except the Egyptian life had been traumatic. The human experience really was out of balance. Tess thought about her life as Penelope in New Zealand; certainly she had been steamrolled by a couple of sword-bearing assailants—but Penelope had also done some steamrolling herself. She wondered briefly about what other traumas had occurred in her other forty or fifty lives on Earth.

"And so, why is she here?" asked Rina, to her guides. "To know where she is going. To know, the deep inside knowing, what her value is. If the things she had been feeling are true."

Tess nodded. "Absolutely, that is why I'm here," said Tess.

"You have a gift, communication with nature. With animals, and nature devas. You've had many spiritual experiences. You are to use these gifts and these experiences to create something. A meditation park."

Tess was taken aback. "A meditation park? What is that?" she asked.

"It is down the road," Rina continued. "You will live your way into it. You are here to have these experiences revealed with time, to live your way into your path. You need to visit other sacred sites, do some research first. But now to restore your balance; your job throws you out of balance, and you are not always on side with what they are doing. You need to spend some time in nature, with animals, in the garden. This is restorative to you."

"I love gardening, but I haven't had the time to get into the garden lately," said Tess.

"Meditation and nature will restore you," continued Rina. "You are a tool of the universe. So far you've taken this journey by yourself. Now they are here to help. They will help you to help others. Take instructions from Spirit and know that you are being guided."

Rina put down her pen and looked at Tess. "This is a unique gift. I thought you were a little different from the others that come here for guidance. Oh—they've got some book recommendations," exclaimed Rina, and she picked her pen back up again and proceeded to write down the titles of a plethora of books for Tess to read over the coming months.

After a few moments she paused, and then looked up at Tess. "There's something about a rose. Do you know anyone with rose in their name?"

"Oh, that's my mother!" exclaimed Tess.

"Right," said Rina. She's here too, and she wants you to do something. She wants you to set up a hammock in the backyard and read—romance novels!" Rina smiled.

"Yeah, that's what I did when I was a kid," Tess exclaimed. "We had one of those hammocks on a steel support because there were no trees in the backyard, and I spent most of the summer in that hammock—reading romance novels!"

"Well she wants you to start doing that again" said Rina. "Or maybe, well, now they are telling me Harry Potter. Yes, the Harry Potter series, or romance novels. Those would be good choices for you to be reading right now."

Tess couldn't understand why on earth she should be reading either romances or children's stories, but Rina had added this to her list of book recommendations from her guides.

"And ..." Rina continued. "You need to learn how to release the emotional burdens of others from yourself. And you need to learn how to block it, and how to protect yourself from it. Spiritual psychotherapy or holistic life coaching would be best to help you with this."

Tess felt good that she'd already been having these sessions with Sam.

"Do you have any questions for them?" asked Rina.

Tess was ready for this. "Yes," she said anxiously. "It's about this spirit that's been visiting me. He first visited when I was thinking about my high school friend Christopher Thomas, and I actually thought it was Christopher's spirit—that Christopher had passed on a number of years ago and was now visiting me periodically."

"Okay," said Rina. "Continue."

"Well I've just recently learned that Christopher is indeed alive, which of course is fantastic, but I'm wondering who this spirit really is and why he allowed me to believe it was Christopher."

"Okay, they're telling me that this spirit has the mind of an inventor engineer, a scientific mind. He is an ascended master architect—kind of an architect of the universe. He has a high level of communication—his energy vibration is high. He has a complicated name, and his mind has an arcane sense to it, which is much like the mind of your friend. That's what he wanted you to know, that he is like your friend."

"But he's not that friend, even though he let me think that he was," said Tess.

"Yes, and he has an inspired and complex mind like that of Einstein and Tesla combined. You will work together on the park."

As Rina described this spirit, Tess could feel the energy of the spirit around her—and suddenly she knew at once his identity, and at the same time she knew that his presence had been around her for some time now. Now she knew why she often wrote her journals from back to front, why she had books containing his writings and paintings on her burgeoning bookshelf; why she had his self-portrait and other of his works hanging on the walls of her house, and why she had been so enchanted by the art of the Renaissance masters! All in all he was going to be a most extraordinary spirit to be working with!

Tess was quite overwhelmed by the end of the session, and after thanking Rina, emerged from her studio in quite a daze. She had a lot of information to absorb. But, she did feel much more peaceful about the sense of purpose that had been nagging her for so long—now she had a focus for her efforts. As Tess pondered all of this new awareness, little did she know that these were just a few small pieces of an even bigger puzzle that was taking shape—events that were being orchestrated around her that would in the near future lead her to a mystery school, the Knights Templar, conspiracy theory experts, and UFOs!

Tess wandered around the shopping concourse but just couldn't settle down—likely because all of the new information she'd received was still integrating somehow. Then suddenly it snapped into her mind—the book list! Yes, she'd visit a bookstore and see if some of the books on Rina's list were there. That would be a good start! In the end she only had time to pick up one, the first novel from the Harry Potter series.

It was a few weeks after her reading with Rina, and Tess was in the middle of her session with Sam. "Huh, Sam? What did you say?" Tess thought that Sam had said that their sessions were over, and her heart had jumped into her throat.

"Tess, I'd like to end our sessions but not our friendship. I'd like to continue seeing you, but as a friend, not a client."

Tess was always amazed at what occurred during her sessions with Sam, and she was thrilled at this turn of events. This was Tess's last session before going on holidays with Stan—they had planned a two-week summer vacation in Prince Edward Island.

"Why, Sam—that would be fantastic!" exclaimed Tess. "We should pick a day to get together once Stan and I are back from vacation." Tess felt a deep connection with Sam, and knew that he felt the same connection—like a soul group connection, but it was deeper than that. Tess was figuring that their connection was that of a wanderer soul group connection, because their energy together was more magical in flavor. It was almost a romantic feeling, but deeper still than that. Like the feeling of two souls who were caught up in an adventure together in a remote corner of the universe, each with their own unique purpose and a common set of experiences to share with each other.

"Tess I'll just get this out of the way right now, but you know that I'm gay, right?" said Sam.

"Yes," said Tess, as she had known right from their first meeting.

"So I'm not looking for that kind of a relationship," he said firmly.

"I know."

"We really do have a cosmic kind of rapport, and I'd love to continue that a little more informally—over coffee or dinner, away from the office. And I'd like to learn more about our soul connection."

"Why don't we ask Btai Paul?" asked Tess.

"Fabulous idea, Tess! Okay, Paul, do you have any insights for us? What should we discuss together? Are we missing any guidance? Is there anything that we should be following up on right now?" Sam's thoughts came out all at once.

Tess sat still for a moment, and then she noticed a visual image in her mind's eye. "He's unraveling something—it looks like a scroll. It is a scroll!" And then Tess started laughing hilariously. What a sense of humor! Btai Paul was pointing to a ridiculously long scroll that he had unrolled so far it was all the way across the room, and he was asking them:

Well, where would you like me to start? It's quite a long list. Shall I begin at the top?

Tess relayed this to Sam and they both laughed together.

Remember the higher self of group souls. Remember, wanderers have two of them.

"Right! Btai Paul is reminding me about wanderers. I might have mentioned them in passing during our last session."

"Yes, Tess, they are evolved souls that have come to Earth, I think you said."

"Yes. Well I think what I'm feeling from Btai Paul is that we, ah, and by the way I think you are also a wanderer."

"I suspected as much."

"Yes, well we then are not only part of the same soul group, but we are a part of the magical or wanderer soul group."

"So there's the Earth soul group and the wanderer soul group?"

"Yes. I think this means that we share the higher self of the wanderer soul group, and this higher self might have a more magical side to it."

"Ah, so that explains it."

"Explains what?"

"Well, these experiences I've been having, very cosmic experiences; they seem to happen most often when I'm with you."

"You mean your visions?"

"Yes, and the tingling—sometimes my head, or more like the area around my head, gets so tingly when we hit on something together. It's like a barometer for a cosmic truth or something."

"Wow, Sam! That sounds like part of your gift, your magical side is coming out!"

"Yes—oh, Tess, we're going to have to stop soon," said Sam, glancing at the clock on his desk. "I have another client coming in."

"No worries, Sam. By the way, I have a book recommendation for you—I'm in the middle of one of the books recommended by Rina."

"Oh, Tess, I meant to ask you how your session went," said Sam, gathering up his notes and putting them inside of his file folder.

"Well, I have to tell you that I probably wouldn't have picked up this book on my own, because I thought it was a children's book. But it's not. Well, it's great for kids, but man, it's really excellent reading for adults too."

"What are you talking about, Tess?" said Sam, now standing beside his desk.

Tess stood up, and Sam walked her to the door of his office.

"Harry Potter, Sam! I'm reading the first one from the series, and it's phenomenal! I've found that reading this book has totally absorbed—and relaxed my mind! The visuals that are created by the writing are fantastic—it's really great reading, Sam. I'll bring it to you when I'm done."

"Okay, Tess, if you say so," said Sam, and he gave her a hug. "Call me when you and Stan are back from PEI, okay?"

"Will do, Sam," said Tess, and sent Sam a huge smile as she ducked through the door.

Prince Edward Island was unbelievably green, and it was entirely covered with what looked like a patchwork quilt of greens and browns. The air had a tropical feel to it, moist and breezy with the fragrance of many flowers all mixing together to form an intoxicating air that made you want to breathe in deeply. And there were flowers everywhere! Tess secretly vowed to revamp her garden the instant they got home. She remembered Rina's guides had mentioned that she was restored by being in nature—and she could certainly feel the stress emptying from her body and mind on this beautiful island!

Stan and Tess had attended the twenty-fifth wedding celebration of friends of Stan's, and had decided to stay on and tour the island afterwards. The renewal of vows took place in a beautiful church perched just on the edge of the ocean in a small town, Mount Carmel, on the southern edge of PEI. Stan and Tess had enjoyed meeting the islanders, who were very down to earth and much friendlier than people from the bigger cities on the Canadian mainland.

They had stayed a few nights in a small farmhouse that was turned into a vacation rental, and it was in this spot where Tess felt a presence—a ghost, in the house. Tess had asked Stan to get up with her around 2:00 a.m. to see if they could capture any photos of the ghost with their digital camera. Tess had recently been fascinated by "orbs," which were round circles of energy that were known to be associated with spirits and ghosts, and they sometimes appeared on the film of cameras and video recorders. With the proliferation of digital cameras, more and more people were finding these orbs in their pictures, and Tess was determined to see if the ghost in their vacation farmhouse would show up on film.

Tess had felt the presence of a small boy, probably around

five or six. He may have died in a fire, because both Tess and Stan caught occasional whiffs of smoke during their stay there. But after twenty minutes of sitting on the living room sofa in total darkness, nothing more than the strobe from the carbon dioxide detector had caught their eye. Stan decided to catch up on his television—there was a satellite dish in the farmhouse, and he turned on the TV. After a few minutes Tess started to notice that her body's energy system had "turned on." Soon her chi energy was running through her body at full tilt! She stood up and paced a bit while Stan caught a bit of a sitcom. Then she noticed something else, swirling energies inside of the room—she could feel and see them as a swirling haze around her.

"Stan, can you shut that off for a minute?" exclaimed Tess, standing still in the center of the room.

Stan grabbed the remote and aimed it at the TV console, and the living room was once again immersed in inky blackness. But Tess could still see the whirling cloud of energy around her—it seemed to be expanding out about twenty feet or so.

"What's going on Tess?" asked Stan.

"I dunno, Stan. My energy system is running full tilt, and I can see this swirling energy around me."

"I can see that something's going on with you," he said quizzically. "Why don't you ask your guide what is going on?"

Tess queried Btai Paul.

It is a tube of energy.

"Wow, Stan, it's some kind of energy tube."

"Oh," said Stan, and yawned mightily.

"Sorry, Stan, I know it's late."

"Well, I'm going to bed. Let me know if you run into any aliens or anything," he said with a wink to Tess, and he headed for the bedroom.

Undaunted, Tess asked for more information about the energy tube. She learned from Btai Paul that in the farmhouse was a "node," or a point, where a few energy lines crossed—energy lines called ley lines that created a system of grids around Earth, much like the acupuncture meridians formed a grid in the human body. The energies in this particular place were more intense when the moon's orbit was close to the island, which it was at that time of the evening. Tess had not only detected these energies, but her energy field had merged with it! Tess wondered briefly about this amazing connection she seemed to have with the Earth and its energy field, and drifted off into a dream-like state in which she saw a myriad of geometric shapes, orbs, and energies whirling around her. She recognized a three-dimensional Star of David, and then just for a moment what looked like her mysterious eye that would appear during her meditations, but it was sitting inside of a triangle, and both appeared three dimensional. Pretty wild stuff!

After ten minutes or so, Stan's voice called to Tess from the bedroom, and she left the swirling energies to resume her night's sleep.

There were apparently over 365 beaches on PEI, and Stan and Tess had visited a number of them. Many were deserted, and it was so peaceful to just walk up and down the hot sand, letting the cold, salty ocean water wash over their feet. In some places the sand was an incredible red color. After a morning of beach hopping, Stan and Tess headed into St Petersburg, a small town in the northeastern part of PEI. They'd spotted a fish and chips spot on their previous drive through and hoped to sample their fare.

They pulled into St Petersburg and slowed down in front of the fish and chips restaurant—it was packed! There was still one parking spot, and Stan gingerly drove in, but Tess stopped him.

"Let's go, Stan."

"Go where?"

"Let's try this one," Tess said, pointing to the restaurant immediately opposite the fish and chips spot.

"Okay, Tess." Stan pulled reluctantly out of the driveway and then prepared to make a right turn into the neighboring driveway where the Blue Schooner restaurant was.

"No, not this one," said Tess suddenly.

"Huh? Make up your mind, Tess," said Stan.

"No. Let's keep going," said Tess.

Stan straightened the car out and slowly drove ahead.

"Well, where will we go now?" he said quizzically.

"There!" Tess pointed to the restaurant in the blue motel to their right.

"Right on!" said Stan. "I'm starving!"

"Me too," said Tess.

Stan parked the car, and they walked over to the motel entrance, which seemed to serve also as the entrance to the restaurant.

A tall, slim woman was behind the reception desk. Tess strode over to the pretty blonde-haired woman. "Hello. Can we get a table for two?"

The woman looked up at Tess and smiled. "Why of course." Then she stopped and looked Tess right in the eye. Tess stared back, feeling something, but she was not sure what. Tess's eyes flickered momentarily down to her name tag, which read "Suzan."

Suzan looked away and turned back to pick up two menus and then swept past them. "Come on in, this way." Suzan led them to a table with four place settings near the window. Tess picked the chair facing the window and Stan moved around to the chair on Tess's left side.

"Oh, he likes to sit to your right doesn't he?" said Suzan.

"What?" asked Tess.

"It feels different for him to be on your left."

Tess looked over at Stan. It did feel different. "Yes, I think you're right. He usually sits to the right of me. How did you know this?" asked Tess curiously.

"I'm sensitive," she said with a smile, and stepped back a few steps. "And you have a very strong aura." Then she turned and hustled over to another table to take their menu order.

They ordered fish and chips, as this had been on their minds since they were on the beach earlier in the morning. Suzan doted on Tess for the entire meal, bring by refills for her water glass, then returning a few minutes later asking if she'd like extra ketchup, or lemons for her fish. She seemed to be very curious about Tess and didn't pay any attention at all to Stan. Stan was giving Tess his raised eyebrow every so often, and Tess smiled to herself. Something cosmic was going on!

After they'd finished, they walked over to the reception desk to pay for their meal, and Suzan looked up at Tess.

"You know, I feel like I am here visiting Earth from another planet, and that you and I are from the same planet," she blurted out. Tess smiled; now she knew what was going on—Suzan had just told her—right out of the blue!

"Have you heard of wanderers?" Tess asked Suzan. Suzan hadn't, and they chatted a bit more, but the restaurant was full, and Tess could see that Suzan had to get back to work. They exchanged contact information, and Tess promised to send Suzan information on wanderers, and then Stan and Tess turned to leave. Suzan warmly wished them well and turned back into the busy restaurant.

Outside, as Stan and Tess walked back to the car, Stan stopped and turned to Tess. "I could feel her energy as soon as we walked in there," said Stan.

"Wow, Stan!" Tess was impressed.

"Yeah." He stood quietly for a moment and looked deeply into her eyes. It was like time had stopped for Tess and Stan. Tess could feel the energy of the universe swirling around them—as if all of the planets and the stars were right there beside them, as if they were a part of both Stan and Tess, and they were also a part of the universe. It was a cosmic moment of time.

"How did you know?" asked Stan slowly, not taking his eyes off of her.

"What do you mean?" asked Tess.

"How did you know to come to this restaurant?" Stan pointed at the entranceway from which they had just emerged. "You knew that she would be here, didn't you?" Now he had his hands on his hips, but his voice was mysterious and low.

"No, I didn't, Stan."

"Yes, you did, Tess. You said no to the fish and chips spot, and you also said no to that spot," and he turned and pointed to the Blue Schooner just next door.

"Yes, I did do that."

Stan turned back to her. "And you said yes to this spot, where Suzan is."

"Yes, I did do that too."

"You knew."

Tess felt that cosmic feeling again; the universe was swirling around them.

"I guess I did, Stan," said Tess slowly, realizing that it was her soul that knew and that her soul had directed them to this restaurant to meet Suzan.

Stan shook his head and took a step toward the car. "That blows my mind, Tess." He looked back and smiled at her.

"Yeah, it kind of blows my mind too," said Tess.

They spent their last night in PEI in a small inn in downtown Charlottetown. They had a wonderful afternoon walking around the shops on the boardwalk; one in particular had a multitude of hats outside the shop on a wire stand. Tess picked up a fabulous purple woven hat with a wide brim that was supported by a wire hidden inside. Stan called it a Tess hat.

They munched on Peking duck flavored mussels at the Flex Mussels restaurant on the dock, and afterwards, when they finally checked into the inn, they found that for some reason their room had been upgraded to an executive suite!

The inn was a renovated old mansion, and the executive suite was what may have been the master bedroom. It was decorated in the old Victorian style and had a four-poster bed with a canopy, and a sunken Jacuzzi and newly renovated modern bathroom. Stan and Tess flopped into the bed, oblivious to the elegance of the room, exhausted and exhilarated from their time together, and both were asleep in no time.

The next morning they had a leisurely country breakfast in the inn restaurant, which had a wonderfully large patio. The sun was just appearing over the huge chestnut trees at the back of the inn, and the waitress had started opening the umbrellas on the patio tables. A beautiful summer's day was ahead, good for traveling! After a hearty breakfast they went back to their room to pack up and head to the airport. Stan had dropped their suitcase onto the bed and was piling their nightclothes into it. Tess was admiring the décor in their room, and had a sudden thought.

"Stay right there, Stan," exclaimed Tess, and she dove into her handbag for the camera. "I'm going to take some shots of this room; it's really quite beautiful. I don't know why I didn't do this before! Hold it right there," she said to Stan, and he froze with a smile. She snapped the picture and then out of habit clicked the preview button to see the photo. She blinked and couldn't believe her eyes! There was a beautiful huge orb just over Stan's left shoulder!

"Stan—look at this!" Tess rushed over and showed Stan.

"Wow, Tess—can you feel anything? Ask your guide who is here."

Tess stood still and took a deep breath, and then let it out slowly.

Your adventure is just beginning!

"Wow, Stan. It's a pretty cosmic answer." Tess wasn't quite sure what she and Stan would be doing next. But she was absolutely certain that it would be interesting!

"I don't doubt it for an instant," replied Stan, thinking that he'd better not ask, and lifted his eyebrow at Tess as he turned back to the suitcase on the bed.

Then he stopped and looked back over at Tess.

"You know, when we got married I just wanted a normal life. You know, a nice wife, good job, work toward our retirement, and, well, maybe travel a little."

Tess looked back at Stan. She was getting that cosmic feeling again; the universe was swirling around her and Stan.

"But we're not going to have a nice, normal life, are we Tess?"

"Nope."

"Well, then." Stan gave Tess a wink. "I guess I can live with a little adventure in my life." Stan hauled the suitcase off of the bed and headed out the door.

Tess put on her purple Tess hat, grabbed her bag and the

camera, and headed for the door, but stopped and quickly turned and looked over at the wall next to where Stan had been standing with the orb. She could feel the cosmic energies from the universe swirling all around her. She smiled, and then turned and followed Stan out the door.